P9-CRI-988

SWEPT AWAY

ALSO BY MICHELLE DALTON

Fifteenth Summer

Sixteenth Summer

A SIXTEENTH SUMMER NOVEL:
Pulled Under

A Sixteenth Summer

SWEPT AWAY

A Novel

MICHELLE DALTON

Simon Pulse

New York London Toronto Sydney New Delhi

This book is a work of fiction. Any references to historical events, real people, or real places are used fictitiously. Other names, characters, places, and events are products of the author's imagination, and any resemblance to actual events or places or persons, living or dead, is entirely coincidental.

ᰔᰔ

SIMON PULSE

An imprint of Simon & Schuster Children's Publishing Division

1230 Avenue of the Americas, New York, New York 10020

This Simon Pulse edition May 2015

Text copyright © 2015 by Simon & Schuster, Inc.

Cover photograph copyright © 2015 by by Goto-Foto.com

All rights reserved, including the right of reproduction in whole or in part in any form.

SIMON PULSE and colophon are registered trademarks of Simon & Schuster, Inc.

For information about special discounts for bulk purchases, please contact Simon & Schuster Special Sales at 1-866-506-1949 or business@simonandschuster.com.

The Simon & Schuster Speakers Bureau can bring authors to your live event. For more information or to book an event contact the Simon & Schuster Speakers Bureau at 1-866-248-3049 or visit our website at www.simonspeakers.com.

Cover designed by Jessica Handelman

The text of this book was set in Berling.

Manufactured in the United States of America

2 4 6 8 10 9 7 5 3 1

The Library of Congress has cataloged the paperback edition as follows:

Dalton, Michelle.

Swept away : a Sixteenth summer novel / by Michelle Dalton. —
Simon Pulse paperback edition.

p. cm.

Summary: While volunteering for the summer at the local lighthouse in her hometown of Rocky Point, sixteen-year-old Mandy Sullivan falls for the grandson of a local artist, and as the two explore all the lovely adventures the seaside town has to offer, Mandy wonders if their relationship is more than a summer fling.

[1. Love—Fiction. 2. Summer—Fiction.] I. Title.

PZ7.D16942Sw 2015   [Fic]—dc23   2014044752

ISBN 978-1-4814-3609-0 (hc)

ISBN 978-1-4814-3608-3 (pbk)

ISBN 978-1-4814-3610-6 (eBook)

For Tom S.

Who possibly knows everything.

And definitely knows more than I do!

June

W hy do lupine flowers have to be such an old-lady color?"

I open one eye, then the other. I squint at my best friend, Cynthia Crowley, who stands in front of the full-length mirror hanging on the back of her bedroom door. She fluffs the grayish-bluish-lavenderish skirt of her formal dress.

She isn't all wrong. If you've ever been to Maine, you've seen lupines. They're the tall, spiky, green-leafed plants that kind of look like corn on the cob on top, but with flowers instead of kernels. They're everywhere. Standing proud like soldiers in gardens, marching along the roadside, reproduced on tea towels, souvenir mugs, and postcards. Even T-shirts—though I don't think any Mainers wear those, just tourists.

Lupine flowers are all kinds of purple in real life. Translated into Cynthia's gown, the color somehow ended up pretty fusty. But that's what happens when the Ladies of the Lupine Festival League sew the dress themselves.

I shut my eyes again and fling my arm over my face to block out the morning light streaming through the bay window. "Why does the Lupine Queen have to begin her reign at the crack of dawn?" I moan.

I hear the rustle of chiffon and fake flowers and know Cynthia is about to pounce.

"Good morning, good *morning!*" she belts out in her "I'm going to be a Broadway star" voice. The song is from one of her favorite old movie musicals, one with lots of singing and dancing, and I can see why she likes it. I guess I kind of like it too. I actually prefer blockbuster action films, but Cynthia thinks they're "juvenile."

I roll away from Cynthia just as she lands on the bed. She bounces on her knees the way we used to in third grade, jostling me so much I grab one of the poles of her four-poster bed to keep from rolling off. The bright blue canopy flutters above us. *Everything* in Cynthia's room is a bright color—and usually bejeweled, appliquéd, or fringed, too.

"Your dress!" I scold. "You'll ruin it!" Only I'm laughing so hard I doubt she understands me.

I pull myself up to a sitting position and lean against one of her many jewel-toned pillows. I rub my face. "How come we both got zero sleep," I grumble, "and you're already dressed and looking camera ready?"

Cynthia gives me one of her coy "li'l ol' me?" looks. "Just the kind of girl I am," she quips in a babyish voice.

She isn't wrong about that, either. When Cynthia wakes up, she's ready to start the day. All energy, enthusiasm, and blond hair. It's why she's had boys pursuing her since they stopped seeing girls as cootie carriers.

Me, not so much. Sure, I've had boys ask me out sometimes, but mostly as a way to penetrate Cynthia's inner circle, since I'm the innermost ring. At least, that's how I figure it.

Cynthia climbs off the bed in a flurry of chiffon. "Seriously,

Mandy," she says in her normal voice. "I have to be there at nine for the kickoff at ten. You've got to get ready."

"I can't believe you're abandoning me for the summer for musical-theater camp!" I pull a bejeweled pillow onto my stomach and punch it. Then I tuck it behind my head and add sulkily, "Even though I'm very happy for you."

I really *am* happy for her. Mostly. I know how much going to camp means to her. She's taken tap, ballet, jazz, and hip-hop dance classes since she could walk, along with voice lessons that were a whole hour drive away. Since I've known her, Cynthia's been itching to get out of "Rock Bottom" (her name for Rocky Point) to pursue her performing-arts dreams. I wish I had such direction. My mom wishes I did too.

I force myself up off the bed and cross to the window. If I get into the exact right position, I can see the lighthouse peeking out of the morning fog, overlooking the restless sea. Red stripes circle its white three-story tower, so everyone calls it Candy Cane. The skinny strips of Maine's jagged coastline reach out like tentacles, as if they're trying to grab the many islands that pepper the waters, with Candy Cane the striped fingernail on the finger that is Rocky Point.

Before there was even a real town here, there was the lighthouse. It was decommissioned long before I was born, another sign, according to Cynthia, of how unimportant Rocky Point is to the rest of the world.

This, she isn't exactly right about. The Coast Guard built a newer, more modern one on Eagle Island farther out into the water back in the 1940s. We can hear Eagle Island's automated foghorn and see the red-light flashes. But Candy Cane is one of the few reasons tourists come to Rocky Point. So maybe it's the *only* important thing about Rocky Point to the rest of the world.

I turn away from the window. I'll be seeing far too much of Candy Cane this summer. Mom roped me into working for the Historical Preservation Society, and the lighthouse is their star attraction. "Working" in the sense I have to show up, not in the sense that I'll be getting paid.

Whomp! One of Cynthia's pillows whacks me in the face. Luckily, it's a fringed one, and not one covered in tiny mirrors.

"Hey!" I complain, tossing the pillow onto the bed. "What was that for?"

"Stop looking so dire!" she scolds. "You'd think *you* were the drama diva, not me!"

I fling a hand across my forehead and clutch my chest. I stumble across the room to gaze piteously at our shared reflection. "I don't know what's to become of me!" I wail in a terrible Britishy accent. "Trapped in the tower as a servant to an evil witch."

Cynthia giggles and flicks me with her stretchy headband. I snatch it and twist it around my wrists. "Save me," I beg, dropping to my knees and holding up my bound hands. "I'm a prisoner! The witch kidnapped me when I was a mere babe. She absconded with me—"

Cynthia raises a honey-blond eyebrow at me. "Absconded? Working on your SAT vocab already?"

"Absconded," I repeat, raising my own dark eyebrow back at her. She gestures magnanimously for me to continue.

"*Absconded* with me to a land where buildings are made of candy canes."

Cynthia's mouth twists as she tries not to laugh. "She used her powers to trap you inside a kiddie board game?"

"Not Candy Land," I admonish her. "A *land* of *candy*."

She holds up her hands in surrender. "I stand corrected." She goes back to frowning at her dress, studying it from every possible view.

I slump against a bedpost. "At first I loved all the fudge, saltwater taffy, and caramel. But soon my stomach hurt all the time, my teeth rotted, and the peppermint scent of my prison gave me awful headaches. Now I desperately await the arrival of a prince with a serious sweet tooth to free me."

Cynthia gives up searching for the elusive angle that would make the dress passable and turns to face me. "You done?" she asks, reaching for her headband.

"For now." I unwind the headband and give it back to her.

She slips it over her head and pulls her hair back from her face. "Maybe one of the summer boys will rescue you."

I snort. "Yeah, right."

"Could happen," Cynthia says. She picks up her signature bubblegum lip gloss and points it at me. "So. Could. Happen," she repeats, using the lip gloss to punctuate each word.

"Are you kidding me?" I flop back onto her bed. "Like who?"

Cynthia narrows her eyes, considering. I can practically see her flipping through her mental file labeled "Summer Regulars." "Someone new," she concludes.

"Would have to be," I say. "Since not a single Regular is even remotely an option."

Rocky Point doesn't have the long, sandy beaches that some

of the coastal communities in Maine have, and isn't close to the big towns with loads of things to do. So we have people who come for the whole summer, mostly because they have ties to the area: They're here visiting relatives, or they grew up here or nearby and keep a cottage as a summer place. They generally come year after year, so we've watched the kids in those families grow up from toddlers to our age.

The only "true" tourists we get are usually on their way somewhere else. They break up the drive by spending the night at one of our two bed-and-breakfast inns because they have the charm and romance missing from the land of suburbia. Or so I figure it. Sometimes we get groups on a Lighthouses of Maine tour visiting Candy Cane since it's the subject of a famous painting featured on Maine postcards. There are also Artists and Artisans tours. Every Maine schoolkid can rattle off the names of the famous artists who painted here: Edward Hopper, Winslow Homer, N. C. and Jamie Wyeth among many others. So tourists check out the art galleries and our genuinely showstopping views that inspired so many paintings, then go on their touristy way. Still, it's Candy Cane that's the star attraction.

Satisfied with her makeup, Cynthia slips off the headband and refluffs her hair. "Your mom's not an evil witch, ya know."

"Not to you, maybe," I grumble. "And now she's my boss. As if she's not on my case enough already. And with Justin gone for the summer . . ."

"Why would anyone *voluntarily* take summer classes?" Cynthia shakes her head.

"I know! Mr. Overachiever Double-Major just makes my

grades seem even more pathetic. Even though they were actually better this past year." I sigh. "I can't believe he's staying at school all summer."

Cynthia gives me a sympathetic look in the mirror. Now that my brother and I have outgrown our childhood attempts to kill each other, I kind of adore him. Mom certainly does. They practically *never* fight. And while Justin was away at college this year, Mom and I got into it more than ever.

Can my summer get any worse? No Cynthia. No Justin. That means no baby steps into the ocean until Cynthia yanks me under with her. No nightly trips to Scoops to try every flavor at least three times before voting for Best New Flavor at the Goodbye to Summer Festival. No action flicks with Justin to relieve the frustration of the third-straight day of rain. And no outings to local theaters to watch Cynthia perform.

Nope. This summer is going to be all me, Mom, and Candy Cane.

"Your mom can't hang around the lighthouse," Cynthia points out. "She has her job at the library."

"She'll find a way," I groan.

"I've done all I can." Cynthia lifts and releases the overskirt in one last attempt to make the dress turn into something wearable, and concedes defeat.

"Aren't you going to freeze?" I ask, frowning at the strapless gown.

Even though the Lupine Festival is the "official" start of summer in Rocky Point, Maine, our first day of summer is chillier than the last. Most of the Summer Regulars haven't even started arriving yet, so it's like one big party for the locals. That's why I like it—there's lots to do, but it's still super low-key. The calm before the summer season storm.

Cynthia picks up a gray-blue-lavender chiffon shawl and drapes it around her shoulders. "I've got this lovely item, to complete the grandma look." She pouts at her reflection. "I can't believe they expect me to wear this to the Lupine Dance tonight too. It will be everyone's last memory of me."

"You're not dying."

She waves a hand dismissively. "You know what I mean. This is how everyone will picture me while I'm away."

"Not with all the selfies you post," I tease.

She sticks out her tongue and goes back to arranging the shawl, before shouting, "Would you puh-leeze get up already!" She tosses my clothes onto the bed. "I have to be there in less than half an hour."

"Okay, okay." I get up, grab my bag with my toothbrush and toothpaste in it, and slump across the room to the bathroom. "But I expect you to keep your eyes peeled for my prince."

*M*y nose wrinkles at the full-on assault. The only downside of the Lupine Festival is that it's a serious fish feast. Last year I couldn't get a decent order of French fries for a week because they tasted like fried clams. My mom swears they don't fry them in the same oil, but I don't believe her.

It's hard to be the only person in Rocky Point who hates seafood. Maybe the only person in all of Maine. It's not just weird;

it's practically sacrilegious, since fishing is a major component of the Maine economy. My English teacher's husband is a fisherman, the Brownie troop leader's son is a fisherman, the Little League coach is a fisherman, my neighbor owns the marine supplies store on the wharf . . . Long story short, fishing isn't only a way of life here, it's *the* way of life.

Music blares from the little stage set up on the commercial pier where a band called the Rock Lobsters performs passable covers of classic songs. I turn away from the food booths on the public pier and keep my face to the ocean. Still briny, but the salty air blowing off the water helps tone down the fish smell. It's a little biting, with a slight chill still in the air, but I love the wide-awake feeling the ocean spray gives me.

I wave at some kids I know from school who are handing out flyers for Whistler's Windjammers cruises. The only takers today are the people with houseguests; locals don't go on the high-priced cruises since a lot of them have boats of their own, or have friends who do. I scan the crowd but don't see anyone to hang with, so I start over to the nonfish booths. At least they had the good sense to separate them this year.

Cynthia will know exactly where to look for me. Salivating in line waiting for my first fried blueberry pocket of the summer. Yum. That's a booth where I can trust the oil is lobster- and clam-free. Pure. Nothing but pastry dough in that grease.

I'm blissfully Mom-free for the festival, so no lectures today on how many are too many pockets. Right now she's standing at the foot of the circular staircase that leads up Candy Cane's tower. I can picture her there wearing her 1840s-style dress that could have been worn by Katharine Gilhooley, the wife of the first lighthouse keeper. Thanks to James and Katharine's large family, the keeper's house beside the lighthouse is pretty big. About ten or so years ago, the historical society did a fund-raiser to turn the house into the Keeper's Café and Gift Shop.

The Keeper's Café is closed for the Lupine Festival but has a booth on the pier with all the others. Mostly for publicity, since their menu is woefully limited. As I pass it, I notice Celeste Ingram selling lemonade. Smart move hiring her. Judging from the boys hanging around the booth, the café might actually draw some local customers this summer.

Celeste is back from her first year at college. Even Cynthia—who can pretty much start a conversation with anyone—has never spoken to Celeste. There's something, well, *celestial* about her. As in, out-of-this-world beautiful, and sort of untouchable. She has flowing white-blond hair in the summer that only darkens a tinge the rest of the year, and wide blue eyes, broad cheekbones, and a sharp, tiny nose that gives her the appearance of an elfin queen.

"Hi, Mandy," Vicki Jensen says as I get in the blueberry-pocket line behind her. "Where's Cynthia?" Vicki and I have had a bunch of classes together most years, but she's more Cynthia's friend than mine.

"Stashing her tiara," I reply. Cynthia's changing into something less formal until the dance, now that she's been crowned and sashed, and has declared this year's Lupine Festival officially open.

"How'd it go?" Vicki asks. "I only got up a little while ago."

"You mean you slept in? Like a normal person the first week of summer vacation?" I pout with envy. "Cynthia insisted I be there with her at the opening ceremony."

"Yeah, I figured." Vicki grins. "What best friends do, right?"

I grin back. Silly as it might seem, it's always nice to hear myself acknowledged as Cynthia's best friend. Once we hit high school, Cynthia roared into the popular crowd, and I worried that our bestie status since elementary school had ended its long run. But Cynthia proved me wrong.

"Hello, Mandy." Our next-door neighbor, Mrs. Jackson, has her twins—rambunctious eight-year-old boys—with her. I get as far away as I can from those two the moment they're armed with pastries. Blueberry stains are impossible to get out.

But Maine is the blueberry capital of the world, which means blueberry stains are an inevitable part of Rocky Point summer life—just like grease spots, fish smells, and mud. I may be considered a traitor for not liking seafood, but no one can fault me on my Maine bloob (my *personal* term for blueberries) loyalty.

"Hi, Mrs. Jackson. Hi, guys," I say, scanning my possible escape routes post–pocket purchase.

"I've been dreaming about these for *months!*" a familiar New York accent cries up ahead of me in the line. Joanna Maroni and her family have been coming to Rocky Point since we were in seventh grade. Cynthia and I usually hang with her and another Regular, Patti Broughton from Boston, all summer long. Cynthia'll be gone, but at least I'll still have Joanna and Patti. But I know it just won't be the same.

When I finally arrive at the front of the line, I reach for the luscious deep-fried fruity treat. A hand suddenly snatches it away.

"Hey!" I spin around, ready to smack the pocket thief. Instead I fling my arms around the culprit.

"Justin!" I crow. This is the first I've seen my brother since he came home for spring break in March. He must have arrived last night while I was at Cynthia's for our sleepover.

Justin grins at me, flecks of piecrust on his lips and purple smudges on his chin. I take a step back and punch his arm. "That was mine! You owe me a pocket!"

"Mmm-mm!" He takes another big bite and rolls his eyes heavenward. "My first pocket since last summer!" He licks his lips. "As good as I remembered."

"It was supposed to be *my* first pocket of the season!" I scold him.

"Watch it!" Justin grabs my arm and yanks me out of the path of a pocket-wielding eight-year-old. The twins are waving their treats around in delight.

"Boys," Mrs. Jackson scolds. "Those are food, not flags."

Justin and I move away from the line, now stretching all the way back to the lobster roll booth. I narrow my eyes at Justin. "Just because you saved my hoodie from the twins," I tell him, "doesn't mean you're off the hook. I want my pocket."

Justin swallows the last bite. "Where's Cynthia?"

That seems to be the first thing everyone says to me if they ever find me without Cynthia by my side.

"She's ditching the gown till later," I tell him. "And you're avoiding the subject. You. Back on line. Now. Must. Have. Pocket!"

He frowns, puzzled. "Gown?" Then he nods. "Oh, right. Lupine Queen. I forgot."

I look up at him, surprised. "You used to be all gaga for the Lupine Queen."

"Don't remind me. I can't believe I'd actually get up at the crack of dawn just to be at the front of the stage for the opening ceremony." He shakes his head at the memory of his younger self.

"So now you think this is all, what"—I gesture vaguely to indicate the whole festival—"dumb?"

"Not dumb at all," Justin says. "The queen thing, though. You've got to admit it's kind of dorky."

"And you're not particularly interested in high school girls, now that you're a big college man."

He grins. "Something like that." He wipes his mouth, then tosses the napkin in a nearby trash can. "Come on, let's get back in line."

"You're the one who should wait in line," I protest.

He grabs my arm and drags me along, and I let him. It will give us a chance to catch up. We stroll along the length of the line, greeting neighbors, classmates—and then I see *him*.

I have no idea who he is. I have definitely never seen him before. I would have remembered.

He's studying the festival schedule, and the first thing I notice is that he's nearly as inappropriately dressed for early summer in Maine as Cynthia was.

He stamps his sandaled feet and shifts from side to side, giving me the impression that he's already regretting the Hawaiian-print board shorts and vintage-looking sky-blue bowling shirt. I figure any minute now he'll admit he's cold (why don't boys ever want to do that?) and untie the dark blue sweatshirt knotted around his waist.

The next thing I notice is his shaggy brown hair, with bangs long enough to flop over his face as he gazes down at the paper in his hands. Then he tips his head back to swing the bangs aside, and sticks his sunglasses on top of his head.

I suddenly stop noticing anything at all.

Anything, that is, other than the lips that look soft and full enough to be a girl's; the high, wide forehead; the sharp chin that seems to be pointing at the schedule in his hands; and his sun-tinged skin that tells me he's come from somewhere a lot warmer than Rocky Point, Maine. And twinkling blue eyes—or are they green?—that suddenly lock onto my own dark ones.

Busted.

I quickly glance away, grab Justin's arm, and breathlessly say, "Come on, slowpoke. They might run out before you get me my pocket."

"The booth's only been open an hour," Justin protests as I practically trot him toward the back of the line. I can't help risking a peek over my shoulder at the mysterious sun-kissed stranger, but he's gone back to studying his festival schedule. Only a tourist would give it such careful consideration.

Is he here for just the day? Or is he—oh please, please, please—a new *Regular*?

I spot Cynthia arriving at the pier, scanning for me, flanked by Joanna and Patti. "There's Cynthia," I tell Justin. "You get me my pocket and come find us. We'll probably be over at the arts and crafts."

Justin shrugs. "You know they're best right out of the fryer," he says.

"Just do it," I order. I weave my way through the snaking lines radiating from the booths. This time I manage to keep from swiveling my head for another peek at Surfer Boy.

I stop dead in my tracks midway to Cynthia, paralyzed by the *worst* idea. He probably thinks Justin is my *boyfriend*! I literally smack my forehead. *How stupid am I?*

I stand there still as a statue, forcing the hungry throngs to swerve around me. Luckily, on Lupine Festival day everyone's always in a good mood, so no one seems to mind. My brain spins on overdrive trying to think of a way to remedy the situation as I watch Patti, Joanna, and Cynthia approach.

Patti looks thinner and for once isn't carrying one of her ever-present bags of chips. Maybe she kept her vow to "eat healthy." The hamburger, two hot dogs, and a lobster roll, along with mounds of potato and crabmeat salad at our Labor Day picnic at the end of last year's season nearly did her in.

The big surprise is Joanna's hair. A spiky short cut dyed a color not found in nature has replaced her long dark mane. Fuchsia is the closest I can figure.

If I wasn't already frozen by my possible gaffe with Surfer Boy, her dye job would have stopped me. All the years the Maronis have been coming to Rocky Point, Joanna and her three sisters have always dressed in the same ultraconservative uniform: pastel sundresses or khakis and polo shirts. Their hair was often styled identically—French braids or pulled back with skinny headbands. Did her sisters dye their hair too, to keep with the matchy-matchy? That I'd have to see to believe!

"Don't worry," Joanna says, holding her sandwich away from me. "We'll stay downwind."

"Thanks." I grin, happy that she remembers my fish aversion. Sometimes it takes a while for us to get back in the swing of things after being away from each other for a year. It's nice to know that my quirks and I don't just vanish, like that town in the musical *Brigadoon*. Cynthia and I have watched the movie a bunch of times—it's about this town in Scotland that appears only for one day every hundred years. Sometimes I feel Rocky Point is like that to anyone *from away*—the term Mainers use for someone who isn't from Maine. To them we exist only while they're here and then vanish back into our famous Maine fog.

"Your summer's going to be great," Patti says to Cynthia. "I know how much you love being in shows."

Cynthia nods, her eyes bright. Every time she talks about going to the Vermont Performing Arts Summer Workshop she gets the same slightly dizzy look—like the very idea makes her head spin. "It's going to be awesome," she says, bending forward from the waist to make sure no mayo falls onto her top from her overloaded lobster roll.

"Yeah, you must be stoked to be getting out of here," Joanna says, just as her front jeans pocket buzzes. She pulls out her phone and reads the text. She types something back, then sighs. "I begged my parents not to drag me here, but no. They want to torture me."

"Torture?" I repeat. Rocky Point hardly qualifies as a method of torture, and for all the summers I've known her, Joanna has loved it so much she cried when she had to leave. Maybe the fuchsia hair dye has affected her brain.

She waves her cell phone around. "I think they did it just to break up me and Sam. He's back in Brooklyn with our friends, and I'm stuck here."

"But you come here every summer," Patti points out. "It's not some new stunt they pulled."

Another buzz, another text. While Joanna's eyes are on her phone, Cynthia and I each give Patti a "what's up with her?" look. Patti shrugs.

Justin appears with my bloob pocket. "Don't say I never did anything for you, Sneezy," he says, holding it out to me. Sneezy is his nickname for me, thanks to my allergies.

"You *didn't* do anything for me," I counter. "You repaid your debt."

I take the paper-wrapped treat from him and tentatively flick it with my tongue to test the temperature. You have to be careful with pockets. They can be treacherous, luring you in with their homey, acceptably hot pastry, then spurting steaming blueberries that scald the roof of your mouth. But this one is perfect. Still hot, but not at a dangerous level. I take a bite, shut my eyes, and inhale deeply, which is the only way to eat a pocket.

"Hi, Justin," Patti says.

"Hey," he replies. I can tell he's trying to place her. Maybe to Justin the Regulars live in Brigadoon, and *we're* the real world.

"You remember Patti," I say, rescuing them both from potential embarrassment. I can be magnanimous now that I have my bloob pocket. "She lives in the green cottage on the bay side past

Second Time Around but before Scoops," I explain, listing two of Rocky Point's favorite spots.

"Oh, right," he says. I know he still has no idea who she is.

I also realize from the way Patti is twirling her hair and smiling that she's into Justin. But she's not even a blip on his radar.

"See you later, Sneezy," he says. "I told Mom I'd fill in for her at the lighthouse so she can grab lunch."

"Great," I grumble. "Suck up to Mom so I seem like an even worse child."

"You *are* the worse child," he teases.

I scrunch my nose at him, since my mouth is too busy with the pocket to bother with a retort. Patti laughs way too loudly, and Joanna never raises her head from her cell phone.

"Are you going to the dance?" Patti asks Justin.

"Gotta see Cyn here dolled up in her Lupine Queen gown, don't I?" Justin winks at Cynthia.

"Ugh." Cynthia shudders, then licks the glob of lobster that fell out of her sandwich off her wrist. "I'm never going to live it down."

"Exactly why I have to see it." Justin salutes us. "Ladies."

I swallow the last bit of pocket and say, "You're going to look lovely in Mom's Mrs. Gilhooley costume."

"Ha-ha," he says, then jogs away.

"Make sure Mom gives you the bonnet, too!" I call after him. I roll up the paper the pocket came in and wipe my face.

"Does he have a girlfriend?" Patti asks, still twirling her hair.

There must have been a lull in the texting because Joanna pipes up, "Forget it, Patti. Why get involved with someone you'll leave at the end of the summer?"

"I think it would be romantic," Cynthia says. I shoot her a look, and she quickly adds, "Not with Justin. I mean, he's a nice guy and everything, but he's like my big brother. Only better," she adds, "since I don't have to share a bathroom with him."

"Yeah, that does suck," I say.

"You really think having a thing with someone who is here only for the summer is actually a good idea?" Joanna presses.

"Why not?" Cynthia says, studying her lobster roll. I know she's trying to decide if she can just pop the last of it into her mouth in one piece. "Sometimes knowing a thing is temporary makes it beautifully tragic." She makes up her mind and in the sandwich goes.

"Ever the drama queen," Joanna says.

"Well, I'm ready for something nice and simple, and a summer fling seems exactly in order," says Patti.

"Forget Justin," I tell Patti. "He's only here for a few days. Then he goes back to the University of Maine for a summer semester."

"I'd imagine a two-day fling is too short for even the ever-adventurous Patti," Joanna teases.

"Two days would hardly qualify as a *romance*," Patti scolds. "And it's romance that I'm after."

They continue debating various definitions of romance as my mind wanders back to the dark-haired boy I saw earlier.

"Ready to buy some mismatched coffee mugs?" Cynthia interrupts my thoughts.

We turn away from the food booths and stroll along Water Street to Main. The Square, as everyone calls it, is the literal center of Rocky Point. The grassy plaza lies halfway between the harbor and the bay. It's also midway between the pointy tip where Candy Cane stands to the south and the beginning of the woods to the north. Mom's library anchors the south side, the middle school the north. Our high school is a few blocks away from the library.

Today's flea market is set up in the parking lot of the middle school. That means we can check out the Artists and Artisans tent in the town square on our way there. We cruise by the shops with sale racks and tables outside.

People sprawl on the benches lining the Square. They're busy eating fried clams out of cheerful red-and-white-striped cardboard cartons from booths on the pier, or sandwiches from Taste To Go, the take-out place on Randolph Street. Kids drip ice cream and giggle or drop ice cream and wail. Mostly they're kept out of the Artists and Artisans area because no parent wants to be forced to buy hand-painted chiffon scarves covered in ice-cream fingerprints or historically accurate sailboat models with suddenly broken masts.

Cynthia and I breeze past the section where framed pictures hang on chicken-wire walls. Candy Cane is a favorite subject, though none of the paintings has the evocative feeling of the one on the postcard. Maybe because those displayed by the amateur artists all depict her (I always think of Candy Cane as a "her") on a bright sunny day, and the painting on the postcard is of the lighthouse in the gloom. To me, that's a more accurate image. Rocky Point's sunny days are nowhere near as common as the rainy, foggy, or cloudy ones. The anonymous artist knew Rocky Point like a local.

"What do you think Brad Ainsley came up with this year?" Cynthia asks. We stroll past tables with handblown glass vases and goblets.

"Something bizarre, I'm sure." Brad Ainsley lives up by the Canadian border and does the whole arts-festival circuit in Maine. The sculptures have some kind of theme each year that's only clear to him.

"Nautical," Cynthia surmises as we study Brad Ainsley's latest creations.

"Ya think?" I deadpan. The sculptures appear to be in two categories: those whose stuck-together pieces create a ship shape, and those made of actual ship or fishing materials.

I lean forward, about to press a button placed on the shoulder of a figurehead, wondering what craziness it will unleash, when I let out a gasp and grab Cynthia's arm.

"What?" she asks. "Did something bite you?"

"No," I squeak. I step in front of her, my back to Surfer Boy. I force myself to speak in a calm, low voice. "Don't look, but there's a boy over by the sculpture with the broken blue mast sticking out of the upside-down hull."

Cynthia's eyes flick from mine to a spot over my shoulder. I know she spotted him when her jaw drops. "He's new."

I nod. "I saw him before when I was in the pocket line."

Her eyes return to mine, and she takes my hands. "We need a plan."

My eyes open wide and my body goes cold, then hot, then cold again. It's some weird combination of fear, exhilaration, and anticipation.

Cynthia's eyebrows rise expectantly. But my usually over-drive brain is on strike. Total blank.

"Uh . . ." is all I can come up with.

Cynthia gives me a little shake. "Don't get stage fright now! This is our chance!"

"What if he's from up the coast and is only here for the festival?" I say weakly, disappointment washing through me as I realize this is the most likely scenario.

Cynthia grins. "Then we just have an awesome day of flirting!" She drops my hands and gives me a hip check. "We could use the practice."

Her hip check jostles an idea loose. "I got it!" I declare. "Follow my lead."

We edge our way around some of Brad Ainsley's more lethal sculptures as our target moves to the last one in the row. I hoped we could position ourselves opposite him, but he's standing right where the tent is tethered to the ground. We'll have to settle for sidling up beside him. Which we do.

Surfer Boy doesn't even look up. He's intensely focused on a piece that I can only describe as Ship-nado. Dozens of small model boats—dinghies, canoes, schooners—swirl around in a chicken-wire funnel.

My plan is to start talking about super-interesting things so that he can't help but check us out. Only now I can't speak. Complete mental freeze.

My eyes flick to Surfer Boy. He's kneeling and peering up inside Ship-nado. I wonder if that's how Brad Ainsley wants us to view his work.

Cynthia keeps nodding her head toward him in sharp little jerks and widening her already wide-open eyes in strange rhythmic bursts, like reverse blinking.

I clutch her hands. "Ask me something," I whisper hoarsely. "Something interesting. It will make him look."

She stops blinking, tilts her head the way she does when she's thinking, then gives a sharp nod. She clears her throat and says loudly, "I think it's wonderful that you're helping the very important Historical Preservation Society with one of its most prized landmarks."

I'm about to give her an "are you kidding me?" glare but then realize if he's from away, he might actually be interested in our little lighthouse. So I quickly turn my glare into an approving "good one" expression.

"Oh yes, Candy Ca— I mean, the Rocky Point Lighthouse is such a great—"

I break off as our target stands up, brushes the gravel from his knees, and strolls away.

Cynthia and I stare at his back. "Can you believe that?" Cynthia fumes. "It was as if we weren't even here!"

My brow furrows. "You know, I think he really didn't have any idea that there were humans around. He was so into this sculpture." I peer at it again. Now that I'm up close, I can see that the ships aren't empty. Teeny-tiny people are inside. It's kind of great and kind of creepy at the same time.

Cynthia shrugs. "Probably just a Summer Snob."

Summer Snobs are a subgroup of Regulars who come here every year but don't want anything to do with the locals. They give parties for each other, browse the art galleries, and visit the antique stores and the weekly farmers' market, but wouldn't be caught dead at Louie's Lobster Pound eating a shredder with their bare hands—even though everybody knows that's the best way to eat your lobster. If you like lobster, of course.

I watch Surfer Boy approach a table of antiques. Once again he's mesmerized. He strikes up a conversation with the woman at the table. I give him one last look as Cynthia and I leave the tent to head for the flea market behind the school. We gave him a chance to talk to us, and he didn't jump at it. Cynthia always says that if a guy doesn't take a little hint, don't bother giving him a bigger one.

I shake off my disappointment and get into my flea market groove. I love flea markets. Not only are the items in my price range, but it's fun to poke through other people's stuff. It's like sneaking into their house and spying on how they live.

I know it's silly, but there's a little part of me that feels bad for the odds and ends, and I always hope they'll find new owners to appreciate them. Sometimes I buy things that I figure will never get bought. Mom just sighs when I show her my latest "pity purchase" and then says, "Well, at least these are the only kinds of strays you bring home." Mom has a strict "no pets" rule.

"Snob sighting just to starboard," Cynthia murmurs.

I look up from the chipped pig-shaped mug that is going to join my wacky mugs collection. Two tables over Surfer Boy gazes intently at a pile of lobster traps. Then he does the same thing at a table selling knot art and handmade fishing lures.

"You know, I don't think he's a Summer Snob," I tell Cynthia, formulating a theory. "I think he's an alien from a planet where no one fishes."

"If the aliens all look like him, you should move there," Cynthia teases. "You'd get to avoid all seafood *and* be surrounded by hunks."

"Definitely not from Maine, that's for sure." It's not just the tan and sandals. His curiosity about pretty much everything on sale at the flea market tells me these are things he's never seen up close before. Things that are part of daily life here.

Then the unthinkable happens.

Blue eyes—yes, they are definitely blue, not green—suddenly meet mine.

And I can't do anything but look back.

I'm as mesmerized by those eyes as he was a moment ago by a tiny ship-in-a-bottle. The weird thing is, I don't do any of the things I thought I would when confronted by the steady beam of a handsome boy's gaze. I don't blush; I don't giggle; I don't faint; I don't anything.

I don't even move.

But weirder? Neither does he.

I have no idea how long we stand like this, both frozen. It feels like forever, until I realize that Cynthia has only just finished paying for her floppy sun hat. In the time it took for Cynthia to pull out her wallet, count out the bills, and hand them over to the ninth-grade algebra teacher, Suzanna Hughes, who's manning the table, something shifted in me. Or rather, *not* shifted. It felt as if I was caught in a fishing net, unable to move, but not wanting to try.

Maybe thirty seconds at most.

Then it's over. Cynthia says something to me, something distracts Surfer Boy, and our eyes drop. Life picks back up, and we each return to our separate worlds.

"You okay?" Cynthia asks, adjusting the hat so that the brim doesn't make it impossible for her to see.

"He looked at me," I whisper.

Cynthia's head swivels, and she spots Surfer Boy down the row. Now he's studying an old sailor's manual.

"And when I say *looked*," I continue, "I mean took in every detail, almost as if he could—" I'm about to say "see into my soul" but luckily realize before the words come out how ridiculous they'd sound.

"As if he could . . . ?" Cynthia prompts.

"As if he had X-ray vision and was checking to see if my brain was still in my skull."

Cynthia laughs. "Well, is it?"

"Not so much," I admit.

Cynthia tips her head back so she can examine my face from under her floppy brim. "Wow. Boy made an impact, did he?"

"He did."

"And you're saying he actually made eye contact."

"And held it," I confirm. "Unless he has such super vision that he was actually trying to see the price tag on the ironing board for sale behind me."

"Well, that bowling shirt *could* use a quick pressing . . . ," Cynthia jokes. She knocks into me with her shoulder. "So . . . go get him."

"I—I . . ." I slump and look down at my feet. One of my sneakers is untied, and I have a big splotch of blueberry on the other one. That's in addition to the blueberry trail down my shirt. I *thought* that pocket was a little understuffed. Now I see where some of the filling had gotten to. "For all I know he wasn't looking at me because he's interested. He could have been staring at my blueberry stains. Or thinking how weird I am for buying a pig mug."

"Hang on." Cynthia grips my arm.

The sudden change in her tone makes my head instantly pop back up. She's openly staring in Surfer Boy's direction, and she looks seriously stunned. I glance over and my jaw drops.

"What is he doing talking to old Freaky Framingham?" I gasp. "And Freaky Framingham is talking back!"

"It's hard enough to wrap my brain around Freaky Framingham being here at all," Cynthia says. "I think my head's going to explode, putting him and Hottie McHottie together."

Freaky Framingham has lived in Rocky Point as long as I can remember. He's that guy whose house you avoid, which isn't hard to do, since it's in a deeply wooded area. The path to his house from the road is just a narrow strip of dirt without a sign to mark it. But everyone in Rocky Point knows exactly where it is. Each year on Halloween kids dare one another to knock on his door.

There are rare Freaky Framingham sightings. He'd usually be in his battered blue pickup. But he'd never wave to pedestrians or other drivers at our few stoplights, like everyone else. He just keeps his hands firmly on his wheel. Though his face is hard to see behind the cracked windshield, we all assume his expression conveys how much he hates everything and everyone. He'd be at Main Street Goods, picking up groceries, and someone would greet him and he'd just grunt. Or he'd mutter under his breath and stalk out.

And now he's standing two tables over, and Surfer Boy is showing him the sailor's manual. Surfer Boy doesn't look nervous or afraid talking to our town grouch. Freaky looks almost presentable for a change. Normally he wears ratty paint-spattered overalls with flannel shirts washed so many times it's hard to believe they're any warmer than wearing tissues. His gray hair is wild and long, and he has the weather-beaten skin of many old-time Mainers, the result of a life lived mostly out of doors, battered by high winds, powerful sun, and cold weather.

Today he's still wearing overalls, but they're cleaner than usual, and the shirt looks close to new. His hair is brushed and pulled back into a low ponytail. He looks almost . . . normal.

"That is seriously freaky," I murmur.

"No lie," Cynthia says, equally mystified.

We watch as if it's some kind of mystery show on TV, and we're looking for clues to explain how these two people wound up talking to each other.

"Do you think ol' Freaky has, I don't know, been to therapy or something?" Cynthia suggests.

"Hard to picture, but something has happened," I say.

"Maybe he decided to strike up a conversation with the only person here who wouldn't know him."

"Could be," I say doubtfully. "But don't they seem like they know each other?"

Freaky's usual dour expression hasn't changed. He just stands there frowning, stroking his stubbly chin while Surfer Boy shows him things in the book. Then Freaky does something totally bizarre. He pulls a wad of bills out of his back pocket and pays for the book. Mr. Cooley, the guy who sells secondhand books at Second Time Around over on Berry Street, looks as shocked as Cynthia and I feel. He takes a minute to register that this is really happening, then accepts the dollar. Freaky Framingham strides away from the table, and Surfer Boy scurries after him.

Cynthia and I turn to face each other, wearing identical "huh?" expressions.

"How could they possibly know each other?" I ask.

"Why would anyone voluntarily spend time with Freaky Framingham?" Cynthia says. "I mean, that boy, that serving of yummy cuteness, just followed him. On purpose."

Our heads turn simultaneously to catch another glimpse of the strange sight.

I don't know if it's because he could feel us staring in complete and utter disbelief, but just at that moment Surfer Boy looks back.

And I'm mesmerized all over again.

Because this time he doesn't just stare at me. He smiles. And lifts his chin in a teeny-tiny itty-bitty greeting.

But it's big enough to make me bang into Cynthia. And that's without even moving. I guess I kind of went a little lopsided. If she hadn't been standing next to me, I might have fallen over.

Cynthia slings her arm across my shoulder and brings her face next to mine. "Seems you made an impression on him, too."

The ginormous smile I feel on my face reminds me of how not-cool I am. There is no way I can play coy, or haughty, or any of the other ways I've seen girls act around the boys they like.

It's just right out there: *I like you*, in screaming neon on my face.

He turns and jogs to catch up with Freaky Framingham. Proof that he actually is with the old coot. If he wanted to escape, he could have, since ol' Freaky hasn't slowed down a bit and is now out of the parking lot.

"I need a bloob pocket," I murmur. "For strength."

"Do you really want to get back in that line?" Cynthia asks. "With all those eavesdroppers? We have some planning to do!"

Happily, the usual table piled with drinks and baked goods donated by the middle school sits again at the exit. The money from these sales goes to the school, so I feel virtuous as I buy a blueberry muffin, an oatmeal-blueberry cookie, and a tall lemonade. Once we have our purchases, we leave the tent and cross the Square. I sit cross-legged on top of a picnic table, and Cynthia lies on the bench, her floppy hat protecting her face from the sun. She says something, but it's too muffled to understand.

I reach down and flip off her hat. "What?" I ask.

She sits up and swivels around to face me. "I said, I just can't figure it out."

"I know!" I gnaw on my lower lip.

"You know what I think?" Cynthia says impishly. "I think just like you're trapped in a candy tower to be a witch's servant, he's under a spell. A spell that can only be broken by a kiss from an innocent year-rounder."

I duck my chin so that she can't see the flush creeping up my neck. I fiddle with my shoelaces, my mouth twisting as I try to keep the smile from spreading. A kiss. A soft, tender brush of those lips on mine.

I haven't had much experience in the kissing department. Last New Year's Eve, Kenny Martin suddenly laid one on me in the middle of a party. I yelped—not exactly the reaction he'd been hoping for—and banged into Cara Michaels and Evan Lawrence when I stumbled backward in surprise. They weren't exactly pleased when I interrupted their dance-floor lip-lock. And there were a couple of awkward good-night kisses when Johnny Carmichael walked me home after a group of us went to the movies. Awkward enough that he stopped trying, much to my relief.

But now . . . I tip my head back and watch the clouds drift. Their soft edges make me remember how soft his lips looked. I'm pretty certain kissing Surfer Boy wouldn't be anything like my previous experiences.

Of course, kissing him would require seeing him again. And talking to him. How am I going to do any of that with Cynthia gone? I'll never have the nerve. If our paths ever even cross again.

"Maybe he'll be at the Lupine Dance," Cynthia suggests.

I brighten at the idea. Day-trippers often stay for the dance. Best of all, Cynthia will still be here to help me get ready, coach me, and provide moral support. A kiss from a day-tripper sounds incredibly romantic. One beautiful night and then just a lovely memory.

Assuming he doesn't bring Freaky Framingham with him.

I sit glumly at the edge of the pier, my legs dangling over the gently lapping water. The moon's reflection quivers with each rise and fall of the peaceful wavelets, and the little white twinkle lights strung on every pillar and post sparkle in the sea's mirror. It looks like fireflies learning to swim. The DJ's music thrums from the loudspeakers, and even though my back is to them, I can picture my neighbors, my friends, and random visitors dancing their butts off.

Over on the other pier, the food booths are now lit with clip-ons so bright that it looks like a movie set. Beside me two tween girls compare notes on a shared enemy, some boy who spent most of the school year embarrassing them. I want to interrupt and explain that it means he likes them, but then I tell myself to shut up. What do I know about boys?

I hear a rustle behind me and glance up at Cynthia. She has put her Lupine Queen dress back on as required for the Sunset Ceremonies, and now her tiara is askew and her sash is crooked. "Scoot over," she orders the tweens. They oblige without protest. After all, she's the queen.

"Your dress . . . ?" I say as she plops down beside me. The skirt puffs up around her, making her look as if she's rising from a lavender-gray-blue cloud.

"They make a new one every year," she reminds me. "One of the perks of being queen." She lifts, then drops, a fistful of chiffon. "I get to keep this monstrosity."

"Everyone get their blue ribbons?" I ask. One of the duties of the Lupine Queen is to dole out prizes for the various competitions just before the dance.

Cynthia nods. "Lorraine Bartley won for her painting of lobster traps."

I gasp in mock horror. "You mean Candy Cane wasn't a prize-winner?" The lighthouse is always a favorite subject.

"I know. Shocking."

I wiggle my toes, trying to ease the ache in my feet—and warm them up. It's still pretty early to be walking around at night in sandals, and I don't usually wear such high heels.

Our preparations were in vain. The high heels and my favorite red sundress with the scalloped hem and seams that give my somewhat boyish figure a bit more curve. Cynthia loaned me her short fake-leather jacket that hits my waist at just the right spot. She helped me with my makeup, and we even practiced possible opening lines. You know, to break the ice and start a conversation. All for nothing, because the mysterious stranger remains a mystery. He never showed up.

"I just don't get it," I say. "Why didn't he come?"

Cynthia tosses a pebble into the water. *Plink.* "I guess he was a day-tripper after all."

"Then why would he be with Freaky Framingham?"

"Good point."

I turn to face her. "He wanted to avoid me."

Cynthia twists her face into her "you're being ridiculous" expression. I know it well. "Why would he want to avoid you? He doesn't even know you. And that smile definitely implied he'd actually *want* to get to know you."

I kick my feet together lightly, still trying to warm them. "Maybe he really *is* an alien," I muse. "And aliens have been experimenting on Freaky all these years."

"That could explain why Freaky is so freaky," Cynthia says.

"Now the alien sent here disguised as a surfer has beamed them both up to the mother ship. Only an alien would dress like that in June in Maine."

Cynthia nods. "Someone got their intel on infiltrating humans wrong."

"Or," I continue, the tale spinning taking my mind off my cold, aching feet and my disappointment, "maybe Freaky Framingham used his terrible powers to turn Surfer Boy into a lobster." Ol' Freaky being an evil sorcerer is a pretty common Halloween story. "Then he chopped him up and served him in one of the lobster rolls."

Cynthia smacks my arm. "That's just gross."

I giggle. "But you have to admit, it's kind of so bad it's good."

"I like the alien theory better," Cynthia says. "Add it to the archive."

The "archive" isn't really an archive, or any actual place. It's just what Cynthia says after I spin a particularly good story.

Cynthia yawns. "I am so beat. Being a queen really takes it out of you. How do the royals do it?"

"They have things like household staffs," I say.

"Oh yeah. Forgot."

"And," I add, stretching, standing, and then holding my hand out to help Cynthia up, "they don't have to worry about getting in the middle of a knock-down-drag-out over at the pie contest."

Cynthia stands clumsily, nearly tipping over into the water when her foot catches on her hem. I right her, and we step carefully away from the edge. "No lie. Mr. Carruthers and Ms. Lynch glared so hard at each other I thought their eyes would fall out of their heads."

The rivalry between Mr. Carruthers and Ms. Lynch over their blueberry baked goods is legendary.

"That's a definite plus to queendom," Cynthia says as we make our way along the periphery of the dwindling dancers. "I get to sample the contenders."

In spite of myself, my eyes still scan for the mysterious stranger. By the time we reach the end of the pier, I have resigned myself to having tortured my toes for no good reason. A wave of sadness washes over me.

Snap out of it, I order myself. This is ridiculous. I'm feeling all this disappointment over a boy I had never seen before and will probably never see again.

*P*ostcard rack? Filled. Brochures about joining the historical society? Neatly displayed beside the cashbox. Xeroxed copies of *The Lighthouses of Maine* map stacked on the table by the front entrance? Done! The oversize lighthouse bank with the neatly lettered sign DONATIONS WELCOME! not very subtly placed? Yep. I've been at my post at the lighthouse for a whole ten minutes, and I'm already bored. How am I going to get through the next six hours? How am I going to get through the next two and a half months?

Cynthia headed off to camp yesterday morning full of anticipation, and all I have to look forward to is imprisonment in Candy Cane. *She'll be back in August*, I reminded myself when I arrived and yanked open the heavy wooden door, years of humidity making it stick.

I survey my domain. In the dark entryway there's a wooden bench, an umbrella stand, and some pegs on the wall. Visitors rarely hang up their coats, but the pegs are used to hang stray scarves, hats, and gloves they sometimes leave behind.

The reception lobby is in the attachment that connects the keeper's house to the lighthouse. Originally the keeper had to leave the house in freezing rains and gale-force winds to tend to the lighthouse, sounding the foghorn, keeping the lanterns lit. So sometime in the 1870s, after enough complaining, the attachment was built so that he could be protected from the weather and still get the job done. Thanks to the distance to the tower from the house, the room is pretty big. There's even a second floor that once housed sailors who'd been rescued, reached by a rickety, narrow staircase in the alcove behind my desk. Now it houses exhibits.

The lobby holds long glass display cases, the reception desk (really just an old table), and the souvenirs I'm supposed to sell. On one side is a door to the original keeper's house, where the café and the gift shop are, and another upstairs exhibition room, though that's closed this summer. On the other side is the entrance to the lighthouse tower. People can climb the three-story circular stone stairs to the top. The actual light was removed when Candy Cane was decommissioned, so there's room up there for three people. It's the spot where people love to take photos. It has an amazing view of the harbor, the bay, and on clear days, the ocean.

I amuse myself briefly by skimming the totally lame jokes in the very slim paperback *Wit and Wisdom from Down East*, then rearrange the souvenir T-shirts. That doesn't take up more than a minute, since we only sell three styles: one with a lobster on it, one with a lighthouse (not Candy Cane), and one with the word "Maine" on the front. On the back it says "Vacationland," something that can be found on a lot of Maine license plates. The *real* gift shop is in the café. Mom had the idea to sell a few things here just in case a visitor doesn't bother going into the café. Since it only takes me one minute to switch the T-shirt order, I switch them back again.

In desperation I start reading the captions of the photos displayed on one of the walls.

"Huh," I grunt. I never knew that the second Candy Cane lighthouse keeper was the son of the first.

I hear the door open behind me. *Unbelievable!* Mom's checking up on me already! I knew she'd never be able to resist "stopping by" on some pretext.

"I'm totally fine," I snap as I whirl around.

Only I'm not anymore.

"Whoa," Surfer Boy says, a startled expression on his face. "No one said you weren't."

I blush all the way from my multihued toenails (leftover from the sleepover with Cynthia) to the crooked part in my hair. If it could, I think my loose braid would go from dark brown to bright red with embarrassment.

"I—I'm so sorry," I sputter, my hand rising involuntarily to fluff my bangs. "I—I thought you were someone else."

"Ooo-kay," Surfer Boy says. Now he goes from startled to

puzzled. He's staring at me like he's trying to place me. Either that or he's deciding whether or not he should just back away slowly and run away.

Or maybe I have something on my face. My hand once again moves on its own, this time to my mouth for a quick subtle swipe. I give it a furtive glance. No crumbs, no stains. I run my tongue quickly across my teeth, feel nothing sticking, and lick my lips. Determining that I'm bloob free, I smile. Big. I need to make up for my rudeness. Hopefully he doesn't think I'm a hostile psycho.

Then I remember: He has been seen in the company of Freaky Framingham. Compared with that curmudgeon, my greeting was as warm as could be.

My smile must have triggered something, because instead of making a quick escape, he smiles back. "You were at the Lupine Festival yesterday."

Ohmigod, ohmigod, ohmigod. He really *did* notice me. It wasn't just my imagination. I finger the tags dangling from the T-shirts on the rack beside me. The plastic hangers make little clicky noises as they bang lightly against each other. "Yeah. Were you?"

Inwardly I wince. Why am I acting as if I wasn't mesmerized by those exact blue eyes? I don't have to admit to the mesmerized part, but I can at least acknowledge I saw him, too!

If he was insulted by my super-cool response, he doesn't show it. He nods and grins. "Great intro to Rocky Point."

My heart speeds up. This is the perfect opening to grill him for information. Why oh why isn't Cynthia here with me?

"You visiting?" Am I only able to speak in two-word sentences?

"Got here a few days ago," he says, finally taking his first real steps into the reception area. He perches casually against a long display case holding odds and ends that were found in the keeper's house during the renovation, things the original keepers had left behind. He crosses one foot over the other at the ankle, and leans on his elbow. I know I'm supposed to tell him not to put weight on the display case, but he looks too cute like that.

"From where?" I ask. Okay. Two-word sentences will have to do for now.

"California."

"Ah." *Seriously, Mandy?* my inner voice shrieks. Now I'm down to syllables.

California explains the tan, the board shorts, and the sandals. I notice today he's far more suitably dressed for early summer in Rocky Point. Dark jeans, flannel over a tee, and sneakers complete with socks.

"So, are you open?" He gazes around at the displays.

"Yes! We are. I mean, I am." *Get a grip!* "That is, yes, Candy Ca— The lighthouse exhibit is open."

He nods and straightens up.

"Here for the summer?" I blurt. "I mean, that would be kind of a long trip for just a few days."

He ambles to my little desk where I sell the tickets. "Yeah," he says, fishing out his wallet. "My mom and me—we're here visiting her dad. I haven't seen him since I was really little and he was out in California."

I take his twenty, give him his change, and try to think of a way to keep this conversation going. Happily, he does that for me.

"Maybe you know him," he says, slipping the wallet back into his pocket. "John Framingham? His house is a bit out of town, back by the . . ."

I never hear the rest of the sentence because my mind is spinning. Freaky Framingham is related to this totally gorgeous, totally normal-seeming hunk of cuteness? His *grandfather*? How is that even possible? That implies a Mrs. Freaky and that they had daughter Freaky who had this very nonfreaky son!

My fingers itch to grab my phone and text Cynthia. But I don't. Mom lectured me on giving the right impression since I'm representing the historical society (and—though she didn't say this—her). Being on my cell isn't proper greeter behavior.

He's looking at me expectantly, and I realize that he has given me information in the form of a question. Which I should answer. "Of course I know him. Everybody in Rocky Point does." I manage to stop myself from saying "he's the town weirdo." I very cleverly finish up with "He's lived here, like, forever."

"Not exactly forever," says Surfer Boy aka Cutest Boy I've Ever Seen aka Freaky Framingham's Freaking *Grandson*. "But close. I'm Oliver, by the way."

That might be the most adorable boy name I've ever heard. I don't know anyone named Oliver. It sounds quirky and old-fashioned and sort of hipster all at once. Special. Not like my name.

"Mandy," I say, wishing it was something more unique. Less bland. It's not even short for anything. Not Amanda. Not Miranda. Not Mandolin or Mandible. Not that I'd rather be named for an instrument or a jawbone.

"So, Mandy," Oliver says, "do you have to stay here at the desk, or can you take me on a tour?"

Suddenly I wish I'd read the mountain of info Mom piled on me about Candy Cane's history. But I'm not going to let a little lack of knowledge force me to pass up this opportunity.

I'm not actually supposed to leave my desk, but it's not like I'm expecting a truckload of tourists to arrive. That never happens, and even if it does, it won't be until after the Fourth of July weekend.

I give him a big smile, and just as I'm coming out from around the desk, I can see that someone's struggling to get the door open. *Really? Now?* I stare at the door, willing the person to give up, to assume that we're not open, anything to get them to go away.

No such luck.

The door gives suddenly, and a tubby man stumbles in, his hand still gripping the knob. "Whoa," he says, righting himself. He straightens his rain slicker. He's dressed as if he's well acquainted with Maine. "That door puts up quite a fight, doesn't it?" he says with a smile.

"Um, yeah," I say. I glance at Oliver. He slips his hands into his pockets and peers at the photos above the display case. *Maybe I can take care of this guy quickly, and then give Oliver a tour,* I think.

"Just one?" I ask cheerfully, already picking up the ticket book.

"Just a second," the man says. He steps back out, carefully propping the door open with his foot, and hollers, "They're open! Come on!"

I watch in dismay as a passel of people pour into the lobby.

There isn't parking at the lighthouse, so I had no warning that three SUVs just unloaded three blocks away in the public lot. There are fifteen in all: two sets of parents, three random adults, and eight kids ranging from toddlers to teens.

By the time I sell them their tickets, answer multiple questions, and field various requests for bathrooms, drinks of water, and suggestions for other nearby attractions, Oliver has vanished. Who could blame him? I wish I could have disappeared too—though preferably with him. Did he go upstairs to the second-floor display area? Into the lighthouse?

More important—will I get a chance to talk to him before he leaves?

He's here all summer! The idea blasts through my bad mood like it's the Eagle Island foghorn.

The family group splits up, some going into the Keeper's Café, others checking out the lighthouse. They seem in constant motion, and the various side doors keep banging open and shut. I finally remember to slide the stopper under the front door to hold it open so that visitors won't have to struggle with it, and—my mom's big fear—assume we're closed.

After the noisy family finally departs, and I write down their purchases in the ledger book (one lighthouse magnet, one lobster-shaped teething ring for a baby), I pull my cell out of my bag. I figure if I hold it in my lap and someone walks in, no one will notice that I'm texting.

Freakiness with Freaky just got freakier!

I wait for Cynthia to respond. I know that once she's actually at camp she probably won't be able to text very much, but right now she's still at her grandparents' place in Vermont. It doesn't take long.

Tell tell tell!!!!!!!

How can I boil it all down into texts? How adorable he looked leaning against the display case, all casual and comfy as if he's been here a million times before. That when he paid for his ticket, I got a whiff of salt air and sunblock, and even though that's how everyone smells in Rocky Point, there was something different about his scent, as if the California air still clung to his clothes. That his smile revealed one front tooth an infinitesimal smidge shorter than the other. That his hand, when he took the ticket from me, has a faded scar on the back of it.

Wow. I had no idea I noticed so much about him.

I decide to stick with the headline:

He's Freaky's grandson.

And then follow that doozy with the really big news: He's here all summer!!!!

Barely a second passes:

OMG!

Then:

OMG SQUARED!!!!

As I'm trying to figure out what to text next, she writes back: How did you find out?

Me: He came to check out Candy Cane.

Cynthia: I guess you're not so mad about that gig anymore!

Me: No lie!

I don't get to read the next text because Mrs. Gallagher

comes in. I'm glad I kept the phone under the table. "Hi, Mrs. Gallagher," I say, quickly hitting vibrate so that the phone won't ring or beep. "What can I do for you?"

"Do you think it would be all right if I leave flyers about the Fourth of July events here?" she asks, holding up a sheaf of bright red paper. Mrs. Gallagher runs the community center and is always looking for a way to spread the word about the summer festivities.

"Oh, sure," I say, then frown. It's not like there's much counter space. "Leave them with me, and I'll find a spot where they can go."

She smiles indulgently at me, that look adults get when they're about to make some pronouncement about you. "You're all grown up. With a job and everything."

I'm not sure this qualifies as a job, and don't know what she means by "and everything," but I just smile as I'm expected to and say, "Yup. Looks that way."

"Well, I don't want to keep you from your work."

We both look around the empty lobby. Mrs. Gallagher smiles again and says in her always-chipper voice, "Hope you'll enter the boat parade this year. Toodles!"

Once she leaves, I riffle the stack of papers, scanning for a spot to put them. I finally just shove them under the cashbox. At least they won't blow away if a gust comes through the open doorway.

I slip one out and look at it. I've always kind of wanted to enter a boat in the Fourth of July boat parade. It's not anything fancy: homemade floats on any nonmotorized boat—rafts, canoes, kayaks, dinghies. Some are as simple as a rowboat strung with Christmas tree lights along the gunnels with costumed kids rowing. Others are far more elaborate, their builders hoping to win one of the prizes.

I slip the flyer back under the cashbox and allow myself to indulge in some serious crushing. "Oliver," I murmur dreamily. I picture us in a cute montage doing all those things summer sweethearts supposedly do: taking romantic walks on moonlit beaches, sharing a lemonade with two straws, riding together on a single carousel horse . . .

Carousel horse? I snort. Where did *that* image come from?

I stand and pace the lobby. My only ideas about romance come from books and movies. I have nothing to draw on but my twisted (Cynthia's word) imagination.

Creaking overhead alerts me to the presence of a visitor upstairs. Then footsteps. I stare up at the ceiling. Those are definitely footsteps up there.

I swallow and tell myself it must be a straggler from the massive family that just left. But I could have sworn I counted fifteen enter and fifteen leave.

Then who . . . ?

I lower myself into my seat, thinking about the ghost of Anna Christine, the sad widow of the lighthouse keeper who was swept away in a storm. She was said to still haunt the lighthouse, waiting for her true love to return. On Halloween there are always a few people dressed as poor Anna Christine.

I grip the edge of the table, ears perked, ready for the piercing wail or deep moan, or whatever goose-bump-raising sound ghosts make.

"Are you open every day?"

I nearly fall off my chair when Oliver comes around the desk. "You've been here this whole time?" I ask.

He smiles sheepishly and shoves his hands into his jacket pockets. "I—I know. I—I'm impossible."

Impossibly adorable.

"Wh-what do you mean?" Are we both actually *stammering*? Is that cute to the nth degree, or are we both so uncomfortable with each other that we can barely get the words out?

He hunches his shoulders in an apologetic shrug. "I drive my friends nuts. That is, the ones willing to go to museums with me. I read every single label, look at every single object. Often more than once."

"That's why you were here for so long," I say. "You're a 'completist.'"

He looks baffled, so I quickly explain. "It's someone who has to own, say, every issue of a particular comic. Or is compelled to absolute thoroughness in a museum. It's what my brother Justin calls our cousin Randy. A completist."

One eyebrow rises. "Oh yeah?"

I grin. "Don't worry. I think there's a twelve-step program for it."

He smirks. "Oh, I don't know. If being a 'completist' is wrong . . ."

"You don't want to be right." I finish the song lyric. Our parents must play the same dorky music.

We smile at each other, and I desperately try to think of something clever to say, something to keep the conversation going, some way to get him to ask me out, to stick around, anything—but my mind is a total blank.

"So, uh . . . ," he begins, but before he can get the sentence out, I see someone in the entrance and abruptly stand. Startled by my sudden movement, Oliver takes a step back.

She's backlit by the bright noonday light, but even without actually being able to see her face, I know exactly who it is. "Mom!"

She steps out of the shadowy entryway. Her eyes flick to Oliver and hold for a moment, and then back to me. "How is everything going?"

"Fine. Great. Splendid." *Splendid?*

She looks at me for a moment then turns to Oliver. "Is this your first visit to the Rocky Point Lighthouse?" she asks.

I can tell her wheels are turning. She's trying to decipher exactly what's going on. Is this boy a distraction? A paying customer? My secret lover?

Ha! I actually snort out loud at that one. Her head swivels back to face me. I look down at the desk and rearrange the souvenir pens and pencils in their holder.

"It's my first visit to Rocky Point, period," Oliver says. "It's very cool." He looks around the lobby. "And this place . . ."

His whole face lights up, as if the photos on the walls, the objects in the display cases, the cheesy gift shop items, fill him with a kind of joy. I watch, fascinated. What does the world look like from inside his bright blue eyes? "Well, it's just great."

My mom smiles, and the lines on her face seem to vanish. *Make Mom's day*, I think. She's looking at him as if she just discovered a long-lost best friend.

"You think so?" She gazes around the lobby fondly. "It certainly holds a special spot in my heart. I'm always glad when someone else sees how special this place is."

I roll my eyes and sit back down. I really hope she isn't going to launch into how much she loves Candy Cane.

"See, Mandy?" she says to me. "This young man doesn't think Rocky Point is boring."

Oliver looks at me, surprised.

"I don't think the lighthouse is boring," I say defensively.

Now Mom looks at me with the same surprised expression as Oliver. "This very morning you said—"

"Isn't the library open?" I ask, cutting her off.

"I thought I'd take my daughter to lunch on her first day on the job."

Oliver takes this as his cue. "Well, I'll see you," he says.

"Wait," I blurt. He and Mom both look at me. *Now what?*

I grab one of the flyers and hold it out to him. "Um . . . you should check this out."

He takes the flyer, smiles, then lopes out of the lobby, tripping a bit on the way out the door. He glances back at us, his cheeks tinged slightly pink. I smile, he shrugs, then he's gone.

"I love it when younger people take an interest in the history here," Mom says.

I rummage in my bag to make sure I have the lighthouse key, then knock the wedge out from under the door and hold it open for Mom. "Yes, I know."

I grab the GONE FISHIN' sign that hangs on the inside doorknob and slip it onto the outside knob.

"Is he a day-tripper?" she asks as I make sure the door is locked.

"No, he's here for the summer."

"Really? Where's he staying?"

I shrug. For some reason I don't want to let on that he's Freaky Framingham's grandson. She'll probably assume he's just as weird as his grandfather, despite their shared love of Candy Cane. "We didn't really get much of a chance to talk." That's certainly true.

Mom leads the way up the path. We've never gone out to lunch together before, not on our own. It suddenly seems weird.

I don't think something bad has happened. When Mom has to break bad news, her eyes and mouth don't match. She smiles a toothy, tense grimace as if she's trying to project "everything will be okay" no matter what she's about to say. But her eyes won't match her lips—they're shadowed, holding a sadness or worry in them. When she told us about Dad's heart attack, even back then, I had already learned to recognize this contradiction on her face. That day, the disparity was sharp, her smile bright but brittle, and her eyes sunk into her face as if they were in retreat. Justin and I perched on the battered vinyl sofa swing on the screened-in porch, and I knew I didn't want to hear whatever she was about to say. Knew with such certainty that I covered my ears before she spoke.

I sneak a peek at her as we walk the three blocks to where she parked the car. Mom isn't exactly a chatterer so we walk along in silence, accompanied by the familiar sounds of our crunching, shuffling footsteps, the *whump, fwump* of seagull wings, and the soft slap of water against the moss-covered boulders. As far as I can tell, Mom's face forms a coherent whole. Her eyes seem kind of tired, and her mouth has a downward slant, but that's been her usual expression for a while now.

We slide into the car, the seats warm from the sun, and buckle up. Her hands on the wheel, she says, "Tiny's?"

I shrug. "Sure."

Tiny's actually *is* tiny. The owner took the space in the alley between the Laundromat and the hardware store on Main Street and created a thriving take-out place. In deference to the local economy there's always one seafood item on the menu, but otherwise it's vegetarian and vegan. More Summer Regulars seem to frequent it than us locals, though it's often quite busy right after New Year's when people making vows to eat more healthily suddenly remember it's there.

By the time we've gotten our salads (lobster for Mom, of course, greens with feta cheese and watermelon for me) and snagged one of the benches lining the town square, the fog has burned away. It's not hot, the watermelon is weirdly delicious in the salad, and Oliver is going to be here all summer. Things are looking up—I even forgive Mom for interrupting my first conversation with him.

Until . . .

"I know you're disappointed that both Justin and Cynthia are gone most of the summer. But perhaps without the usual distractions, we can spend some time thinking about your junior year."

"Seriously, Mom?" I put the plastic fork back into the take-out container. "Summer vacation just started. You really want to talk about school?"

"Next year is crucial for your college applications," Mom says. "Your grades improved this past year, but . . ."

I sigh, long and loud. "I know. I'm not perfect like Justin."

"Now, Mandy," Mom says, "I'm not comparing you two."

"Of course you are. Just like all my teachers who say '*You're* Justin Sullivan's sister?' as if they can't believe Mr. Straight As could be related to the B Queen."

"I'm sure you're exaggerating. And you got several B-pluses this year."

Here's my thing with school. If it's about concepts, I've got it nailed. So I'm good in English, and even things like social studies. But when it's about stuff that has to be memorized and super detailed, not so much.

Before he died, Dad was the one who used to help me with my homework. The strongest impression that stays with me is how patient he was. Both Mom and Justin would try to help me later, but Justin would get bored (who can blame him?), and Mom just got frustrated.

"Okay, Frowny-face," she says in her teasing tone. It's what she's called me since I was a little girl and would pout. "I get it. It's a bit early to start in on school." She pats my hand. "And you're showing real maturity and responsibility taking on the greeter job at Candy Cane."

Wow. A compliment. I give her a small smile as we pack up our trash and toss it into a nearby receptacle.

After parking in the lot, Mom walks me back to Candy Cane, and as I struggle to get the heavy door to unstick, I hear her sigh behind me. "Another thing to fix," she mutters. The door suddenly gives and I stumble inside. I slip the wedge into place to hold it open, then turn to say bye. She smiles that oh-so-bright smile and says cheerfully, "Just add it to the list."

What's this about? I wonder. Her worried eyes don't match the chirpy tone. *Something* is *wrong*. "Um . . . ," I begin.

She turns slightly so that the breeze off the water stops blowing her hair into her face. She smooths it down with one hand and jiggles the car keys with the other. "I'd better run," she says. "Caroline is alone with the new volunteers, and sometimes having the help isn't any help at all."

"Thanks for lunch," I call after her. She waves without turning around, and I watch her slim back as she heads toward the car. As I take my seat behind the desk, I wonder what she's worried about, then remember that she basically worries about everything. It probably isn't anything specific, just her general "I'm a mom and so I worry" thing.

Other than a completely imaginary return visit from Oliver, no one comes to the lighthouse for the rest of the day. Cynthia must have been somewhere with her family in a cell-phone-free location, because I texted her a few times and never heard back. I played a few games on my phone, one eye to the door at all (okay, most) times in case Mom came back or someone did wander in. I stuck my head out the door to remind myself that the town actually still exists, restraightened every single flyer and brochure, and finally, finally, finally it's four o'clock and I can go home. And look forward to another dull and endless day tomorrow.

The lobster boats are back where they belong in the harbor, the catch unloaded long ago and already being delivered to restaurants or sold to walk-ups right at the dock. People really go gaga for that—fresh off the boat, right out of the trap. Me, I have to look in the other direction. The squirmy, crawling creatures give me the jeebies.

I dismount at the steepest part of Weatherby Hill and push my bike to the top. This isn't going to be big fun come late July and August when the sun beats down and the humidity skyrockets. Hopefully, though, the daily bike ride will get me into better shape. I'm not exactly the most athletically inclined person. I'm more of a couch-inclined person, something Justin and Cynthia rag on me about, sometimes simultaneously.

I'll show them, I think with a grin. I hop back on the bike and pedal hard for about two blocks, and then decide it's just too much work. This is vacation, right?

After dinner I call Cynthia. With all we have to discuss, texting just won't do.

"Don't leave out a single anything," Cynthia says. "How did you find out about the freaky Freaky connection?"

I tell her everything—about Oliver's arrival, how cute he looked, how we were bonding, and how Mom might have ruined it all by almost revealing my lack of interest in Candy Cane, which he seems to love as much as she does.

I flip over onto my back with an awful thought. "He might not come back to the lighthouse. I mean, he already spent all morning looking at what takes most people fifteen minutes. Twenty, tops."

"Because he likes you and wanted to hang around," Cynthia insists.

Sadly, I have to tell the truth. "Not exactly. He spent all the time upstairs looking at those exhibits. I didn't even know he was up there."

"Huh." Now I can picture Cynthia's "working on it" expression. The face she makes when her brain is trying to come up with a solution, a plan, or an explanation for something. "Well, maybe now that he knows you work there, he'll come back!"

"Maybe . . ."

"Come on, Mandy! The way he looked at you at the festival! That was the face of a boy who seriously liked what he saw. It was as if I wasn't even there at all."

I sit straight up at that. She's right! Cynthia was standing right next to me, and *I* was the one he smiled at, who he remembered. A giant grin spreads over my face.

"What is with me?" I moan. "All day I've been mood swinging. Elated. Miserable. Happy. Sad. Panicked. Calm. What is up with that?"

"Hormones," Cynthia says, perfectly imitating her mom. That's what her mother says to explain the inexplicable things Cynthia or her sisters do. Part resignation, part exasperation. Turns out it's a pretty convenient excuse. Cynthia started using it herself to get out of trouble, particularly with her dad, who turns seven shades of pink at the mere mention of hormones. It's become our favorite catchphrase to explain the unexplainable— everything from a teacher suddenly getting strict to extreme shifts in the weather.

"Hormones," I agree, giving the word the same treatment. This sets us both laughing hysterically.

Over my cackling I can hear Mom calling up the stairs. "Hang on," I tell Cynthia. I open my door and pop out my head. "Yeah?"

"Shouldn't you be getting ready for bed?" Mom says from the foot of the staircase. "It's another workday tomorrow."

"Gotta go," I say into the phone.

"Keep me posted," Cynthia says.

I nod at Mom and return to the privacy of my bedroom. "As if I wasn't going to send you hourly bulletins if I ever see him again."

"You will."

That's the thing about Cynthia. Her confidence is contagious. At least for a little while. Long enough for me to go to sleep excited about tomorrow.

As I coast down Weatherby for my second day of Candy Cane duty, the breeze coming off the water blows strands of hair into my face. They keep sticking to my lip gloss, but I'm in such a good mood I don't care. I simply flick them away each time it happens. I just hope I'm not wiping off the Blushing Rose gloss each time I do. I forgot to toss it into my bag, since I don't usually travel with makeup, much to Cynthia's constant annoyance. At least the shadow, mascara, and shimmer face powder won't wear off. I'm not so certain about the shimmer. It might be a little much for sitting in a lighthouse all day, but I can always wash it off once I get there.

Even though I know it's unlikely that Oliver will come back, I took care not just with my face but with the rest of me too. The jeans that fit great and a cute top Cynthia picked out for me last month to "enhance my assets." Not exactly sure what assets those might be, but whatever. If Oliver really is a "completist," then he might come back today to make sure he didn't miss anything.

I hope!

I open up, humming a sea chantey that had been blasting from the open doors of Ahoy, a swimwear shop on Main Street. Once the season really gets under way, Rocky Point goes overdrive on the fishy and Maine Americana. It's as if summers send Rocky Point back in time, and that's the way the Regulars like it. They seem to come here to get back to the "good old days," but truth to tell, I don't see what's so great about them. How people lived here in the winters before good heating, television, and cars is beyond me.

Today as I look around Candy Cane, I try to understand what Oliver finds so appealing. Is he a history buff? Into lighthouses, specifically? Drawn to all things sea-related? I've met all of those types of visitors, and I guess I'm even related to one, since Mom loves all that stuff. I can't remember if Dad did too, but since all my memories are of them happily together in never-ending conversations, I guess he did.

By noon there have been no visitors, and my stomach is growling. I poke my head out of the lighthouse door. No one. Not Oliver, not a tour bus, not even Mom to take me to another lunch.

That's probably a good sign, I tell myself. It means she doesn't feel the need to check up on me. But it also means that I'll have to settle for whatever's on the menu at the Keeper's Café. Luckily, I don't have to pay for the overpriced fare since it's a "perk" of the job, but I should really start thinking about bringing lunch.

I hang the GONE FISHIN' sign on the door and lock it. Then I walk around to the main entrance of the café, the one you can enter without having to go into the lighthouse.

The café is supercute, with lots of Maine-related decor and old photos, but the menu's limited to what can be prepared on a hotplate or in a microwave. The idea had been that the café would offset some of the costs involved in maintaining the lighthouse, but I don't see how that's possible. No year-rounder or even Summer Regular eats there since the menu is so limited and, frankly, pretty bad. And tourists to Rocky Point are only a trickle, not a deluge.

I've only taken a few steps inside when I realize there's someone sitting at the counter, talking to Celeste Ingram.

Not just someone. Oliver.

I spaz out. I freeze, and the screen door bangs me in the butt, making me yelp and drop the magazine I'm carrying. My scrunchy bag slides down my arm and lands on the floor with a *thwump*. All this commotion makes Celeste look up and Oliver swivel on his stool at the counter.

Invisibility spell now! I plead silently.

"Mandy, hi," Oliver says, a smile lighting up his face.

I give him a weak smile and an even weaker wave. *A wave? I'm waving at a boy just a few feet away?* Oliver seems to bring out the utter dork in me.

"Hey there, Mandy," Celeste says. "You meeting Cynthia for lunch?"

This is even more shocking than seeing Oliver a second day in a row. Celeste Ingram not only knows my name, but she also knows I'm best friends with Cynthia? Not possible! Then I realize that it's more likely she knows who Cynthia is and recognizes me as the sidekick.

They're both looking at me, waiting. Right. Words. They're those things that come out of your mouth. "Actually, Cynthia's away till August," I say, taking a few tentative steps into the café.

"Working today?" Oliver asks.

I nod and keep approaching the counter. Slowly. They don't seem mad about my being there, but I still have the awful fear that I interrupted something. Once a boy has Celeste's attention, his own stays pretty riveted on her.

"Lunch break, huh?" Celeste picks up a menu and drops it onto the counter right beside Oliver. Not that I need the single laminated page. Still, I take this as a sign that she completely expects me to sit there.

I like that assumption.

"You two have met?" Celeste asks.

I slide onto the stool and pretend to study the menu waiting to hear what Oliver will say about our encounter.

"I was in the lighthouse yesterday," he explains.

The bare facts. Oh well. I suppose he doesn't want to admit to the celestial Celeste that we shared some serious eye beams at the festival, too.

"Can I have a veggie burrito?" I ask. "And a lemonade."

"Sure."

Celeste picks up the menu, slips it back beside the cash register with the others, then pushes through the swinging doors into the small kitchen.

Alone with Oliver, I'm stumped for things to say. He seems equally stymied. He just smiles at me. There's no plate in front of him. Did Celeste already clear it away, or did he come here just to see her? The Keeper's Café opens at eleven. Has he been here a whole hour already? Even a completist would have completed checking out the café decor and gift shop by now, since the upstairs exhibit area is closed.

"Here ya go." Celeste returns with the burrito and lemonade. Microwaving doesn't take much time.

I feel Oliver looking at me. I turn to face him as if I'm capable of conversation. "Why are you eating *here?*" I blurt.

Celeste looks at me in surprise. My mom would be so pissed if she heard me bad-mouthing the café to a potential customer. "I mean, it's kind of far for you," I add lamely.

Celeste has a new kind of surprise on her face. This isn't an "I can't believe you just said that" expression. This is a "you already know his deets?" face.

I busy myself trying to figure out the best way to eat the soggy burrito. It may be free for me to eat here, but I am *so* going to start bringing my own lunch.

"I was checking out the grounds," Oliver explains. "When Celeste opened up, I realized it had been a long time since breakfast."

Of course. He took one look at Celeste and followed her inside like a baby duckling after its mama.

A woman with steel-gray hair cut in a short bob pops her head into the café. "Do you know when the lighthouse opens up again?" she asks.

I turn around, still chewing the big bite I took of the burrito, and say, "I can open up if you want."

"Oh, I wouldn't want to interrupt your lunch," she says, but her tone broadcasts she really wishes I'd hurry up already and let her in.

I take a swig of the lemonade and stand. I hastily wipe my mouth with a napkin, wad it up, and toss it onto the plate.

"Thanks," I say to Celeste. I pick up the lemonade. "I'll bring the glass back later."

"Sure. You want me to wrap up the burrito?"

"No thanks."

I start walking toward the woman, who stands half in, half out of the café doorway.

"Hang on, Mandy," Oliver says behind me. "I'll come too."

I spin around in disbelief to see Oliver picking up a sketch-pad that he had stashed under the counter. He's going to leave Celeste and come hang out with me?

But once I struggle with the door and take the woman's admission fee, it becomes apparent he's not there to hang out. He's back to visit the lighthouse again. "I thought I'd do some sketching, if that's okay," he says.

"Sure. Just . . . if a group wants to go up to the tower, give them room."

I refuse his five dollars; it seems like a lot to pay since he was just here yesterday, and I'm hoping maybe it will encourage him to keep coming back.

I don't see Oliver—or anyone else—the rest of the afternoon. That's not strictly true. Oliver came down from the tower and then walked around outside, sketching Candy Cane from different angles. What's so fascinating?

When I lock up for the day, he's still outside, sitting at one of the picnic tables behind the Keeper's Café. My heart sinks. Is he waiting for Celeste? He doesn't look up when I cross to the shed to get my bike. Our great romance is over before it begins.

I slam the shed shut and yank the padlock closed. I walk my bike along the gravel path, the tires spitting up little pebbles. In case Oliver looks up, I don't want him to see me awkwardly mounting the bike. I've never quite mastered accomplishing this gracefully. I force myself not to look his way.

"Hey," I hear him call. "You done for the day?"

I glance over. He's standing now, and heading toward me.

"Yup," I say.

"Okay if I walk with you?" he asks.

There go those hormones again: from doldrums to delight. "Sure," I say.

We fall into step, me pushing the bike, him carrying his sketchpad. I'm glad he doesn't have a bike too. I don't want him watching me huff and puff up Weatherby. I'm living proof you can be slim and not exactly be fit.

"I'm meeting my mom at the library," he says. "You know where that is?"

I laugh. "I should. It's where my mother works." Good. I'm managing sentences of more than single words.

"Have you lived here your whole life?" Oliver asks.

I nod. "Have you lived in California all yours?" There. A question about him. That's what the dating guides Cynthia and I pore over say to do to keep a conversation going with a boy.

"In Cali, yeah, but not in the same place. When my parents got divorced, my dad moved to Sacramento, where he works, and Mom and I moved to the suburbs not too far away."

"Was that a big adjustment?"

The instant I ask I want to take the words back. It's such a personal question. Oliver just shrugs. "We were living in the suburbs before, we just moved closer to the city. The divorce part . . ." His voice trails off. I wait. "It was weird that it was suddenly official that dad wasn't living with us. But they had hardly spent any time together for a long time. Mom's job can take her practically around the clock, and Dad often had business trips."

"When did they split up?" It's kind of amazing that he's so open about all this. Maybe it's a California thing.

"A few years back. I think they'd been planning it for a while but wanted to wait until it was time for me to start high school. You know, because of the move."

We start the incline up Weatherby. I nod a greeting at Vicki Jensen and her dad standing outside Second Time Around. Vicki's eyes are huge, taking in the sight of me with a new boy. She makes the universal "call me" sign. I'm glad Oliver doesn't notice. He's too busy watching the ferry chugging toward Hubbard Island.

"So . . . you're visiting your grandfather." Once again I have to stop myself from calling him Freaky. "How come you've never been here before?"

"Partly the distance. And Mom gets antsy if she's too far away from civilization."

"And Rocky Point isn't exactly civilized."

He turns his head to look at me full-on. "I think it's great!" he protests. He stumbles over the curb, turns pinkish, and brings his attention forward again. "Mom, though. She grew up in Cranston and couldn't wait to get out of Maine."

Cranston is a town just a ferry ride away. Or a circuitous drive to the next-door peninsula.

"Like me and Cynthia," I say.

"Who's Cynthia?"

"My best friend. She's away for the summer. She practically has a calendar in her head where she's x-ing out the days until she gets to leave 'Rock Bottom.'"

"This place is so beautiful," Oliver argues. "It's like it says on that sign we passed on the highway." He holds up his hands as if he's creating a banner in the sky. "'Maine: The Way Life Should Be.'"

"The way it should be for a few weeks a year," I counter. "If you were here year-round you'd get insanely bored. There's a reason so many people in Stephen King's books go nuts in Maine."

"Maybe. But this is so much better than the suburbs. Except for the weather." He gives me a grin. "See, I'm not *totally* swept away by all the beauty here."

I blush. I think I know what he really means, but I can't help imagining what he means is me.

"Back home, it seems to be all stress all the time," he continues. "Mom's job is wacky big. Like, millions of bucks at stake."

"What does she do?"

"Matches investors with new tech. So she stays on top of everything that's out there, and tries to nab big money before anyone else can."

"Intense."

"No joke."

"So why now?"

"Why now what?"

"Are things less busy at her job now?"

"She doesn't actually *have* a job. She *is* the job. But, well, some stuff happened that made her want to see her old man. So here we are."

I wait, but he doesn't elaborate. It's probably too personal. I don't care what the reason is; I'm just glad that it brought Oliver here.

We reach the south end of the Square, where I make the turn onto Berry to go home. "Well," I say, "this is where I get off."

Oliver shakes his bangs out of his face, then pushes up his sunglasses. "So, see you around."

I watch him as he walks toward the library. Why doesn't he actually ask me out?

And I'm back down in the doldrums. "The doldrums" is a sailing term. It refers to a spot in the Atlantic Ocean where there can be long stretches of no wind. If you're in the doldrums, you aren't going anywhere. Which is exactly how I feel. Going nowhere.

*O*liver is waiting at Candy Cane when I arrive the next morning. That's three days in a row! No one can love a lighthouse this much! He *has* to be here to see me—or Celeste, I remind myself as a way to keep from giggling giddily. I skid to a stop, spitting gravel. I climb off the bike, vowing to practice so that I can do it with ease.

He smiles sheepishly. "I'm back."

"So I see." I smile, then stash the bike. When I turn back around, Oliver's up and waiting at the door.

"Awfully eager," I tease, jiggling the key in the lock. The tumblers turn, but the door doesn't budge. Dang! Stuck. I let out a puff of air to get my bangs out of my face and push harder.

"Let me," Oliver says.

I take a step back. "Be my guest."

Oliver rattles the doorknob, then puts his shoulder against the door. It groans, but doesn't open. Oliver steps back again. "Are you sure you unlocked it?"

"It's sticking worse than usual," I offer. I think maybe he's a little embarrassed that he tried to go all macho and failed. "The humidity."

"Must be it." Oliver runs a hand through his hair. "Okay. On the count of three?"

"Sure." I step up and stand sideways to the door, figuring we'll both have to use our shoulders. Oliver moves into place behind me.

I shut my eyes and feel his warmth against my back, and

sense his chin just above my ear. I smell that scent again, part laundry detergent, part ocean, part something unidentifiable. I grip the knob, afraid I'll lean into him instead of into the door.

"One. Two. Three. Now!" Together we shove hard against the door. It swings open and we stumble through. Oliver grabs my elbow to keep me upright, but our momentum is too much. We land on the floor in a tangled clump.

We're laughing so hard, we just lie there, my arm trapped under his chest, his leg across my hip. Once we catch our breath, we quickly scramble back up to standing, straightening our clothing and not looking at each other. I think we both sensed the moment had gone on a tad too long.

To recover completely, I lean against a display case and cross my arms. "Okay. What is it about the lighthouse you love so much?" I'm genuinely curious, and there's more than a teeny-tiny part of me that hopes he'll say something like "it's not the lighthouse, it's the lighthouse keeper." Mushy I know, but I figure it would sound a lot better coming out of his mouth than rattling around in my brain.

Oliver looks around the lobby, his eyes dancing from one photo to another. "I don't really know," he says.

Not the answer I was hoping for.

"When I was really little, we lived near the water," he goes on. "I don't really remember it, but there are pictures of me dressed as a pirate. Maybe that's when the whole seafaring fixation started."

I smile, picturing him as a little pirate boy. "And continues," I say, remembering the way he studied the model boats in the Artists and Artisans tent at the festival. Now that I know he's a completist, his behavior that day makes more sense.

"You must know a lot of great stories about this place," Oliver continues.

I shrug. "Some, I guess." My mind spins as I try to recall a single bit of lore from Mom's files, but I draw a blank. I never am good under pressure. I don't know how Cynthia manages, getting up there in front of everyone when she performs.

"I love a good ghost story," Oliver admits. "Or just weird history. Lighthouses and places like Rocky Point are great sources. Not like the boring suburbs."

Those things I'm actually into. It just never occurred to me before that maybe Candy Cane qualifies. I gaze around the lobby with new interest. Maybe I'll take another look at Mom's files while Oliver is . . . My face scrunches in confusion. *While Oliver goes around measuring things?* He has pulled out a professional-looking tape measure and eyes the archway that leads to the stone stairs.

"Mind if I . . . ?" He jerks his pointy chin toward the stairs.

"Go ahead."

He smiles, and I wave away his wallet. What the heck is he doing? I can't ask, because a group of kids all wearing bright orange camp T-shirts barrels in, followed by two frazzled teen counselors (the younger sisters of a couple of boys at my school) and two even more frazzled adults. Usually the camps bring kids on rainy days, so I'm surprised to see them.

"Plumbing issue," the chunky older woman in khaki shorts and camp T-shirt explains with a sigh. "We have to find things to do with them all day while repairs are made. We missed the first ferry to Hubbard Island, so we're here until the next one."

That explains the frazzle. "Do you want me to let the café know that there's going to be a group?"

"We brought our own lunches, but thanks."

Too bad. Mom would have been thrilled to have such a crowd so early in the season. "You could always grab a cup of coffee," I suggest.

"That would be great, but these munchkins are a handful," she replies.

She's not wrong. The kids make so much racket that Oliver comes down from the tower to see what's going on. Good thing, too, since several kids make a beeline for the stairs, a teenaged counselor trotting after them. Oliver flattens himself against the wall to let them by.

"Only three fit in the tower at a time," I call after them. I catch Oliver's eye and give him a rueful smile. He gives me a "what can you do?" shrug. He mouths "Later" and leaves, nearly tripping over two kids rushing to the mini-gift-shop area. I'm disappointed but seriously, I can't blame him. It's as if Candy Cane has been invaded.

Once they leave and I've restored order to the lobby, it's time for lunch, which I forgot to pack. It's Keeper's Café again.

And once again, there's Oliver, sitting at the counter, chatting away with the intimidatingly beautiful Celeste. I try to back out before they can see me, but Celeste, perfect in all ways including as employee, looks up immediately. "Hey, Mandy."

Oliver swivels and grins. "Survived the hordes, I see."

"All in one piece. And so are the displays, thank goodness." I hover in the doorway like an idiot, again unsure if I'm interrupt-ing something.

"Meeting someone?" Celeste asks, grabbing some menus.

"Oh! Nah." She must think if I'm still standing at the door I want a booth. Oliver smiles at me, his legs stretched out, one sneakered foot over the other. That's the way he stands, too, one leg slightly over the other, ankles crossed. Must be some kind of laid-back California posture.

"Know what you want?" Celeste knows I can recite the menu as easily as she can.

The burrito was pretty close to awful, so I decide to try some-thing nonmicrowaved. "Salad?"

"Lobster, crab, chicken, or just greens?"

"Chicken, please. And a lemonade."

She slips a tall plastic glass under the lemonade dispenser, then places it next to Oliver. I guess that's where I'll be sitting.

"Oliver said you got a big crowd," Celeste says, placing the rolled-up napkin holding my silverware on the counter as I settle onto the stool. "You think they'll come over here?"

"Sorry," I tell her. "They're a camp group that brought their lunches."

She rolls her green eyes. "Of course they did. Hang on, and I'll get your salad."

"She must be as bored as me," I say as she pushes through the door into the kitchen.

"Not just bored. She's not making any tips if there aren't any customers," Oliver points out. "She's worried about school expenses."

So she spilled her woes to him. They're getting close. When he came to the lighthouse, he was so busy measuring and sketching he never really talked to me.

I slouch, letting my hair fall like a curtain, masking the sides of my face. I don't want that flashing neon sign that always reveals what I'm thinking to show Oliver my jealousy. But seriously, why *wouldn't* he be into her? And why wouldn't she be into him?

Although . . . Celeste's in college. Isn't he going into his junior year like me? The thought cheers me up enough to restore the appetite that I lost when I first walked into the café.

I hear that boy Oliver has been spending time with you," Mom says.

My fork doesn't make it to my mouth; it just hangs there, scrambled egg dangling through the tines. Once a week we have breakfast for supper, and tonight's the night.

This was Mom's late day at the library. Even though school's out, the library stays busy. Summer Regulars always run out of books to read because they forget how often it rains here. And the library has the best Wi-Fi in town, and the only truly consistent cell signal.

I shovel the scrams into my mouth, buying some time to get my various reactions under control. Shock that she knows, annoyance that everyone knows everything about everybody in this tiny town, and a teensy thrill at the idea that it's *me* people think Oliver is there to see.

"Not with *me*," I say after I swallow. "He's in love with your lighthouse."

Mom chuckles. "I guess I do kind of think of it as mine." She reaches out and pats my hand. "And now yours."

New thought: Does she know that I haven't been charging him? That would probably bug her more than the idea of Oliver trying to have his way with me up in the tower.

"If he's really interested in the history of the lighthouse, you should send him over to the library."

The historical society's office is on the top floor of the library. The building is her home away from home. I think if she didn't believe a mom has to be present with a teenage girl in the house, she'd happily move there.

"I'll mention it," I say, although I know I probably won't. If he's at the library all day, that means he won't be dropping by Candy Cane as often.

"Do you spend much time talking to him?"

I sigh. "Don't worry, Mom," I say, pouring syrup onto my bacon. "I'm greeting everyone just the way a greeter should."

My tone must irk Mom, because she bristles and says, "Good to know, but that isn't why I asked." She taps a finger on the table, the way she does when she's getting ready to head into tricky territory. "I was wondering if you know anything about him."

Uh-oh. How to play this? Is she genuinely asking me, or does she know already that Freaky is his grandfather? And if she does, would that mean she'd ban me from seeing him, if I ever get the chance? Outside of the lighthouse, that is.

"Not a lot," I say warily. "Do you?" It only just occurs to me that Mom could be a good source of intel.

She takes a sip of decaf, her concession to this breakfast being of the supper variety. "Rumors. You know how Rocky Point is."

Do I ever. "So . . . ," I say as casually as I can. "What have you heard?"

"The one thing that seemed the most unlikely turned out to be true. He's John Framingham's grandson. He's here visiting with his mother."

So she already knows.

One of her eyebrows rises. "You don't seem surprised."

"Actually, he told me. And I saw them together at the Lupine Festival."

"That's right, there *had* been a Freaky sighting."

I gape at her. She smiles. "What?" she says. "The adults find him just as odd as you kids do."

"How'd you find out?" I ask.

"Oliver's mother came into the library. She needed to use our Internet connection. I'm not surprised there isn't one up at the cottage."

"Yeah, somehow the world's crankiest recluse doesn't seem the type to use social media," I say. "So what's she like?"

"A little intense. You know, one of those high-powered types who want everything yesterday. She tried to cover it, but I could tell that our connection wasn't fast enough and that 'relax' isn't a word she's very familiar with. But pleasant enough."

Mom sneaks a piece of syrup-soaked bacon from my plate. "I wonder what it was like to have John Framingham as a father," she muses. "She mentioned she grew up in Cranston, so we may have actually been to some of the same events."

"Freaky didn't always live up on Evergreen, right?" I ask.

"He moved here just around the time you were born, I think."

"Did she say how long they're here visiting?"

"Hard to say. I think the plan is the whole summer, but I don't know how long she'll last. She seemed pretty frustrated by her cell service too. She made jokes about it, but I don't think this is actually vacation time for her."

My heart sinks. I might never get a chance to really get to know Oliver if they leave soon.

*J*ust near closing time Oliver walks into the lighthouse. He no longer bothers to attempt to pay since I always refuse to take his money (don't be mad, Mom!).

I'm doing the end-of-the-week tally: number of visitors, what items were sold, anything we need to restock. Pretty easy since it's been slow.

He holds his sketchbook in front of him, as if it's a protective shield. He looks different. Shy. Insecure. Not the look he usually wears.

"Um. . ." He tosses aside his bangs and clears his throat. He tries again. "Um, so I bet you've been wondering what I've been doing."

"Maybe a little."

He takes another step closer. What's he being so tentative about? I don't really care. It makes him look all cute and vulnerable.

He lays his sketchbook on my desk. "Take a look," he says.

I give him a quizzical glance and force myself not to rip it open. I've been dying with curiosity to see what he's been spending all that time doing.

I'm still not sure. The first page has xeroxed pictures of Candy Cane taped to it. Mystified, I turn the page. Here there's a sketch of Candy Cane with notations and conversions: *1/8" = 1 foot*, that kind of thing. My eyes flick to his face then back to the page. He did these? They're amazing.

Other pages have different views of the lighthouse along with close-up details: the portholelike windows in the tower; the different doorways, both inside and out. There's what looks like a floor plan, along with sketches of the Keeper's Café.

"These are so good," I say.

I get to the last of the impressively accurate and detailed drawings and shut the pad. I'm relieved there aren't any romantic portraits of Celeste. But I don't understand why pictures of our lighthouse make him so shy.

"I figured out the scale, then drew up what I thought would be best," Oliver says.

"Best for what?" Is he planning to build a replica of Candy Cane for his yard back home in California? That would definitely stand out in the suburbs.

"Oh, right. Like usual, I forgot the most important part. Mom says I work up to things backwards."

I still look at him uncomprehendingly. "Are you ready to start from the front?"

"Fourth of July." He taps the red flyer peeking out from

under the sketchbook. The pile is still nearly as thick as when Mrs. Gallagher dropped them off. Business hasn't exactly been booming.

I wait for him to continue, because even though he seems to think he's explained everything, I'm still completely clueless. Whatever's obvious to him isn't at all clear to me.

"The boat parade! We should make a replica of the lighthouse and enter it. Pops already said I could use one of his dinghies. Whaddya think?"

What do I think? Did I actually hear him say "we"? As in *we* should do this together. Oliver and me. Me and Oliver. Sharing a common goal. And spending loads of time together.

My fantasizing comes to an abrupt halt when I see the disappointment on Oliver's face. "Sorry," he mumbles, reaching for the sketchbook. "You gave me the flyer. I—I thought you'd be into it. I shouldn't have assumed—"

"I am! I am!" I slap my hand on top of his to keep him from picking up his pad. "I'm completely interested."

Was that too enthusiastic? I don't care. Our eyes meet, and I feel his hand under mine. I don't want to move it. I get the sense he doesn't want me to.

For one glorious moment we smile at each other, then the nerves kick in and we each back off.

"We'll need to get started right away," I tell him. "We have less than three weeks."

"I kind of already got started," he tells me. "But yeah. The pressure's on. Do you have to work here every day?"

"No," I say. "I'm here four days a week, and Janet Milner is here the other two we're open. And it stays light late, so we can still work after my shift. Right?"

"Right. When's your first day off?"

"Tomorrow," I tell him, never more happy to use that word before in my life.

*I*t's really happening," I whisper hoarsely into the phone. "Tomorrow!"

"What?" Cynthia says. "I can barely hear you. Where are you?"

I pace and glance up and down the street from the screened-in porch. I'm too antsy to sit still. I'm keeping an eye out for Mom; this is a conversation she can't overhear. Neighbors either.

I'm about to do something big—go to a boy's house, a boy I like, without telling my mom. And the reason I'm not telling my mom is the biggest part of the story: The boy's house is actually the home of Freaky Framingham.

"I'm home," I say in a more normal voice. "But this is radioactive news."

"My favorite kind!" Cynthia says. "What's going to explode?"

"Me! And"—I lower my voice again—"possibly my mom."

"Oooh." I hear rustling. I can picture Cynthia getting comfy, settling in for a long session. "Spill."

I pause and wave back at Mr. Martin, who's walking his dog, Thunder. Or more accurately, Thunder is walking *him*. Mr. Martin smiles at me and continues trotting down the street.

"Hello?" Cynthia says. "You still there?"

"Just waiting till the coast is clear."

I tell her every single word Oliver and I exchanged, because of course I have them memorized. For once, Cynthia doesn't interrupt me. "You wouldn't believe how adorably awkward and shy he was leading up to his Fourth of July proposal. I mean, proposition," I correct myself hastily. Wait, that sounds even worse. "I mean, *request* to work together," I finish lamely.

There's a brief silence, then Cynthia says, "Whoa."

"Yeah," I agree. "'Whoa' barely covers it."

"But I don't get the mom part," Cynthia says. "Why can't you tell her? I mean, just because you haven't really dated before doesn't mean—"

"You forgot the critical fact!" I squeak. My eyes dart back and forth, ensuring my solitude. I lower my voice again. "Remember who we're talking about. Who he's *related* to . . ."

I hear a sharp intake of breath. "You're right. That's practically nuclear."

"So you see why I can't tell Mom. She might not let me go. Since we have to build the boat at his house. Since that's where the boat is," I add, though I know I'm stating the super obvious. But since Cynthia forgot the Freaky part of the equation, I figure I'd better spell things out.

More silence.

"Hello?" I check the phone. Not a lot of bars, but that's standard. Certainly enough to still have a connection.

"Just thinking."

Good! I'm counting on her to come up with one of her winner schemes to keep Mom from freaking out and forbidding me from going up there.

"Maybe . . . ," she begins, and then stops.

"Yes . . . ," I prompt.

"Maybe this one time your mom's right."

I blink. Twice. That is so not what I thought she was going to say.

"I mean, who knows what kind of crazy you'll find."

"Oliver isn't crazy," I say hotly.

"That's not what I'm saying," Cynthia says. "But do you really want to be up at Freaky's Haunted House of Horrors with a boy you barely know, where there's, like, no road and no cell reception?"

"You make it sound like an episode of *Supernatural*."

"I'm just saying . . ."

"Freaky may be weird, but he's lived here all of our lives, and there's never been anything really strange happening up there—"

"That you know of . . ."

"Are you kidding me? If they found even a dead mouse on his property, the whole town would know about it."

"There's always a first—"

I cut her off. "It's really mean to call it Freaky's Haunted House of Horrors. He's a person. He has a right to live how he wants without everyone going all judgey."

Now this is weird. I'm standing up for Freaky Framingham.

"Mandy, I'm trying to look out for you. You're so nuts about this Oliver that you—"

"You know, I thought you'd be excited for me. I finally have a boy who likes me. Who I like back."

"Look, I saw him. He's supercute. But—"

I don't want her to finish that sentence. "Mom's coming up the street. Gotta go."

For the first time ever I hang up on my best friend.

As I bike up Evergreen Road toward Freaky Framingham's house, Cynthia's voice yells at me in my head. Is she right? No one knows where I'm spending the day. If I disappear, will anyone know where to look?

A twig snaps in the woods off to my right, and I nearly swerve my bike into the bushes. *Get a grip!* I order myself.

How could Cynthia do this to me? I fume. Until that awful phone call last night I was utterly delirious about today. Now I'm completely on edge: nervous about what will happen if Mom finds out; worried that Cynthia's right and that I'm making a terrible, terrible mistake; and actually scared of woods that I've known my whole life.

I had a text from Cynthia this morning—an order to text or call the minute I get home. *If I don't hear from you by 7pm I'm telling your mom.*

Unbelievable.

Though as the woods grow deeper around me, it begins to seem like a pretty good idea.

Freaky's house is on the same side of the peninsula as the harbor, but farther inland, where the woods start. There are winding roads here, so you can't see very far ahead, and it's kind of hilly. Big houses peek through breaks in the pines. Mailboxes line the road to mark where the turnoffs begin. Some mailboxes are super plain—others are pretty hokey. One has a lighthouse perched on top; another is shaped like a big clam.

As I bike up yet another hill, the trees grow more and more dense. The sun's rays hit my face through the small patches between countless trees. The summer warm-up has begun, and I know to be grateful for the shade, but it feels overly symbolic. "If this were a movie," I murmur, then force myself to shut off my overly active imagination.

I round the curve where we gather on Halloween to dare one another to knock on Freaky's door. This is my last chance to back out.

I see movement through the bushes, and I'm so startled I nearly topple off my bike. I right myself, my heart pounding. Then it pounds harder when I recognize the figure loping around the bend.

Oliver.

Over the last week I've gotten to know that loose-limbed gait, the toss of the head to get the bangs out of the way. He smiles and waves, and I pedal toward him, thankful for the dark of the woods that just one minute ago spooked me.

"I thought I'd meet you so you wouldn't get lost," he says as I dismount. "Finding the right road can be tricky. Mom missed it three times when we arrived."

"Thanks." I don't confess that I know the spot well. That pretty much every kid in Rocky Point does.

"Come on," Oliver says. "We have a lot of work to do!"

I push the bike along the rutted path, Oliver strolling on the other side of it. "Is your . . . mom around?" I had been about to ask about his grandfather but switched at the last minute.

"At the house. And Pops is in the shed. He said he'd help."

Help? I'm not sure which is more shocking, that I'm actually going to have a face-to-face encounter with Freaky—a bit like having a conversation with a yeti—or that he's actually on board to help us.

The path isn't nearly as long as it seems on Halloween. Very soon a two-story house with an attic appears through the bushes, Freaky's familiar blue pickup truck parked off to the side of the patchy lawn, a shiny silver car beside it. In daylight it's easier to see how ramshackle the house is—missing shingles on the roof, peeling paint, a sagging porch. It has the look of a place no one really cares much about. I wonder what it's like to be staying here.

"We're set up out back," Oliver says. "Let's grab some sodas first."

I nod, too nervous to speak. I brace myself for whatever I might find: shrunken heads, voodoo candles, stacks of newspapers towering to the ceiling, dust bunnies as big as a T. rex. Heck, maybe even an actual T. rex.

Oliver opens the screen door and I follow him inside, carefully arranging a smile on my face, determined to play it cool no matter what I encounter. I stop after just a few steps. It's nothing like I expected.

The spotless room is large, with just a few pieces of well-worn furniture. A sofa. A big easy chair by the front windows. I realize that this is the first time I've seen the curtains open. There's a low coffee table in front of the sofa with a coffee mug and a newspaper on it. Behind the sofa are a table holding two lamps and some books. There's a fireplace with a large stack of wood piled beside it, obviously well used, judging from how blackened the bricks in it are. Between the front windows is a large oil painting, a gorgeous rendering of what looks like a foggy Rocky Point Harbor. Maybe that's the view Freaky looks at when he keeps the curtains drawn.

Narrow stairs near the front door lead upstairs, presumably to the bedrooms. A doorway minus a door on the other side of the room reveals a sunny yellow kitchen. Not a color I would have expected from Freaky. There's a door in what looks like a newer wall, some kind of addition, that isn't visible from the front. The original house is so big I wonder why he'd need more space. Maybe that's where he keeps the bodies. . . .

Stop it! I order myself, following Oliver across the room. Still, I can't keep from peeking through the door's window into the addition. All I can glimpse are rolls of what look like canvas.

"Hey, Mom," Oliver says as we enter the kitchen. "This is Mandy."

If the front room surprises me, the kitchen shocks me. The giant old stove taking up a whole lot of space makes sense; it looks like it's been in the house since dinosaurs roamed the earth. But the super-expensive fancy-pants pots and pans do not compute. The cappuccino maker Oliver's mom is using matches *her*, but not Freaky. Does she crave her version of caffeine so badly that she brought it along?

She glances up from foaming and smiles. "Hello, Mandy. Your mom's the librarian, right?"

"That's right." I grin. Oliver must have told her that. Which means he talked about me.

Then it hits me. There are no secrets in Rocky Point. Oliver's mom will mention my being here to my mom the next time she needs an Internet connection.

She spoons the foam into her cup and sprinkles cinnamon over the top. Even with her back to me, I can see what Mom saw. A trim, pulled-together woman who radiates a kind of coiled energy, like she's bursting to do something and there isn't enough to do. If I were wearing her crisp, navy linen slacks and the equally crisp white top, they'd be wrinkled and stained almost as soon as I put them on.

She turns and leans against the counter. "You know, that boat parade has been around since I was a kid," she says. "Are motors still outlawed?"

"Yup," I say. Then I realize I should probably say more. This is Oliver's mom! I want to make a good impression.

"Too bad," she says. "It would be a lot easier to make elaborate floats if you didn't have to worry about rowing."

That problem occurred to me, too. I've seen enough rowboats tip over and oars tear apart decorations to know that rowing will be an issue. It's super funny when Cynthia and I watch from shore. No one ever really gets hurt. Wet and cold, yes, but the parade is too well monitored for anything bad to happen. But now I'll be someone who could wind up in that water.

"I think it's cool," Oliver says, opening the fridge and pulling out two sodas.

"I know. You love a challenge," his mom says, smiling at him. She reaches up and ruffles his hair as he passes her.

"Mom," he complains. He hands me my soda and smooths his hair back down.

"Well, I won't keep you. I know you two have a lot of work to do."

"Nice to meet you, Mrs.—" I stop, realizing that she's divorced now and I have no idea what name she uses.

"Call me Alice," she says. Wow. A grown-up asking me to use her first name? She is *so* not from Rocky Point.

"Well, thanks, Alice." It feels awkward but also very adult.

"There's Pop's leftover lobster mac and cheese, and salad, and cold cuts if you get hungry," she tells us. Then comes the whammy: "Is the library open today?" she asks me.

"No," I reply. Luckily, it's true. Mom's there taking care of historical society business, but the library itself is closed to the public.

Mrs. . . . *Alice* sighs. "I guess I'll be driving over to Franklin. Let me know if you want me to pick up anything."

"Will do," Oliver says.

Made it through round one: meet the mom. I think I passed. Now onto round two: meet Freaky.

Maybe we've all been wrong about him, I muse. *The house is so . . . normal. Maybe Freaky is too.*

We go out the kitchen door. The backyard is much bigger than the one in front, though just as unattended. There's a big shed that's practically the size of a small cottage. A picnic table with benches sits under a shady tree; grass and weeds curl around the table legs. Right in front of the shed stands a worktable with an attached vise and a saw lying on it. I can smell that sweet scent of freshly cut and sanded wood. Sure enough, there are several pristine planks stacked beside the table.

"Pops?" Oliver calls. "You back here?" Oliver starts for the shed as I take a swig of soda and settle onto the picnic table bench.

"Don't need to holler." Freaky Framingham emerges from the shed carrying a roll of chicken wire. He squints at me.

"Pops, this is Mandy. She's going to help with the boat."

"Hi," I say. I have to force myself to not say "Hello, Freaky."

Freaky just gives a sharp nod, then leans the chicken wire against the shed. "Getting you your materials," he tells Oliver. "That's the way to start. Everything to hand."

"Right, Pops," Oliver says. "We got much more to haul out?" He crosses to Freaky.

"Enough."

They head toward the shed, and I stand and put the soda can on the table. Just as I start to follow them, Freaky calls over his shoulder, "We'll handle it."

"Uh. Oh. Okay." I sit back down. Does he think that because I'm a girl I shouldn't be around tools? Or does Freaky not want me in his shed?

I take another sip of soda. The fog has burned off, and now the outside of the can is sweating. Soon I will be too.

Oliver and Freaky come back out, Oliver carrying a tool-box, with his sketchbook tucked under his arm. Freaky has a staple gun in one hand and coiled wire in the other. Looking at them side by side, I can see the resemblance. They're both long limbed, with narrowish shoulders. Neither would ever be mistaken for a football player. Freaky wears his standard flannel shirt and paint-spattered overalls. Today, maybe because he's been working, his wild gray hair is held back not only in a ponytail but a purple bandanna as well, hippie style.

"I'll leave you to it," Freaky says. "Going fishing. Tell your mother."

"Okay," Oliver says.

Freaky goes back into the shed. Oliver lays the sketchbook on the picnic table and opens to a diagram of the structure he wants us to make. It's a little intimidating.

"So I think I took care of all the math," Oliver begins, but stops when Freaky comes back out with his fishing gear. Now he wears a battered canvas hat and has exchanged the flannel for a T-shirt, revealing muscular and tan arms. Skinny, but muscular. "Sinewy," I guess is the word. The flannel is now tied by the sleeves around his hips. He nods as he passes but doesn't say another word. He goes around the house, and in a few minutes we hear the truck start up.

Oliver fiddles with the pencil he's holding. "Um, so, my grandfather doesn't really talk very much. Don't take it personally."

"I don't."

I wonder if Oliver has any idea of his grandpop's rep in our town. Should I tell him, or will that make him not like me?

"Pops helped me figure out what materials we'll need," Oliver says. "He had a lot of stuff already."

"So how is this going to work?" I ask.

He points to the sketchbook page. "We'll use the planks as the base. Pops already cut them to the right size. We'll build the lighthouse on top of that."

"Out of chicken wire," I surmise.

"Exactly. It's lightweight, so it should work."

"Yeah," I say with a laugh. "It would be pretty embarrassing if a lighthouse made a boat sink. It's supposed to prevent that!"

He grins, then returns to the page. "Once we've got the shape, we'll cover it with papier-mâché and paint it."

"What about the hat?" I ask.

"The what?" His eyebrows knit together.

My cheeks flush. "That's what I call the spot up on top where the light used to be. That would be hard to construct out of chicken wire."

"Oh! The lantern house," he says. "I was thinking maybe balsa wood? It's super lightweight. I use it to make models all the time."

So he's a model maker. It tips him a bit into the nerdy category, but somehow that just makes me like him even more.

"What kind of models?" I ask.

He flushes. "Oh, you know, the usual. Old-fashioned airplanes. Whaling ships. That kind of thing."

"That's what had you so interested at the festival."

"You saw that, huh."

"Kinda sorta," I say, and he grins again. I don't know why, but it gives me a supreme lift being able to make him smile so easily.

Oliver puts the boards on the worktable. "I figured out a scale that will work on the boat but still be big enough to sit inside."

"How will you row?" I ask, trying to understand what he has in mind.

"Who said I'm going to be the one rowing?"

I gape at him. "You roped me into this project so that I can be the one doing the hard work?"

"Kidding!" he says. "Though . . ." He studies the boards. "You'd probably fit better than I would."

"Let's make sure the thing is seaworthy before I even think about volunteering for that job."

He shows me the mini keeper's house he already started making, then we spend the morning working on the lighthouse tower. We hammer the boards together to make an open square, then use staple guns to attach the chicken wire to it. Oliver is very precise about everything, so it takes forever. He had noticed that Candy Cane narrows toward the top and insisted our chicken wire version do the same. It's not easy to do, especially since it's my job to hold the ends together while he checks the measurements and his drawings. The wire digs into my hands, leaving deep, red grooves. He's rapidly going from cute to annoying.

Once we have the basic shape down, Oliver steps back and announces, "We need a break."

"That's for sure." I use my arm to wipe the sweat off my forehead, and open and close my hands, trying to stretch them out. I never knew you could sprain your palms.

"How about we eat down by the river?" he suggests.

"Sounds good." Maybe my cranky will vanish once I'm sitting in the shade and don't have to worry about making sure my nails go in absolutely straight, or that the staples are evenly spaced. And I thought Mr. Forester the science teacher is exacting.

I follow Oliver back into the house. Freaky hasn't returned. The silver car is out front, so his mom is still around somewhere.

"So . . . lobster mac 'n' cheese doesn't really seem like picnic food."

"Not so much," I agree, relieved I don't have to confess my antiseafood stance. I also realize I'm starving. A quick glance at the clock tells me we worked way past my usual lunchtime.

"How about . . ." He rummages in the fridge and pulls out a paper-wrapped packet. "Turkey?" He tosses it onto the counter. Then he reaches in and pulls out another packet. "Or ham." He tosses that onto the counter too. "Or that old classic, PB and J. The J being Maine wild blueberry of course." He pulls out the jars and places them on the counter, then peers into the fridge again. I have the feeling if I don't stop him, he'll empty its entire contents.

"Ham," I declare, just as he holds up several plastic-wrapped cheeses. I cross and take what looks like Swiss from him. "And cheese."

He grins, and in the brightness of his smile all of my annoyance vanishes. "Mustard? Mayo? Lettuce? Cornichons?"

"Cornichons?" I repeat. "Who has cornichons?"

He shrugs as he holds up a jar. "Pops is kind of into fancy food."

"You're kidding me!"

"That's surprising to you?"

"He—he just never struck me as the gourmet type." I frown. "Except this kitchen looks like it belongs to someone who knows food."

"Yeah. He's definitely a better cook than my mom."

"I heard that." We both glance up and see his mom standing in the doorway.

"Uh . . . sorry, Mom."

I notice she has the same twinkly blue eyes as Oliver. "Don't be. I agree with you. He likes cooking; I don't. Though I can't remember him doing any cooking when I was a kid." Her voice changes as she adds, with less warmth, "It was a later interest."

She eyes the counter, now piled high with all the choices Oliver pulled out. "Hungry?"

"Just being a good host," Oliver explains. I can see that he and his mom get along and they like teasing each other.

"Planning on eating the peanut butter with a spoon?" She crosses to the sink and places her cappuccino cup into it.

Oliver and I both look at the counter. He smacks his forehead. "Bread! I knew I was forgetting something."

"That's so something I would do," I tell him. "Including the head smack."

He smiles again, obviously appreciating my mini confessions. It's cool to meet someone I can tell embarrassing things to, and instead of making fun of me (yes, Justin, I mean you!), he thinks they're endearing. At least, that's how it seems.

"How's the project going?" Alice asks.

"We're going to apply the papier-mâché after lunch," Oliver says. So that's what's on the agenda for the afternoon. Excellent! Something I know how to do. And very difficult to screw up.

"Sounds like you've got it all under control."

"Where's the cooler?" Oliver asks. "We're going down by the river."

"Don't track the mud in," she warns as she steps aside and opens a very well-organized pantry behind her. She pulls a Styrofoam cooler from a shelf. "You know your grandfather."

"Outside is outside, inside's in," Oliver says, sounding as if he's quoting a well-worn saying. He takes the cooler from her and tosses in some cool-packs he pulls from the freezer. Only he drops them twice before they land where they're supposed to. I pretend not to notice.

"Exactly." Alice opens a cupboard and takes out a plate, then narrows her eyes at the counter. "I'll wait till you're through in here." She returns the plate to the shelf and once again tousles Oliver's hair as she leaves the room.

Oliver rolls his eyes and smooths his hair back down. "Moms, right?"

"Don't I know it."

We make our sandwiches—ham and cheese for me, turkey with, *ooh la di da*, *cornichons* for him—then stash them in the cooler. Oliver adds two sodas, a pair of peaches, and some cookies. We head outside, wind around the shed, and take a downhill path Oliver tells me leads to the river.

"I found this spot the first day I was here," Oliver says. "You'll love it."

I glance up at him and watch the cutest blush spread across his face. *That's right, buddy*, I think with pleasure. *I didn't miss that little assumption you just made there. That I'll love it 'cause you do.*

"I mean, I *think* you'll love it." He shifts the cooler to the other hand. "That is, I hope you'll like it."

"I'm sure I will," I assure him, letting him off the hook. "Even if I didn't go for the cornichons, I feel I can trust your judgment."

The woodsy part of Rocky Point has a completely different

feel from the harbor and the bay. Those are wide open places, where sound travels and light glints off the water. On sunny days, anyway. I always want to whisper in the woods; the tree canopy overhead and the dense brambles make it seem like a place for secrets. The smells are different too—not the salty tang of sea-water but a darker smell of damp earth and pine.

"It gets narrower and steeper here," Oliver says. "We should go single file."

He moves in front of me, and I have to say, I do enjoy being able to watch the cute habit he has of tapping the bushes as he passes them, almost as if he's petting them. And the way his T-shirt shifts across his shoulders as he ducks under a low tree limb. Not to mention the curve of his butt in his cutoffs.

I'm paying too much attention to Oliver and not enough to my own feet. I trip over some roots and stumble into him. I fling out my hands to catch myself and wind up with a fistful of his T-shirt. This makes him lose his footing too, and we flail about and then land in the dirt.

"Sorry, sorry, sorry!" I say as he turns to look at me.

"You okay?" he asks.

"I should have warned you. I'm kind of a klutz."

Weirdly, a total look of relief takes over his face. "Seriously?"

"Uh, yeah. Why do you look like I just told you your bout of plague is in remission?"

"It's just—I'm a total klutz too!"

"You are? But you didn't do any dumbhead thing building the tower."

"I'm good on the micro scale," he explains. "But macro? The

only reason I haven't slammed into a tree yet is because I'm concentrating super hard."

"That's great!" I exclaim.

We stare at each other for a moment. It's one of those "I'm seeing you for the very first time" kinds of deep looks. Then I spoil it by bursting out laughing.

"What?" he asks, looking wary, like maybe I was only pretending to be a klutz so that he'd make this confession.

"We're both super happy that we have clumsiness in common. But we're working together on a project that requires us to not just use tools and build something, but to navigate down a river."

He lets out such a contagious laugh that I start laughing again. We shake our heads as we smile at each other, and for a minute I think he might kiss me. He doesn't lean in, though, and I suddenly feel self-conscious. I stand and brush off the back of my shorts. Then I hold a hand out to help him up. He takes it, and I feel the warmth of his hand, its solid palm but slender fingers. It's the hand of someone who can do fine detail work, not the hand of a sports guy or a fisherman.

I drop it the minute I realize I've held it a beat too long. "Lead on," I say in a bright voice worthy of Cynthia in one of her perkier performances. "I promise not to trip you again if you promise not to lead us directly into the river and drown us," I add in my own voice.

He cracks a grin that makes the slightly longer front tooth poke out over his lower lip. Adorableness. "Deal."

He turns back around, and we carefully make our way down to the water's edge. This part of the river is pretty wide, and it

moves with the laziness of a turtle. The only noticeable movement is where boulders poke up sharply and the water has to
slap around them.

I scan the area, searching for a dry place to park ourselves.
Like so many places in Maine, there's very little shore, and what
there is here consists primarily of muddy grass. We didn't bother
bringing a blanket, which suddenly seems like a serious oversight.

"I'll show you my favorite spot," Oliver announces.

He pushes aside the branches of a thick bush, revealing a
large flat rock. A large, *dry* flat rock.

"Looks good," I say. He squeezes past the bush, then holds it
back so I can make it through without too many scratches.

We settle onto the rock, the surface nicely warmed by the
sun, but still cooled by the breeze off the water and the shade of
the trees overhead. Oliver unpacks our lunch, and I try to find the
most flattering position to sit in. I decide stretching out my legs
ensures that there's no awkward possible over-revealing. I really
should have checked out my outfit in every posture imaginable.
Another thing Cynthia would have helped me with. There's so
much that I rely on her for. My heart sinks a little remembering
our fight last night.

But then it lifts again. Oliver is kneeling beside me and holding
out my sandwich. I take it from him, and he shifts around to grab
the sodas. He pops his can open, then clinks mine. He holds up the
can like he's making a toast. "To a good morning's work," he says.

"Without any casualties," I add, tapping his can with mine. I
wish he'd made a more personal toast, but it's still sweet.

We each take sips, then get down to the serious business of

eating. I'm not one of those girls who pretends she's not hungry when she gets around a boy. Food should never be betrayed that way. Unless it's fish, of course.

"Nice, huh?" Oliver says. He finished his sandwich and is now lying with his arms under his head, gazing up at the treetops.

I swallow the last of mine, then stretch out beside him. "Definitely," I agree. The leaves overhead rustle with the breeze. Each time they flutter, a bright patch of blue sky appears then vanishes again.

"It's funny," I muse. "Each part of Rocky Point is totally different, like there are four distinct towns."

"What do you mean?" He rolls onto his side, leaning on his elbow.

I keep my eyes on the leaves above me, all too aware of the closeness of his face. I also don't want to spoil the moment by becoming *over*aware of the smear of mustard in the corner of his mouth.

"Well, there's here, all woodsy and rivery. Then there's the harbor."

"Where the food booths were for the festival."

"Yup. To me, the harbor is kind of the heart of Rocky Point. The *real*est part. That's where the fishermen work and live and keep their boats. The shops there aren't the touristy kind."

"There's that lobster shack," Oliver points out. "I even read about it in a tourist guide."

"Yeah," I concede. "But it's there even when tourists aren't. It's a super-convenient way for the lobstermen to unload the lobsters that aren't already tagged for restaurants."

"What are the other parts? To you."

"There's the bay side," I continue. I'm enjoying being a tour guide, particularly since I can do it lying down. With a boy. A boy who is not only Cute with a capital C, but also seems to be completely interested. Though I'm still not sure if the interest is in me or in Rocky Point. "That's where you can go for a beach fix with actual sand. It's not very big, but there are beachy shops, beachy views, beachy things to do. Beach houses . . ."

"Beach umbrellas, beach volleyball . . ."

I giggle and continue the game. "Beach dunes, beach grass, beach . . ." I run out of things to add, so Oliver picks up.

"Beached whales. *Beach Blanket Bingo*. The Beach Boys."

I smack him in the chest as I laugh. "And then there's the Square," I say. "The town square," I add, so he knows what I'm talking about. "Around there it's like a small town you might find pretty much anywhere in New England. What makes Rocky Point unique, though," I say, just now realizing that I actually believe what I'm telling him, "is that you can experience all these different Rocky Points in a single day. With just a bike."

He smiles. "You love it here."

I sit up and turn to look down at him. "You know, maybe I do."

He sits up too, rummages in the cooler, then hands me a cookie. I take it from him, frowning as I think.

"Something wrong?" he asks.

"I was just thinking I should thank you."

"For what?"

"For a couple of things, actually. One, for making me see my own town in a different way. Making me realize I don't actually hate it here." I take a bite of the oversize cookie. Oh my. Probably the best oatmeal chocolate-chip cookie I have ever tasted in my entire life.

"Add thank you for this cookie!" I say, spitting crumbs. My hand flies to my mouth. "Sorry," I mumble behind my hand.

"Thank Pops," he says with a grin. "Like I said, he knows his way around the kitchen."

"No lie." I take a swig of soda to wash down the crumbs, regretting washing away the flavor of the cookie as I do. Happily it's a really big cookie, so I'll have plenty more tastes.

"What was the other thing you were going to say before the cookie distracted you?"

"Thank you for asking me to make the float with you. I've always wanted to take part."

"So why haven't you?" he asks, taking a bite of his own cookie.

I shrug. How can I explain it just never seemed right? Cynthia wasn't into it, and no one ever invited me to join a team. He'd think I'm a friendless loser.

I turn away, trying to think of a way to change the subject, and my eye catches something floating downriver. I swing my legs around and kneel for a better look.

"See something?" Oliver asks.

"Just some twigs tangled together," I say. Something about the sticks in the water reminds me of something.

"Doll rafts," I murmur. My throat feels thick, and my breath feels tight, as if someone's squeezing my chest.

"What?" Oliver sits up and scoots beside me. I turn away.

I know these symptoms. I'm about to cry. *So not cool!* I yell at myself in my head.

I clench my jaw and jam my teeth together. I swallow, trying to get the lump to melt.

"What's wrong?" he asks, alarmed.

I don't want to use the "hormones" line on him—that would be more embarrassing than crying.

I shake my head, which, to my horror, makes tears actually drop out of my eyes. I cover my face.

"Mandy?"

I inhale sharply, squeeze my eyes shut behind my hands to wring out any remaining tears, then force myself to face him. "I don't mean to be a total weirdo," I say. "I just—it's just that . . ."

He's looking at me with such soft concern I glance away. Keeping my eyes on a tree limb sticking up against a boulder in the middle of the river, I say, "I had a memory. It snuck up on me."

"A bad one?" His voice matches his concerned expression.

I sigh. "No. A good one. One of me and my dad."

"And that upset you?"

I shut my eyes again and give a little laugh. "Right. You're not from here. You don't know everyone's history from the moment they were born." I open my eyes again and twist to face him. "My dad. He died when I was eight. There was something wrong with his heart."

The concerned bewilderment is replaced by sympathy. "Oh," he says softly. "Sorry."

"Yeah, thanks." I bring up my knees and hug them. Using a twig, I make little trails in the dirt. "Mostly it doesn't get to me.

You know? It's part of who I am. But every now and then a memory jumps out and grabs me."

"And the river pulled a sneak attack?"

"Yeah." I sense my tiny smile and realize the memory now feels good, not sad. "I don't really hang by the river much. I guess being here now . . ." I raise my head, but I'm still not quite ready to look at him, so I glance back to the water. Using the stick, I point at the clump of twigs that set me off. "That bunch of twigs for some reason made me think of the rafts my dad and I used to make. Toy-size. He called them doll rafts because I insisted on putting passengers on them. And then, of course, he'd have to go rescue them because I'd get hysterical when they'd float away."

"Sounds like a good guy."

"Yeah." It comes out as a sigh. I look down at the ground again. "Yeah." I remember something else. "Sometimes he'd make up stories to go with the rafts, usually about someone being rescued by the Candy Cane keeper."

"Wait—like a Christmas elf?"

I laugh. "It's the lighthouse. Candy Cane. Because of the stripes. Not the official name, of course."

He smiles. "I like it."

"I think there was a story he told me so I'd stop being upset about a toy he wasn't able to catch in time. . . ." I try to remember the details, but they don't come. I shrug. "Anyway, being here. It suddenly brought it back."

"It's a nice memory, though, right?" Oliver asks. "I mean, I'd hate . . . I wouldn't like . . ."

"It's a nice memory. Yes." I put my hand lightly on his arm. "Another thing to thank you for."

He puts his hand over mine. "My pleasure."

Something jumps from the shore into the river, making a loud splash. Startled by the sound, we drop our hands to look. Just like that the moment's over. Thanks to a frog.

Oliver reaches up and pulls a leaf off the bush and pulls it into strips. "I miss my dad too. But at least I know if I want to I can call him. See him."

"Was it bad?" I ask. I know some kids whose parents got divorced, and it was sometimes kind of nasty.

"Bad?" He thinks it over. "Not really. It never got ugly. They never fought—at least not in front of me. When they broke the news to me, they said it was a mutual decision, and I believed them. Now Mom says it was because they had each changed."

"What do you think?"

He shrugs. "I just saw them as Mom and Dad. If they were different from when I was a little kid, I never noticed. But . . ." His eyes drift as his thoughts take him somewhere else. I wait, not wanting to rush him, letting him figure out whatever he's figuring out in front of me.

"The way we lived had changed," he says finally. "Around the time I started middle school, Mom got super successful and super busy. We had more money, but I could tell there was more stress."

"How? You said they didn't really fight."

"Not yelling and screaming, no. But now looking back, maybe all that quiet was significant. You know what I mean?"

I nod. My brother's ex-girlfriend Fiona gave him the silent

treatment for a whole week when they were dating. It wasn't pretty.

"Mom says they ended up wanting different things," Oliver continues. "She's actually really happy being this powerhouse. She stresses when she doesn't have enough to do, not the other way around. Her brain's always on overdrive. I think that's part of what drove them apart. Dad's one of those guys who works hard but wants to kick back, too. She didn't come installed with that button."

"Which one are you like?" I ask.

"You tell me," he says.

I study his face. The humor in his bright eyes. The uneven front teeth. The soft-looking lips. "Jury's still out," I say, my voice a little shaky. The close scrutiny unnerves me. "But if I had to guess right now, you're a mix of them both."

"Sounds right." He laughs. "At least, that sounds better than hearing I'm a driven workaholic or a slacker party boy."

"Your dad's a slacker party boy?"

"Nah. But he *is* more into vegging in front of the TV or inviting the whole neighborhood over for a barbecue than Mom."

"Opposites might attract, but then they wind up driving each other crazy," I say.

"Hey, your doll raft floated away." Oliver points to the water.

I swivel my head to look. He's right. The boulder's clear of debris now. "It's on its way to Candy Cane."

"I guess we should get back to work."

I don't want the picnic to end, but I help him pack our trash in the cooler.

He picks up the cooler and leads the way back to the path. We're both quiet, but it's a nice quiet. I'm not trying to come up with things to say, and I don't think he is either. We just feel . . . calm. Relaxed.

Visitors talk about how being by water puts them into a zone. It doesn't matter if it's the bay, the ocean, the river, or the harbor. Something about negative ions. Or maybe it's the hypnotic effect of moving water. Could be there's something to it, and that's why Oliver and I are so comfortable lazily strolling silently side by side. I feel like we're two different people leaving the woods from those who entered. Or at least our relationship is: We know each other better; we've both revealed ourselves a bit more to each other, maybe more than either of us had expected.

Once out of the woods I can tell by the angle of the sun that our picnic lasted a lot longer than we'd planned.

We step into the kitchen, and he drops the cooler on the counter. His mom must have been in the living room, because she pops her head in, a quizzical look on her face.

"There you are. I thought we might have to send a search party after you."

I back up against the door, totally embarrassed. She probably thinks we were making out this whole time. When we never even kissed.

"We were at the river," Oliver says. He rummages in the fridge and pulls out a soda. He holds it out to me. I shake my head no.

He shuts the fridge and pulls the tab on the soda can. I glance at his mom. She's got that look on her face like she's trying to figure out if we've been up to anything. Oliver is totally oblivious, but I recognize it immediately.

Maybe it's a look parents only use on their daughters. Or maybe boys are just clueless about this kind of thing.

Oliver tips back his head to take a swig, and his eye catches the clock on the wall. "Is that the real time?"

His mom crosses her arms. "That's the real time."

He completely misses her tone. Her "this is why I'm curious about what you were doing" tone.

"Oh man." He puts down the soda and rakes his fingers through his hair. "I guess we should call it a day," he says to me. "I didn't realize it was so late. It doesn't make sense to start doing the papier-mâché now."

"Okay," I say. "I should probably be heading home anyway."

"Would you like to stay for dinner?" Oliver's mom asks.

I would, but I should let my mom in on the news that I'm hanging with Freaky Framingham's grandson before I announce I'm already at the house. But there's another reason I have to say no.

"The service here isn't great, right?" I say. "I'd have to let my mom know."

Alice frowns. "That's right. And Pop never put in a landline. Another time, then."

"How about tomorrow?" Oliver pipes up. A worried look crosses his face. "You're coming back tomorrow, right?"

"I have to be at Candy Cane," I tell him, noticing Oliver smiling at the nickname, now that he's clued in. "But I can come after four. If that's not too late."

"Any time you can spare will be great," Oliver says.

"Okay. I'll ask Mom about dinner." I hope she'll let me. In fact, I hope she'll let me out of the house after hearing I spent all day at Freaky Framingham's without telling her.

We walk through the living room. "So what's in there?" I ask, pointing to the door of the addition.

"That's Pops's studio," Oliver says. "He's an amazing painter. He has some things stored there, but it's always where he works when he's not painting *en plein air*."

"Plain what?" I ask, crossing to the door.

"That's what it's called when an artist paints outside."

"Can I see?" I put my hand on the doorknob, but Oliver quickly puts his hand on my arm and stops me from turning it.

Oliver looks nervous. "Actually, no. It's the one room we're not allowed in when he's not here. It's the major rule."

I pull my hand back, disappointed.

"But no one says we can't peek," Oliver adds with a grin. "Take a look."

I step up to the window in the door and crane my neck. By getting into weird positions I can see different parts of the room. I catch the corner of a painted canvas on one side and cans holding lots of paintbrushes on a worktable. I wiggle a bit more and spot paintings stacked against a wall. I step back. "It looks like he's a really serious painter."

"He is." He turns me around and points at the painting over on the wall opposite the fireplace. The one of the harbor in fog that I noticed when I first came in. "That's one of his."

I step up close to it. I don't know how he did it, but he captured the strangeness of fog, the wetness, the way light looks through it. Tiny little brushstrokes in unusual colors that when I step back again form into a very recognizable Rocky Point Harbor.

"That's really good," I say. "Does he sell them?"

Just then Freaky strides through the door, looks at us suspiciously, nods at Oliver, then disappears into the kitchen. He grunts a greeting to Oliver's mom—at least I think that's what the sound is—and then I hear the back door bang.

"Tools!" I hear him yell from the backyard.

Oliver flushes. "Gotta go. Pops is a stickler about taking proper care of his tools. If he's not happy, then he won't let us use them anymore."

"Go, go." I wave him away. "See you tomorrow."

I'm in such a good mood when I get home that I'm not angry at Cynthia anymore. In fact, I'm grateful to have a friend who worries about me. Cynthia is more like a sister than a friend, and this is just another example.

I punch in her number. She answers on the first ring.

"So I guess you're still alive," she says flatly.

Okay. She's still holding on to her mad. I'm not going to let that rile me up. "I know you were just concerned," I say.

"Don't use that mom speech on me," she says.

"I'm not!" I exclaim. "Anyway, *you* were the one doing the mom thing—" I stop myself and start over. "We were totally wrong about Freaky."

"He's not a freak?"

"Well, I wouldn't go that far. He's not exactly bursting with people skills. But his house is totally different on the inside than the outside."

"Yeah?" She's using her interested voice.

"Yeah. He's like this gourmet chef. Your mom would kill for his kitchen."

"No lie?"

"But here's the headline." I pause for dramatic effect. I've learned a lot from Cynthia over the years. "He's a painter. Seriously good. He's got all these canvases stacked up in a studio he built onto the house."

"That *is* headline news."

"So, come on, Cyn. Let's not be in a fight."

"We're not in a fight," she protests.

"I know, let's not go over it again."

"You have to understand—"

"La-la-la-la-la-la-la," I sing over her.

That gets her laughing. "You are such a child."

I can't really fault her on that since it's what we used to do when we were little kids to stop someone from speaking. Though we usually did it to others, not to each other. Still, I say, "No I'm not. I'm just . . ." I pause to let her brain catch up with mine.

"Hormonal!" we shriek at each other over the phone.

And with that, everything's back to normal again.

S o, um, Mom, you know that boy Oliver?" We're digging into take-out fried chicken at the dinner table. Have I mentioned

Mom's not so keen on cooking? I have the funniest image of her getting cooking lessons from Freaky.

"The lighthouse fan," Mom says with a smile.

Good. The first thing that comes to her mind is what she likes best about him.

Just come right out with it, Mandy. "His mom invited me for supper. Tomorrow night."

Mom looks up from her side dish of corn niblets and cocks her head. "When did you see his mother?"

Oops. I didn't prepare for that question. All I've got is the truth without any prep time to figure out the best way to present it. So I just present it. "Oliver and I are working on a project together. For the Fourth of July," I add quickly. She likes it when I participate in community events. "All about Candy Cane," I put in for good measure.

She frowns and puts down her fork. I now have her full attention. I prefer her in her more distracted state.

She folds her hands in front of her. "You're working on what exactly?"

"A float for the boat parade," I respond with huge enthusiasm, hoping to get her on board.

"Where exactly are you working on it?"

Uh-oh. Two exactlies in a row. Bad sign. And here's where the fight will begin.

"Up at, uh, Mr. Framingham's house." I figure it would be better *not* to call him Freaky when I'm trying to convince Mom how normal everything is with Oliver. "His mom was there the—"

She cuts me off. "Let me get this straight. You went to a

stranger's house. Where there's no cell reception. Possibly not even a working landline. Without a word as to where you were going. Or asking my permission."

"He's not exactly a stranger," I counter, trying to keep my temper in check. A big blowout is not in my best interests.

"Mr. Framingham isn't just a stranger; he's *strange*," Mom responds angrily.

"That's unfair!" Okay, there goes my plan to keep a cool head. But it *is* unfair. "You just know stupid rumors. And that isn't even what I meant."

She raises an eyebrow. At least she's still letting me talk.

"I meant that *Oliver* isn't a stranger. You've even met his mom. You've talked to her a bunch of times this week. That's all you ever ask about when I go anyplace."

This argument actually seems to work. Not bad for an improvisation. Her face changes from her "you are about to be punished" expression to something neutral. That I can't read.

"Let me think about it" is all she says, then goes back to eating her niblets.

I sigh. Well, at least it's not a no.

All day at Candy Cane I replay yesterday with Oliver. I can't believe I got weepy with him! But the most shocking part of this is that I don't feel embarrassed about it. The little crease that formed between his eyes when he was afraid he'd upset me, the soft tone of voice he used—it makes me swoony even now. Between his opening up about the divorce and my brush with tears, there's no denying we are truly getting to know each other.

It's weird, I think as I lock up. This getting-to-know-you thing. I've basically known my friends forever. Even people I'd categorize as acquaintances I've known pretty much all my life. I haven't had to . . . *learn* someone in ages.

Scary.

But deliriously exciting, too.

Mom finally relented. She said I could go to Oliver's to work on the boat and today for supper, but she insisted she drive me over from the library. She claims it's because she doesn't want me riding my bike home after dark. The woods along Evergreen Road are pretty dark, thanks to the thick groves of Christmas trees the road is named for. There's a reason the state flower is a pinecone. But it's *really* so she can check out the situation. Secretly I'm glad. It's a long haul by bike from the tip of Rocky Point where the lighthouse is to Freaky's house in the woods.

I ride to the Square and lock my bike in the rack in front of the library. Mom's as klutzy as me, so she didn't want the hassle of getting the bike into the car. I didn't want to waste time going home, so we compromised. She'll drive me back here tomorrow morning, and I'll bike the rest of the way to Candy Cane. Bonus: It cuts my ride in half.

The library's AC isn't the best, but the dark wood cabinets and high ceilings at least give the impression of being a lot cooler inside. The library is nearly empty. A dad with a baby in a Snugli is trying to convince a toddler that it's time to go. An older woman sits at a computer terminal. A high school boy sits with his head down on a table, obviously asleep. From the curly hair

I identify him as Marshall Beamer. Must have summer school. I flip through some paperbacks in a revolving rack as I wait.

"I'm sorry," I hear my mom saying. "There's just no way we can swing that."

I glance up and see her walking down the stairs with Mr. Garrity, the other historical society bigwig.

Mr. Garrity sighs and takes a handkerchief from his jacket pocket. He uses it to wipe the back of his neck. "I know. We're going to have to take a hard look at the budget. And soon."

I replace the book so that the minute Mom lands on the ground floor we can leave. Oliver's waiting.

"There's my daughter," Mom says, noticing me. "We'll discuss this more."

"I'm sure we will," Mr. Garrity says sadly, then disappears through the STAFF ONLY door.

"Anyone come in today?" she asks as we leave the library.

"Not a single one," I complain.

"No one at the café, either?" We climb into the car.

"Actually, there were some customers," I say as Mom maneuvers around jaywalking tourists. "Guys." I give her a sidelong glance. "Is that why you hired Celeste?"

"What do you mean?" She gets off Main Street and begins the twisty route toward Evergreen.

"So local boys will go to the café."

She gives a little laugh. "No, but if that's a side benefit, I'll take it. We hired her because she's the only one who applied."

I can see why. Everyone knows you don't make much money there. I wonder why Celeste wanted to. "Is she a lighthouse lover too?" This would give her something in common with Oliver. Dang.

It's darker now that we're in the woods, and Mom keeps her eyes straight ahead. I do too, so that I can tell her when to turn onto the right path.

"Actually, I think she needs to make some money but still be able to study. I'm guessing she has plenty of downtime during her shifts. She's doing some kind of online course."

Come to think of it, I did notice thick textbooky books near the cash register at the café.

"This is it," I say when I spot the turnoff.

Mom's eyebrows rise as she navigates the narrow and bumpy path to Freaky Framingham's. "Doesn't exactly scream 'welcome.'" Her eyes flick to me. "Did you feel . . . comfortable when you were here?"

"Yes," I say forcefully. Then, so she has no doubt that I'm telling the truth I add, "Not at first. But definitely by lunchtime."

She pulls up to the house, and I see her look of dismay.

"It's totally different on the inside," I assure her, unbuckling my seat belt and opening the car door before she can frantically drive us away. "Wait till you see."

We trudge up the sagging steps, and I open the screen door, then knock.

Alice appears, tossing a dish towel over her shoulder. "Hi, Mandy. Hello, Marjorie. Nice to see you."

That's right, they've met. Good. Even though Oliver's mom told me to call her by her first name, it still would have felt weird to say "Alice, this is my mother, Mrs. Sullivan."

"I drove Mandy over," Mom explains. "I don't want her to bike back in the dark."

At least the excuse sounds reasonable. It would be terrible if Alice knew the real reason was so Mom can make sure they're not a family of cannibals or something.

"Come in, come in," Alice says, stepping aside and holding open the door.

"What time should I pick her up?" Mom asks as we walk inside. Her eyes dart all around, and I hope Alice doesn't notice how surprised she is by what she's seeing.

"You're welcome to stay," Alice offers.

Please say no please say no please say no.

"Another time," Mom says. "I have a lot of paperwork to get done with the Fourth of July events coming up."

"Have enough time for a cup of coffee? Or tea?" Alice asks.

Mom smiles. "That I can do."

"Oliver's out back," Alice says as she leads us to the kitchen. "Hard at work. I was washing up so that everything will be ready for when my dad gets back."

Mom's eyes nearly bug when we arrive in the kitchen. "Mandy wasn't kidding when she said this was state of the art."

Alice gazes around fondly, then pats the giant stove. "I wouldn't exactly call this up to date, but Pop won't hear of replacing it. He's the cook in the family, not me."

"We have that in common," Mom says, leaning against the marble counter. "Mandy's father did most of the cooking in our house."

"He did?" I say.

She slings an arm across my shoulder. "But I'm proud to say you preferred *my* overcooked carrots."

She's not wrong. I liked the burned bits. Still do.

"Where *is* your father?" Mom asks. I can't tell if she's hoping he's home or hoping he's not.

"Grocery shopping. He doesn't trust me to do that, either. Which is fine by me."

The back door opens and Oliver steps in. His T-shirt is soaked with sweat, pebbles and dirt cling to his knees, and his work gloves look too big for him. He's wearing a bandanna Freaky-style across his forehead. Not exactly glamorous, but insanely appealing.

So is the big smile that appears when he realizes I'm here. "Hallelujah! Reinforcements!" he exclaims.

"Oliver, this is my mom," I say. Then I smack my forehead. "D'oh! You already met."

"At the lighthouse," Oliver says. He holds out his hand for a handshake, which seems kind of over the top, then pulls it back sheepishly when he notices the work glove. "So, hi."

Mom has that annoying "aren't children adorable" look on her face. "Hi again. Any friend of the lighthouse is a friend of mine," she says.

"I'm glad to see you decided to listen to me and your grandfather and wear the gloves," Alice comments.

He scowls at his hands. "They make everything even harder."

"Maybe so, but I'm guessing you've cut down dramatically on the cuts and scratches."

"Whatever," he grumbles, and crosses to the fridge. He pulls out a bottle of Gatorade and takes a long swig. I watch his Adam's apple bob with each chug.

"We should get to work," I say. I want to get out of the indulgent-mom-smiles zone. It feels as if we're specimens to be studied. Since I'm still trying to figure out what's going on between Oliver and me, it's extra uncomfortable to have the scrutiny.

Oliver grabs a second bottle of Gatorade and holds it up to me. "You okay with blue?"

I nod, then we traipse out the back door.

"I hope my mom doesn't tell your mom embarrassing stories about me," I say.

"Back atcha," Oliver replies.

I stop and stare at the structure. "You did the windows!"

There are now evenly spaced holes cut into the chicken-wire tower, three on each side, just like Candy Cane. On the work-table I spot a small balsa-wood structure next to the keeper's house replica. "And the lantern room!"

"That was a lot easier than the windows," Oliver says. "Chicken wire fights back."

"So what should I do?"

"How about you tear the newspaper into strips. The papier-mâché is the next step."

"I can handle that." I sit beside a stack of newspapers and begin tearing. Oliver is very organized. He has a box set up for me to drop the strips into so they don't blow away or get dirty. As I rip, I watch him using wire cutters to bend back the edges of the windows.

"I cut them bigger than they actually are," he explains as he works. "That way we can use the papier-mâché to keep the edges of the chicken wire from biting us."

"Biting *you*, you mean," I say. "Remember, you're the one who's going to be doing the rowing." I stop tearing. "What about a door?" I ask.

He keeps working, his back to me. "What door?"

"How are you going to get inside?"

He stops, his wire cutters midair. Without turning around, he finally says, "We'll bring it to the river, you'll lower it down on top of me, attach it, and presto, I'm inside and ready to row."

I'm really glad his back is to me. I don't think he'd appreciate the way I'm looking at him. But my mouth just reacts. "That's crazy!"

He stops what he's doing to face me. "I've worked it all out," he says a bit testily.

"Oh yeah?" I smirk. "You worked it out? Just this minute when I pointed out the fact that there's no door."

He's about to argue, then laughs. "You caught me."

I laugh too. "I thought you were Mr. Precision."

"I am," he insists. "But there's no door in the lighthouse, so there can't be a door in this."

"There used to be," I point out. "Before they built the attach-ment."

This stops him a moment, then he shakes his head. "No. A door big enough for me to get through won't be to scale. It's supposed to be an accurate replica."

I'm about to argue but zip my lip. After all, this is *his* baby.

Still, my mind works hard as I rip newspaper after newspaper. I have serious misgivings about his plan.

He tosses aside the wire cutters, yanks off the gloves, and wipes his hands on his shorts. "Okay," he declares, turning around. "Time to get messy. I'll get the stuff to make the glue."

When he goes into the house, I stand and stretch. My hands are covered in newsprint. I spot a spigot on the side of the house and rinse my hands.

The spigot is under the window of the addition. When I stand, I see a big painting leaning against the wall inside. It's breathtaking—a boy playing in a river, so focused on his toy boat that he's oblivious to the deer watching him from shore. It's painted in such a way that I can practically feel the cold water on my own toes, sense that it's about to rain and that the boy's playtime is nearly over, and understand both the boy and the deer are equally transfixed. It makes me want to be quiet so I don't disturb them, while also wanting to warn them to take cover. Freaky Framingham is a freaking incredible artist.

Oliver comes back out carrying a gigantic bowl, a sack of flour, and a pitcher of water. He puts everything on the ground beside the chicken-wire structure, then tosses me the apron he had slung over his shoulder. Not a frilly apron, but a serious workman's apron.

"That should take care of most of you," he says. "You're a lot smaller than Pops."

I slip it over my head, then tie the ties. "He's okay if I borrow it?"

"Yeah." Oliver laughs. "Anything to keep us out of the kitchen while he cooks, I think."

My stomach clenches. I haven't mentioned my fish aversion. What if Freaky is whipping up some kind of gourmet seafood dish? Will I be able to get down at least a few bites?

"Hope you like Indian food," he says as he sets up. "Pops said you're probably sick of seafood since you live here."

"I love Indian food!" I exclaim. I'm not even sure if I do, but as long as there's nothing that swam in the water on my plate I'm willing to try. Saved by Freaky!

Oliver mixes the flour and water. "We need to be sure there aren't any lumps," he says. "Have you done this before?"

"Not since grade school, but it's probably like riding a bike, right? Once you learn . . ."

We get to work, dipping each strip into the glue mixture until it's supersaturated. Getting the strip onto the chicken wire is harder to do than you might think. Those suckers like to wrap around things: my fingers, the wrong part of the wire, themselves. Oliver wants us to lay them all in the same direction, but overlapping. This way, he says, we'll know if we've covered each section the same number of times.

It's a gooey and goopy task, and my legs are getting sore. I'm getting in a squats workout from all the bending and stretching.

And the time just zips by.

"'My father was the keeper of the Eddystone Light,'" I sing when it's my turn. We're making the time pass by telling pirate stories (complete with pirate lingo, arrrrgh!) or singing sea chanteys. This is an old folk song that pretty much any kid in Rocky Point knows. Duh, there's a lighthouse in it. "'He married a mermaid one fine night!'"

"'From this union there came three,'" Oliver joins in. "'A porpoise and a porgy and the other was me!'"

I gape down at him. "You know it!"

"Sure! Even us lighthouse-deprived types know songs about the sea."

Oliver is carefully wrapping a strip around the bottom window to help defang the chicken wire. After all three layers are applied, the sharp edges should no longer be lethal.

I crouch by our bowl of flour paste and dip in another strip. Oliver drops down to his knees and sticks in a strip too. I watch our hands swirling the paper, never quite touching, moving as if choreographed. It's how we've been working together too. Like we've been doing it forever, with a matched rhythm. I'll duck under him just as he reaches above me; he'll go one way as I go the other, like we're reading each other's minds.

We pull out our strips and run our fingers along the length of them, squeezing out the excess. Then we both stand and, for the first time all afternoon, bang into each other as we reach for the same spot.

"Oopsie," I say as I carefully peel my strip off his arm. Little white flecks of glue stand out against his tan.

I feel something sticky on my shoulder. That's where Oliver's strip landed. His hand hovers just above it.

"I guess I'm stuck on you."

My head pops up at the husky tone in his voice. He's looking at me so sweetly, the way you might look at a kitten or puppy. I start to say something, but my brain goes blank when his lips are suddenly on mine.

It's a soft, tender kiss, but it shoots through me like a summer thunderbolt.

It's only a moment and then it's over. He pulls back so quickly my eyes have only just closed. I open them slowly, and he's searching my face, wondering, I suppose, if the kiss was welcome.

Before either of us can speak, before either of us can back away, retreat, freak out, or stammer, I place the back of my hand on his cheek, not wanting to get glue on that gorgeous face. I stand on my tiptoes, taking care to not knock over the bowl of glue, and I kiss him.

Me. Mandy Sullivan.

I.

Kiss.

HIM.

And it's wonderful.

July

There are only three days left before the boat parade, and I have discovered something else Oliver and I have in common. We don't work well under pressure.

We're behind schedule. Our classic Maine weather hasn't helped. Luckily, Freaky is a freakishly accurate weather predictor, so Candy Cane Jr. (Oliver's adorable nickname for our float) has never been caught outside, no matter how sunny the weather forecast is on the news. But the rain, the humidity, the general dampness that is Rocky Point slowed down our progress. A lot.

We're supposed to wait twenty-four hours between layers of papier-mâché, but it stayed sticky longer than that. And until that's dry we can't paint it.

But don't worry. We found ways to fill the downtime. That first flour-paste-covered kiss changed everything.

Kisses. Kisses that last forever and not long enough. That keep me occupied in my daydreams and as I drift off to sleep. I don't even text Cynthia. It's as if the kisses exist in their own perfect world. A world so private, so delicate, I'm not ready to share it with anyone. Not even her.

I've never had a single experience—certainly not one this big—that she hasn't in some way been part of. We dissected, analyzed, and categorized everything together down to the most minute detail. As exacting as Oliver is with his measurements.

This is different. For once I don't want to overthink. I just want to . . . be. To . . . discover. To find out what this bright and shiny new energy is.

It's not that I'm keeping a secret from her. It's that I have no words to describe how I'm feeling. What our time together is like. The expression on his face when he confesses what he misses about predivorce days. How he holds my hand without a word and just lets me talk about Dad. Complain about Mom. How we make the work go faster by making up ridiculous sea chanteys or impossibly complicated stories. What it's like to have him casually sling his arm across my shoulder as he points at something on Candy Cane Jr. as if of course that's exactly where his arm is supposed to be. The way I just as casually slip my hand into his back pocket, lean into him, and just listen, happy to be exactly where I am.

Is this what it's like to fall in love?

Only I'm not feeling a whole lot of love today. For the past week stressing over Candy Cane Jr. has made us pretty snippy with each other, and after yesterday's not very successful work session, I'm mostly irritated, annoyed, and exasperated. I thought this project would bring us closer together, but if things keep going the way they have, it might actually make us stop being friends—or whatever—altogether!

The rain outside completely matches my mood. It's also brought in more Candy Cane customers than normal, so I'm actually a little bit busy. Also good, otherwise I'd stew all day long.

I finish counting out the change for one adult, two kids' admission prices, then as the visitors move away, I spot Lexi Johnson hovering at the entry. She's flanked by a skinny boy with hair as red as hers, and a chubby little girl who looks like a kindergartener.

"Hi, Mandy," she says as she approaches the desk. "I heard you were working here."

"Mom," I reply. It's enough of an explanation. Everyone knows about my mom and the historical society.

"Babysitting," she says with a nod toward the two kids. "Cousins."

"I don't need a babysitter," the boy protests.

She rolls her eyes. "I know, I know," she assures him. "I'm really just babysitting your sister."

"Right," the boy declares emphatically.

Lexi pays for their tickets, and the kids wander to the gift shop area. "How's it going?" she asks.

"Not so bad." Then my eyes open wide. "Lexi! Are you making a boat float this year?"

She frowns. "No. We were away the beginning of the summer so I missed the chance to join a crew."

"Want to join mine?"

She looks surprised. "You're making a float?"

"Yes, and we are so behind, and my . . . friend, well, just yesterday he asked if I knew anyone who could help. You'd be perfect!" Lexi is always part of the group building sets and props for school plays.

Her eyes travel to her cousins, who are now crawling under the display tables. "I think you may have just saved my sanity. Now Lara will have to take over the babysitting." Lara is Lexi's younger sister. She grins at me, dimples showing in her heart-shaped face. "Thanks for the rescue!"

"Believe me, you're the one rescuing me! I need the reinforcements!"

*L*exi slows her bike to a stop as we arrive at the turnoff to the house in the woods. "You didn't tell me you're building a boat with Freaky Framingham!"

It's finally sunny, and although I filled Lexi in on most of the details, I confess I did leave out the location. I told her we should just head there together from my house. I was afraid she would back out.

"Don't worry," I assure her. "It's totally fine. And it's not Freaky . . ."

"Oh. My. God." She straddles her bike and stands staring at me. "The new guy! Freaky's grandkid or something. Everyone's been wondering where he disappeared to! He's been with you!"

I blush. "We started working on the boat only a few weeks ago. I think he spends every waking moment working on it or praying for it to stop raining."

We resume biking. Lexi has always been pretty quiet, rarely speaks up in class, isn't one of the girls who spread gossip—or is the subject of any. Cynthia knows her better than I do, because of their school-plays connection. She once told me Lexi's shy, but speaks her mind when she has ideas for designs or how to do things. Right now I'm grateful she's not the type to pry. She probably has a million questions but is too polite to ask any.

We lean our bikes against the porch, and I lead her inside, calling out, "We're here!"

I sent Oliver a text last night saying I was going to bring a helper, but with his spotty cell service I have no idea if he ever got it.

There's no answer, so I head for the kitchen. Then I realize Lexi's no longer following me. Just like my mom, and me, she is dumbstruck in the living room.

"I know," I say impatiently, "different on the inside. But come on. Times a-wasting!"

"Right . . ."

Oliver is out back, of course. Even though I'm braced for more arguments, I can't help smiling. He's kneeling by a can of paint, stirring. We're finally going to begin painting. I'm not sure if I should just launch into my plan to get him to see reason, or if I should work up to it slowly.

"Cool lighthouse," Lexi says, walking over to the tower sitting near the shed.

"Oliver, this is Lexi," I say. "Lexi, this is Oliver. He's the mastermind."

"Thanks for doing this," Oliver says. "We still have loads to do."

Lexi studies the structure. "So is this going in the stern?" she asks.

"In the center," Oliver responds.

Okay, I guess we're getting into it now. I'm glad it's Lexi raising the subject and not me this time.

She glances at him, puzzled. "Where you row?"

"Yup." Oliver stands and carefully lays the wooden stirrer on the lid of the paint can. "It's going to be cool. I'll get in the boat and then the lighthouse will be lowered over me." He crosses to the tower and points at the bottom windows. "See? At this scale, they're big enough to put the oars through."

"Uh-huh." Lexi walks around the lighthouse structure, studying it.

"Lexi does a lot of building for the school plays," I say. "She's even been in the boat parade before."

Oliver looks a little uncomfortable. I know what he's feeling. This is his baby, and now someone—a stranger—is assessing it. I suddenly want to protect him.

"The lantern house looks great!" I say.

"The light works," Oliver says. "It's one of those battery-operated candles. I think from a distance it will look like a lantern."

"Definitely." I glance at Lexi. "Uh, he wants it to be as exact a replica as possible."

I had already told her about the problems: that he won't cut a door, that he'll be rowing through the windows. But the most ridiculous issue is the one I'm hoping she'll solve. The fact that he won't cut eyeholes.

"There aren't any windows on the side you'll be facing?" she asks.

"No." There's a hard tone in his voice. His "don't argue with me" voice. I've heard it more than a few times. "And I'm not cutting any," he says. I know this is meant for me because I've hounded him about it all week.

"But how will you steer?" I ask for the ten thousandth time.

"You sit backwards to row anyway," he says. "So what difference will it make?" He turns away from us and opens up another
paint can.

I throw up my hands and give Lexi a "see what I'm dealing
with" look.

"I totally respect your commitment to accuracy," Lexi says.
"But, dude, you have to be able to see."

Oliver just keeps stirring.

I walk around to the front of the lighthouse, then into the
shed where the boat we'll be using is stored. I climb into it and
sit on the middle bench, where Oliver will be sitting.

I really want Oliver to be able to stick to his vision. But I also
don't want him to be insane. It's not like he's an expert rower to
begin with.

My eyes travel up to a small painting hung above one of the
tool cabinets. I don't know why Freaky hung one of his paintings
out here, but I don't know why Freaky does anything. A little girl
stands at the front of the painting with her back to the viewer.
Way in the background, looking tiny, is a barn. An equally tiny
man leans against the barn wall, but even as small as he is I can
tell he's looking at the little girl. Because she's in the foreground,
she's huge in comparison.

An idea forms.

I clamber out of the rowboat in my typically clumsy way and
rush out of the shed. "I've got it!"

Oliver and Lexi both look at me. They're on opposite sides of
the tower, painting. It looks like a somewhat uneasy truce. I hope
Lexi isn't mad at me for pulling her into this. I hope Oliver isn't

mad that I dragged someone in who might challenge his plans.

"I'll be your eyes!" I declare. "I'll sit in the bow and guide you!"

"But—"

"Hear me out. I know you're worried about scale. But perspective!"

Oliver looks at me blankly, and Lexi's eyebrows scrunch together. Then it's as if a lightbulb goes on over her head. "Perfect!"

Oliver looks from me to Lexi. "What? What are you talking about?"

"I got the idea from the painting in the shed," I explain in a rush. "It's okay if I'm bigger than I should be, because of perspective. It will be as if I'm in the foreground. I'll be the first thing anyone sees—even if just for a second."

"I don't know . . ." I can tell Oliver wants to find a solution, but his perfectionist side is resisting.

"I know!" Lexi says, putting down her paintbrush. "I can make you a costume that will make it look as if you're much smaller."

"What do you mean?"

"Come on," she says. Oliver and I share a quizzical look and then follow her into the shed.

"Get in the bow," she instructs me. I do. "Lean forward." I do. She turns to Oliver. "I'll make a kind of bib for Mandy. With feet on the bottom. She can lean forward so that the feet will touch the edge of the boat."

"I love it!" I exclaim. "And the dress for the bib can be old-fashioned. I can be Mrs. Gilhooley, the wife of the first lighthouse keeper."

Oliver still looks dubious. "But the illusion won't work when the boat is seen from the side."

Lexi and I look at each other. Then we look at him. Then we look at each other.

I fling my hands into the air. "You can't row without being able to see!"

"You gotta give in a little," Lexi says more calmly.

Oliver slouches and stares down at his sneakers. "Okay," he mumbles.

"You guys paint," Lexi says. "I'm going to try to find a doll's dress that will work for the bib." She claps her hands together. "Come on, people! We have work to do!" She points at each of us, then rushes away.

"And I've always thought of her as shy," I say once she's gone.

"Shy?" Oliver says. "She's like a general." Then he grins at me. "But in a good way."

I'm relieved that he's not angry. I'm even more relieved that he's listened to reason and won't wind up crashing into the shore.

He steps up to me and wraps both arms around me and squeezes. "I'm sorry I've been such a jerk." Then he takes a step back. "Thank you," he says. "It means a lot to me that you care so much about our project."

I tug at the hem of his T-shirt, my eyes down. "It's important to you. So it's important to me."

He lifts my chin with his finger, and I look into those blue eyes that always make my breath catch. He brings his lips to mine, and I taste salt and a hint of peanut butter. But more, too. I shut my eyes and melt against him and detect the flavors of trust, and happiness, and gratitude, and I imagine I taste the same to him.

We pull apart and I lay my face against his chest, listening to his pounding heart. His chin sits on top of my head as he plays with my braid. "I guess we should get back to work," he murmurs.

I nod, making his chin bounce. I take a step away from him, and his hands clasp behind my back, keeping me close. I peer up at him with a grin. "So what now, boss?"

He glances over his shoulder. "The paint needs to dry. Let's finish painting the keeper's house."

We release each other and go into the shed. "Have you decided what color scheme to use?" I ask. Over the years the keeper's house has been painted different colors.

"Well, now that you're going to play the role of the light-house keeper's wife, we should paint it the color it was when Mrs. Gilhooley was there."

"Makes sense." I eye the stack of paint cans in the corner. "Any idea what that would be?"

"Not so much, no," Oliver admits.

"I'm sure the info is at the historical society," I say. "Should we go to the library?"

He taps his chin the way he does when he's thinking. I know he's toting up how long it will take to get there, look around, and get back. Then he holds up a finger in his "eureka!" gesture. "The attic!"

"Yeah . . . ?"

"There's a filing cabinet up there full of historical society newsletters and old photos, and other stuff about Rocky Point," he explains.

"There is?" Every day I seem to discover something new and confusing about ol' Freaky.

"See what you can find while I get set up down here."

I salute him. "Yes, sir!"

The house is quiet when I go through the kitchen. A peek out the living room windows shows an empty front yard. Oliver's mom and Freaky are both out. I'm a little relieved—it only just occurred to me that either of them could have witnessed our mini make-out session a minute ago.

The attic is crowded but fairly organized. The filing cabinets are against the back wall, and I manage to get to them without knocking anything over, tripping on anything, or banging into something. Oliver's waiting, so I force myself to keep from poking around, even though my flea market mentality is itching to see what odds and ends live up here. Unfortunately, my eyes start itching too. Dust allergies.

I riffle through the files, and though I don't find any color photos, I do discover a newsletter all about the keeper's house through the years. A quick glance tells me that there are several paragraphs devoted to its various paint jobs.

Mission accomplished. As I squeeze sideways through a narrow aisle, I notice a stack of framed paintings leaning against the wall, their backs facing out.

Curious, I wiggle over to them. I pull the first frame toward me, stirring up a huge dust cloud. They must not have been moved in a while. I let out three gigantor sneezes, then peer down. Even upside down I can tell it's a beauty. I lean it against my legs and pull the next one forward.

"What are you doing?"

I whirl around, making the paintings clatter.

Freaky stands in the doorway glaring.

"I—I'm sorry. Oliver wanted me to find these." I hold up the historical society newsletters.

He just continues staring.

I turn and straighten the paintings. "These are so good," I say. "I bet a gallery would snap you right up. You should enter them in the Fourth of July art show."

"Little know-nothing girls should mind their own business." He storms out of the attic.

What'd I do? I count to ten to make sure I won't run into Freaky on the way down the stairs, and hurry back out.

The screen door bangs behind me and Oliver turns. "I think I made your grandfather mad," I say.

"You didn't go into his studio, did you?" he asks nervously.

"No, it was up in the attic. All I said was that he should put some of his paintings in the art show. He got super angry."

"He's really touchy about his art," Oliver explains, crossing to me. He tucks a strand of hair behind my ear. "Don't let him upset you."

"But I was complimenting him."

"I'm not really sure what the deal is," Oliver explains. "Mom says he was kind of famous for a while, but then he got really bitter about the art world. Mom doesn't even know much."

Just when I think Freaky isn't so freaky, it turns out that maybe he is.

*E*ven though I'm *so* not a morning person, I wake up at the crack of dawn on the Fourth of July. Actually, I woke up every few hours all night, so around six a.m. I decided I might as well just get up. Spinning-brain syndrome.

Justin came home yesterday, and I immediately coerced him into joining Team Candy Cane Jr. The float is finished except for one crucial part: attaching it to the boat. Thanks to Oliver's nutty scheme, that can only happen once we're down at the river.

Today not only are my two favorite guys going to meet, it could also be the day that I drown. Oh yeah—and reveal to gossipy Rocky Point that I have a boyfriend.

At least I think I do.

I'm sniffing the can of coffee Mom left on the counter when Justin comes into the kitchen. I don't like the taste of coffee, but I do like the smell. I'm hoping that I can inhale some of the caffeine to help me wake up.

"What are you doing up so early?" he asks, taking the coffee away from me. He fills the filter basket, asking, "Aren't you the one who always wants to sleep in?"

"Couldn't sleep." I eye him, already dressed in running gear. "What about you? You usually sleep till the crack of noon when you're home from school."

"I'm running in the Red, White, and Blue Five-K Run," he says, "then I'm going to check out my buddies playing at the noon concert." He pulls a coffee mug from the dish drainer and uses it to fill the coffeemaker, then hits the on button. "Where's Mom?"

"Already gone when I got up." I nod toward a note on the fridge. "There's her to-do list."

Justin scans it just like I did a few minutes ago, checking to be sure we aren't on it. She knows all about the boat parade, of course, but it's possible that because it doesn't start until later in the day she expects us to help with historical society events.

The July Fourth celebration is like the Lupine Festival, only on steroids. It's the *true* summer season kickoff, and all the locals know it. This is the first opportunity to catch the eyes (and dollars) of the Summer Regulars. Everyone—year-rounders, Regulars, day-trippers—is trying to cram as much as possible into these two short months, and the frenzy starts today. People who haven't seen each other all year catch up in the town-wide party atmosphere. We're all happy; we're all celebrating together. Sure, a lot of locals are working their butts off today, but even so it's celebratory.

"Free and clear," Justin announces.

"For now," I say, giving him a warning glare. "Remember, you're driving me and Lexi at four."

He leans against the counter, crosses his arms and grins. "So. You and Freaky Framingham's grandson."

"His name is John Framingham," I say, "not Freaky."

Not that I've ever managed to think of him as anything other than Freaky myself. Still working on that.

I narrow my eyes at him. "You're not going to embarrass me, are you?"

"No promises, Sneezy."

We don't officially have to check in until five, but with all we still have to do our plan is to meet Freaky and Oliver at the launch site at four thirty. I asked Oliver if he wanted to enjoy the festivities beforehand, but he begged off, saying he still had fine-tuning to do.

Am I a bad girlfriend for not offering to help? I'm afraid if I go over there we'll get into a fight—we're both so tightly wound about this project. I figure it's safer to hold off until the last minute.

Which brings me back to the question: Am I an actual girlfriend?

Is it possible to sprain your brain? All this going around in circles in there has me dizzy. I need to lie down. "I'm going back to bed," I tell Justin. "I need to start this day over at a more reasonable hour." I shuffle out of the kitchen. "Don't be late!" I order over my shoulder.

"Yeah, yeah, yeah," he mutters, scrounging for cereal.

The whole day I'm antsy. No matter how many times I lie down, I only manage to get in a few twenty-minute catnaps. In between those completely unsatisfactory mini snoozes, I changed my outfit and fixed my hair twice, phoned Cynthia three times (voice mail), and arranged with Patti and Joanna where we should all meet to watch the fireworks tonight. By late afternoon I'm crawling the walls.

I nearly jump out of my skin when my phone rings. "Are you heading over?" Oliver asks nervously.

"As soon as Justin gets here, we'll pick up Lexi." I pace in front of my window, scanning the street for Justin's car. "He was going to the concert, but that ended ages ago. I'll text you as soon as we're on our way."

"Maybe you should call him to make sure he's—"

"There he is!" I click off, then realize I just hung up on him without even saying good-bye. Oops.

I grab my bag and race out the door. "Took long enough," I snap at Justin as I scramble into the car.

"Whoa," Justin says. "I'm doing you a favor, remember?"

"Sorry, sorry, sorry." I drum my fingers on my leg, trying to will myself to settle down.

Justin gives me a sideways glance. "You okay?"

"No!" I blurt. "And yes!"

Justin laughs. "All righty, then."

At Lexi's I get out and help her load her supplies into the trunk. I slide into the backseat. My nervous energy needs space. Lexi joins Justin up front.

Justin and Lexi are talking, but I'm not capable of following their conversation. My head is too crammed with all the many things that could go wrong. I just hope I'm not the one to cause them.

The launch site isn't too far from where Oliver and I had lunch down by the river. Up past Freaky's house is the spot where the river branches. One part continues on down the hill to the harbor, the other forms an inlet where the boat parade takes place.

Justin parks next to Freaky's pickup. The boat is already off the trailer and down at the shoreline, the keeper's house replica still intact in the stern. I must say, Candy Cane Jr. looks awfully sweet perched up there in the truck bed. Then I hear cursing and realize that Oliver and his grandfather don't think Candy Cane Jr. is all that sweet. More like a major pain in the patootie.

Justin swings out of the car and into action. "Let me help with that!"

As he trots over to the truck, Lexi and I unload two bolts of fabric and stacks of newspapers. I carry the bib I'll be wearing and the toy lantern I bought as a "pity purchase" at a flea market. From a distance no one will notice that one side is missing a pane and the other side is cracked. The important thing is it looks like Mrs. Gilhooley might have carried it, and with a new battery it actually still turns on.

Once Candy Cane Jr. is off the truck, it's a lot easier for them to manage. The three of them carry it to the shoreline, but only place it on the ground once Lexi and I spread newspapers to keep it from getting muddy.

"Gotta say, it looks pretty darn spiffy," Justin says, taking a step back. Then he frowns. "But how—"

I cut him off. "It's all under control." I don't want to have to get into the whole "how are you going to row, much less see?" argument again. "Oh—Justin, this is Oliver," I add, realizing I hadn't introduced them.

"Didn't I see you on the other side of a lighthouse?" Justin jokes.

"That was me." Oliver smiles. "Unless you mean my grandfather. Mr. Framingham."

Freaky just grunts a hello and continues laying out tools on the newspaper beside Candy Cane Jr.

My sneakers sink a bit in the muddy bank and make little sucking sounds each time I lift my feet. Maine being Maine, we had a brief shower this morning, but thankfully, both the weather girl on TV *and* Freaky have declared that the rest of the day and the evening will be completely clear.

Oliver bounces a little on his feet, looking nervous. "Let me show you Lexi's brilliant idea," I say to distract him.

I glance around and spot a large boulder. "Over there," I say to Lexi. She follows me with a roll of fabric. I duck behind the boulder and attach the bib. I put on Mrs. Gilhooley's hat that Mom generously loaned me (after multiple promises to jump in the river after it if it blows off my head) and pick up the toy lantern. Then I rise up to the point where the scuffed doll shoes tap against the top of the rock.

"I'm Mrs. Gilhooley," I announce. "My husband the light-house keeper asked me to say hello."

Justin bursts out laughing, but in a good way. Oliver grins and applauds. Even ol' Freaky seems amused.

"I know you're worried about what it will look like from the side," Lexi says, "so come around here."

As Justin and Oliver head over, she pins the dark brown fabric to my shoulders and fans it out along the grass. "See?" she says. "We'll cover the inside of the boat with this. That way no one will see Mandy, and it will look as if Mrs. Gilhooley is standing on the ground."

"Brilliant!" Oliver exclaims. "This is what you two have been whispering about!"

I stand all the way up. "We wanted to surprise you."

Oliver brushes my lips with his. "I love it," he says softly. "Thank you."

I'm embarrassed for Justin to see me kissing Oliver, so I duck my head. "It was really Lexi who came up with the idea," I confess.

"But I'd rather kiss you," he whispers. As an enormous grin practically eats my face, he adds in a louder voice, "Thanks, Lexi. You've been awesome! We never could have done it without you."

"Well, you haven't exactly done it yet," Lexi points out. "We can celebrate after you manage to get the boat past the judges' stand."

Gulp. Rowing is Oliver's job. Navigating is mine. And we're both novices. Not to mention self-proclaimed klutzes.

As if reading my mind, Justin says, "This should be interesting."

"Suit up and do a test run," Freaky says. "I know you've been practicing, boy, but the load is going to be different from when it's empty."

I force myself to not stare. That was probably the most I've ever heard from him at one time.

"You're right, Pops." I can feel Oliver tense beside me. He's got a lot riding on this. Neither of us really cares about winning. But we don't want to be humiliated, either. This was all Oliver's design—mostly, anyway—and Lexi and I gave in to his insistence that he can row blind. We're about to put all that bravado to the test. And we all know it.

As Freaky walks back to the truck, he rolls his shoulders a few times and shakes out his hands. I have a feeling lifting and hauling Candy Cane Jr. was his own brand of bravado.

Oliver goes to the rowboat and stands there, assessing. He calls to Freaky, "Do you think I should get into it on land?"

Freaky shrugs. "Safer on ground. But how strong are your friends?"

Oliver glances over at us, worried.

"Come on, help us get Oliver into the lighthouse," I say to Justin.

Oliver sits in his spot in the middle seat. For a moment we all just look back and forth between the rowboat and the lighthouse. "That won't build itself," Freaky says as he ambles over with the clamps we're going to use to attach the lighthouse to the rim of the boat.

"So how are we going to do this?" I say, worrying as the time keeps passing and people start arriving.

To my astonishment, Freaky takes charge. "Ollie, scrunch down. Once we give the okay, slowly straighten up. Mandy, get in the boat and guide the lighthouse down over him. What's yer name, tall girl?" He snaps his fingers at Lexi. "You, me, and the boy there"—indicating Justin—"will hoist the thing. High."

"Got it," Justin says. Under his breath he mutters, "Hope you got your measurements right."

"We tested it," I snap. It's true. When we finished the chicken-wire tower, before we put on the papier-mâché, Freaky, Oliver's mom, and I lowered it down over Oliver. It worked on land. I just hope we can manage it once it's on the boat.

I clamber into the boat, Oliver scrunches, and the three of

them raise the lighthouse. I reach over to help them get it above Oliver and centered. I shove it a bit more to the left, and Oliver disappears inside the tower.

"You okay in there?" I ask.

"Yeah," comes his muffled reply.

"Are you sitting all the way up?" Freaky asks.

The lighthouse shifts and wiggles but it doesn't flip over. "I am now." We all exhale loudly with relief.

Freaky, Justin, and Lexi step away delicately as if any sudden movement might topple the structure.

"Does it look straight?" I ask them.

Lexi walks all the way around it. "Looks good. Time to clamp it on."

Freaky and Justin get to work as I climb out of the boat and help Lexi with the blue-green fabric we also brought. Once they're done, we cover the wooden platform and metal clamps with the fabric, the idea being that it will look like waves.

"Still okay?" I ask.

"Excellent," Oliver replies.

"Let's get this baby in the water!" Justin says.

Freaky has returned to his truck and leans against it, arms crossed. I guess he's done. Justin, Lexi, and I grunt and heave and shove, and finally get the rowboat into the water. I hop into it, making it tip.

"What's going on?" Oliver calls from inside his prison.

"All okay, just getting settled," I assure him.

"Oars?" Oliver asks.

"Coming!" Justin calls. He and Lexi slip oars in through the portholes. I'm relieved when they begin to move rhythmically, which means Oliver not only has a good grip, but actually has been practicing as he promised.

We immediately ground.

"What happened?" Oliver shouts.

"Sorry, sorry, sorry!" I say. "I wasn't navigating. Don't do anything until I get set up."

"Hang on," Justin says. He wades into the water and holds the rowboat still. I am going to owe him big-time. Except no one seems annoyed. In fact everyone seems to be having fun. Even, I realize, as I take a quick look, ol' Freaky Framingham.

"I'm getting into position," I tell Oliver, being his eyes. "Lexi is tying the bib on. Now she's pinning the fabric."

I sit still as Lexi arranges fabric in the bow so it will look as if the doll shoes are standing on a boulder, and then brings it around me to hide my body.

"Done!" Lexi declares. She moves all around the boat in the water, taking photos.

"Is the lantern lit?" Oliver asks.

"I'll get it," Justin calls, rushing forward. "There's going to be a kind of a lurch," he warns. Lexi holds the boat steady.

Justin carefully gets into the boat. It tips side to side, but the lighthouse holds. Yay, clamps! Justin flicks the switch on the battery-operated candle in the lantern room. "All set."

That reminds me to do the same to mine. I click on the toy lantern.

"Adorable," Lexi declares.

By now the boat parade official, Mr. Saunders, has arrived. He quickly wades into the shallows. "You're not supposed to launch until it's your turn," he tells me.

"Do we have to get out of the water?" I ask plaintively. I *really* don't want to have to ask Justin, Lexi, and Freaky to haul us out and then put us back in again.

"What's happening?" Oliver's stifled voice asks.

Mr. Saunders looks startled. "There's someone in there?"

I want to ask him if he thinks Candy Cane Jr. is rowing herself, but I don't since we're asking him to bend the rules for us. I put on a pathetic face and say, "It will just be too hard to pull us out and then bring us back in."

"What number are you?"

"Five."

He glances at the people arriving with their boats. He looks down at his clipboard. "You okay if we make them third?" he calls out to them.

There's a brief stomach-tightening moment as the entrants confer with each other. Then I see shrugs and hear "Sure!" and "Fine," and "No problem," and I relax again.

Well, relax-ish.

"Get over as far as possible to make room for the first two boats," Mr. Saunders instructs.

"Thank you SOOOOOO much!"

Freaky ambles back down to the boat, then slips a hefty pair of wire cutters under the brown fabric by my feet. "Just in case," he says. He jerks his head toward the invisible Oliver. He lowers his voice and adds, "Lad can be stubborn. Can't imagine where he gets it from."

Then he winks, pats the boat, and stands. "Have fun." He gives the boat a little shove so that we move more out of the way, then heads back toward the truck.

I have the astounding impression that I might have just gotten a glimpse of the "real" Freaky. And that this was his way of letting me know he's not really mad at me for the other day in the attic.

The first boat isn't fancy, but has cuteness going for it. A dad wearing typical lobsterman gear rows a boat with lobster traps hanging from bow and stern. Four little kids wearing homemade fish costumes wave. A mom sits in the stern holding a baby dressed as a lobster—a popular infant Halloween costume around here. It takes them a while to launch because all kinds of relatives insist on taking videos and snapping pictures.

Next up is a boat full of scantily clad mermaids, and I'm secretly glad that Oliver can't see anything from his spot inside the tower. My brother Justin happily helps the girls get the boat launched. I have a feeling this boat is going to be a hit with the boys lining the banks.

Then it's our turn.

"Showtime," I tell Oliver.

"Now?" Oliver asks.

"Now!"

My stomach clenches. I've just realized that even though Oliver is the one powering the boat, I'm really the one in charge. It's all up to me to get us through this.

Oliver's oars hit the water with a splash. "Hey!" I yelp.

"Sorry! Sorry!"

He gets the oars under control, and we glide away from shore. First challenge: get around the bend without snagging on any boulders or low-hanging trees, or going aground.

"Straight," I instruct Oliver. "Straight." I keep my voice calm and even. Almost singsong. Our first task is to get far enough away from shore to make the turn without disaster. But not so far that the spectators won't be able to see us.

"Turn!" I call out.

"What?" I hear Oliver ask.

"Turn!" I screech.

"Which way?" Oliver shouts back.

It just now occurs to me that we should have practiced the route. Not to mention tested our ability to hear each other since Oliver is *inside* Candy Cane Jr. sitting backward to row—and facing *away* from me. Too late now.

"RIGHT! RIGHT! RIGHT!" I holler.

Oliver adjusts quickly (points to Oliver!), and we move into the correct position. Up ahead the first boat is getting *awwws*, and the boatload of gyrating mermaids is getting a lot of whoops and catcalls. I'm hoping they don't totally eclipse us and we glide by the shore without anyone even noticing.

I underestimated our fan club.

"Candy Cane!" someone screams onshore. I think it's Lexi.

"Look!" a voice sounding suspiciously like Justin's shouts. "It's Mrs. Gilhooley!"

A rhythmic cheer goes up. "Candy Cane! Candy Cane!" I detect a strong Brooklyn accent in there. Joanna must have stopped texting her boyfriend long enough to join in.

I grin from ear to ear. It's amazing to hear the applause and chanting and know it's for us. I suddenly understand the rush Cynthia says she feels onstage.

"What's happening?" Oliver asks.

"They're cheering for us!"

I think he says "Cool," but it's hard to tell under all that papier-mâché and chicken wire.

Then the sound changes. The clapping falls off, there's a bit of a hush, and then I hear Justin yell, "Mandy! Watch out!"

I snap out of my reverie. Oliver is a righty, and with no visual cues he's rowed us more toward shore than keeping a straight and centered heading. We're closer in than we should be. Here there are rocks and debris—all just waiting to snag our boat and topple Candy Cane Jr.

"Pull left," I yell.

But he doesn't hear me. The next boat must have appeared behind us because a new section of the crowd starts applauding.

"Left, Oliver! Left!"

"What?" Oliver calls through the papier-mâché.

"Left! Left!"

I turn to yell it directly at the tower, ripping up the fabric, Mrs. Gilhooley's dress flapping and feet kicking as I swing around. "LEFT!"

People onshore join in. "Left! Left! Left!" they shout.

The boat finally straightens back out, and there's loud applause again. I swivel in the seat and rearrange my various pieces, though I know it looks totally sloppy compared to Lexi's careful job. *Oh well*, I think. We already passed the judges before this little mishap, when we were still looking good. I silently vow to ignore the shore and pay attention only to navigation.

"We're starting the curve now," I instruct Oliver. We'll have fewer cheerleaders here—this section tends to fill up with families living on the west side of the inlet. That'll make it easier for me to concentrate.

We row around the inlet and land just opposite from where we began without any further incidents. It's only been about a fifteen-minute trip, but I know Oliver must be exhausted. And hot. And if he is anything like me, totally stressed. Maybe even claustrophobic.

We safely make it to where we can get out, and thankfully, a bunch of people come help us the minute we reach shallow water. Someone detaches the fabric from my shoulders, and I undo the costume bib. I drop Mrs. Gilhooley into the boat and leap out. I hold it stable as three dad types unclamp the lighthouse and lift it off Oliver.

He's drenched in sweat, his hair plastered to his face. Someone hands him a bottle of water, which he accepts gratefully. He's too winded to speak or even climb out of the dinghy. I lean over and fling my arms around him anyway, tipping the boat a bit. "We did it!"

He's still breathing in gasps but says shakily, "I'm totally gross."

I stand back up and hold out my hands to help him. "Yeah, you are!" I say with a laugh.

Once Oliver is out of the boat and we've stumbled through the shallow water, the same dad types drag the dinghy out of the way of the arriving boats. I know we should be helping, but given our natural clumsiness and Oliver's exhaustion, I figure we're doing them more of a favor by standing still.

Oliver pours the rest of the bottle of water over his head and rubs his wet face. He takes in a long breath, then blows it back out.

"I wish you could have seen them," I say. "They were clapping and cheering for us."

"I *kind of* heard it," he says with a rueful smile. He shakes his head hard, like a puppy, spraying me with water.

"Hey!" I scream.

"Sorry!" Oliver smiles and lays a wet arm across my shoulder. I don't mind. "As much as I hate to admit this," he says, "I really should have listened to you. And Lexi. Eyeholes would have helped. And rowing from inside was no fun."

"Well, we survived," I say. "That's all that matters."

Oliver twists to look at Candy Cane Jr. "Yeah . . . I guess. . . ."

"I've figured out something about you," I tell him. "It's like you once said to me. You're excellent on the micro scale. But when it comes to macro . . ." I shrug as I trail off.

"What do you mean?" Oliver asks, turning back around. When I don't answer, he bangs his hip into mine. "Come on, you can't leave me hanging."

I hope he doesn't get mad, but I continue. "Your measurements were perfect. Your staples absolutely evenly spaced. The lantern house, the stripes, it's all just right, all the little details."

"But . . . ?"

"But let's just say the big picture kind of gets crowded out."

"Like giving up the ability to see in exchange for a completely accurate model," he says with a sheepish grin.

I give him a little squeeze. "Don't feel bad," I tell him. "I'm good at the big picture, and totally sloppy in the details." I frown. "I guess that makes us opposites." That seems like maybe it's a bad thing.

"I'd say that makes us complementary, not opposites. It's why we make such a good team."

He leans down and kisses me, but I step back. This is a bit too public, with the other parade entrants coming and going. Not to mention any minute now Freaky's blue pickup will appear.

I glance up the slope and spot the truck pulling up. Freaky climbs out and ambles down the hill.

"Good job," Freaky says. Oliver beams. I can see his grand-pop's approval means a lot to him.

Together the three of us load Candy Cane Jr. onto the truck and the boat onto the trailer. Oliver climbs into the truck cab, then leans out the open window. "See you at the beach for the fireworks," he says.

"Near the dock," I remind him.

He taps my nose with his finger, then settles into his seat. I step back and watch the truck drive away.

I glance around and realize people are staring. This has to be the biggest Freaky sighting all summer. I wonder if they think I'm a big weirdo because of it.

I have a momentous realization: I don't care. Not only do I like—maybe even more than like—Oliver, I've actually grown fond of Freaky. Hopefully, instead of his freakiness rubbing off on me, my total and complete ordinariness will rub off on him. At least in the eyes of the Rocky Point gossipers.

I text Justin I'm ready for him to pick me up. Then I watch a very elaborately decorated boat coming toward shore. A canopy made of netting hangs over the top, the poles disguised with seaweed. "Under the Sea" from *The Little Mermaid* blasts from hidden speakers. The guy rowing is dressed in a scuba outfit, and three people manipulate larger-than-life-size puppets: a jellyfish, a lobster, and a crab. Glow sticks nestled in the netting and seaweed give it an otherworldly, underwatery look.

"Amazing," I murmur. "I bet I know who'll win first prize!"

I hear a horn honk and see Justin pulling up. I scramble up the muddy little hill. "You did great!" Justin says as I get into the car.

"Yeah," I say, "I'm kind of astonished we survived."

"We all are, believe me," Justin says. "So where to? Back to Freaky's?"

I give him a look.

"I'm sorry," he says, shrugging. "I don't know what else to call him."

I sigh. "Me either. But we have to come up with something!"

"How about *Mister* Freaky?" Justin jokes. "It sounds more respectful."

I smack his arm, but I'm laughing.

"He's different from what I thought," Justin says. "Freaky, I mean."

"I know, right?" I already told Justin about Freaky being an artist, and also about how touchy he was about his paintings. "Just drop me off at home so I can shower and change, please." I bite my lip as I watch houses decorated with flags and red-white-and-blue bunting go by the window. "And Oliver?"

"What about him?" he asks as he makes the turn onto Dumont.

"Is he . . . different from what you thought?"

A sneaky little smile crawls across his face. "Mandy has a boy-friend," he singsongs. "Mandy has a boyfriend."

"Stop it!" I protest.

But he keeps singing. "Mandy and Ollie sitting in a tree. K-I-S-S-I-N-G!"

"Cut it out," I shriek through my giggles.

Justin switches to making kissing noises.

I poke his side. "You." Poke. "Are." Poke. "Evil."

He laughs his sinister-villain laugh. The he waggles his eye-brows at me. "You better be nice to me, sis. So far I haven't spilled any of your secrets—"

"I don't have any."

"Or interrogated him about his intentions, or questioned him about his weird attachment to Candy Cane or—"

"Okay! Okay! I get it. You are the best brother ever and I am lucky to have you and when are you going back to school already?"

He laughs and stops to let a bunch of parents with little kids with balloons and painted faces cross the street. There were kid-die events all day in the Square, and now these kids are probably on their way to find a spot for the fireworks. Or grab some food on the piers, though there will also be booths set up near the docks, too. Yep, another seafood extravaganza.

As Justin pulls into our driveway, a thought rattles through me. I'm making my debut tonight as Oliver's girlfriend. Or maybe *he's* making *his* debut as my boyfriend.

If that's what we actually are. We haven't discussed our "status"—we've been too busy building the float and, okay, kissing, to talk about what the kissing means. *Don't overthink*, I order myself.

Between Candy Cane duty and building the float I haven't had a chance to see or even talk to anyone. Not Patti, not Joanna, not any of my school friends (well, mostly they're Cynthia's, but whatever). None of them know about Oliver and me. And now we're about to go public.

I think I'm more nervous now than I was before the boat parade.

I run my fingers up and down my seat belt. "So, um . . ."

Justin stops with his hand on the door. "What?"

I flush. This is embarrassing, but I really do want to know. "So do you like him?"

"Freaky? Yeah, he's aces."

I roll my eyes again. Justin brings that out in me.

"Yes, sis, I like Oliver. And what's more important, you like him. And probably even more important to you"—he pokes me—"is that he likes you."

I lean back in my seat and feel the tension fall away, like it's being swept out to sea. "He does?"

156

Justin scoots out of the car. "Don't go all girl on me, Sneezy. You know he does. Don't pretend you don't."

I'm about to protest, then realize he's right. Oliver likes me. I know it. And he knows I like him. And that's exactly how it should be.

*T*he barge that sets off the fireworks is stationed between Rocky Point and Hubbard Island, so pretty much all sides of the bay provide good views. And all sides get crowded, particularly the U-shaped sandy beach that creates the cove. The band and the officials use the two ferry docks on the bay, so no one gets to sit there, but they make a great meeting point. That's where I head to find Patti and Joanna when Mom drops me off at the wharf.

I pass the same food booths that were at the Lupine Festival, but now that the Summer Regulars have arrived—and a whole lot of day-trippers have invaded— it's *really* crammed. I forgo my bloob pocket just in case Oliver and Lexi beat me here. I don't want him to have to face Joanna and Patti without me.

Music blasts from the loudspeakers, and the whole wharf has a party atmosphere, with lots of people sporting red, white, and blue. It's mega packed even as I make my way down the rocks to the shore. I hope I can find my friends in all this! Light spills from the docks, and the booths illuminate part of the beach, but it's still fairly dark as I get closer to the water.

I had nothing to worry about. I hear Joanna's unmistakable Brooklyn accent and use it as my guide. I try to avoid stepping on any toes or fingers as I pick my way carefully through the people perched on mossy rocks and sprawled on the sand. It's like a human obstacle course.

"I can't hear you!" Joanna's yelling into her cell phone, one hand covering her other ear. "We should text. TEXT!"

Joanna sits on a portable beach chair that holds down one corner of a blanket. Patti lounges on another edge, her legs stretched out in front of her. What's interesting is the guy Patti's leaning against. As I approach, she lifts her face to him. He bends to kiss her, then she gets up and kneels to rummage in a cooler holding down another corner of the blanket.

So Patti found herself her summer romance. Interesting.

"Hey, everybody!" I greet as I drop onto the blanket.

"Mandy!" Joanna cries. "Little Miss MIA!"

"Sorry," I say. "But between working at the lighthouse and building the boat float, I've been super busy."

Patti swings around with her back to the water. "Mandy, do you know Kyle Marcus?"

I look at Kyle, who's now sitting cross-legged next to her. His face is familiar. Curly blond mane. Freckles. "Were you on the soccer team with my brother? Justin?"

"You're Justin Sullivan's sis?" He grins. "Cool. Is he coming?"

"He's around here somewhere," I say, scanning the crowds. "We might run into him. So what have you vacationers been up to while I've been slaving away?"

"Well," Patti says, "Grumpy over there has spent most of the time at the library checking e-mail and gazing at pictures of her beloved Brooklyn. Not to mention her beloved."

Joanna scoops sand at Patti. "I haven't been that bad."

"That's true. We were able to pry you away from Wi-Fi long enough for a trip to Hubbard Island." Patti looks at me a bit apologetically. "We were going to ask you if you wanted to come, but we know you're not all that into the biking and hiking."

"And sneezing and itching eyes," I agree. "My allergies kick in around now, so being in all that nature isn't exactly big fun."

"You looked like you were having a good time in the boat parade today," Joanna says. She holds up her soda can in salute. "Excellent float!"

"Thanks," I say. "It was all Oliver's idea."

Joanna swivels her head. "So where is this mystery man of yours?"

Patti scoots forward. "Is he really Freaky Framingham's grandson?"

"Word really gets around in this town," I say.

"Another reason I miss Brooklyn," Joanna mutters.

"He'll be here," I say. I rise up on my knees and scan the crowd.

"Talking about me?"

Hands appear on my shoulders. Oliver's hands.

"You found us!" I say, glancing up. I'm so relieved that I hadn't said too much. He would have heard every word.

"With Lexi's help," he says, settling next to me. "She's talking to some friends over by the dock. She'll be over in a minute, she said."

"So you're the genius behind the mini Candy Cane," Joanna says.

"I don't know if 'genius' is the right word," Oliver responds. "'Nut job,' maybe. Though I think Lexi and Mandy might refer to me as Pain in the Butt."

"Guys, this is Oliver," I say with a laugh. I nod toward my

friends. "The one clinging to her cell phone is Joanna; that's Patti and her friend Kyle."

"Hey, man," Kyle says. He stands and stretches. "I'm off. Gotta go sell some lobster."

Patti stands and gets up onto her tiptoes to give him a quick kiss. "Later," he tells her.

"You bet."

To us he adds, "If you get hungry, stop by our booth. It's the second one in at Main Street and Water. Don't you dare go to Jake's. And say hi to Sully for me."

"We promise!" I call after him as he heads off.

"Who's Sully?" Oliver asks.

"Justin. One of his many nicknames."

The minute Kyle is out of hearing range, Patti grabs my hands. "So you know him? Tell me everything!" she demands.

"Looks like you already know plenty," I tease.

"But you're here with him all year! And by the way, where have you been hiding him?"

"I guess you just hadn't been paying enough attention," I say.

"Well . . . ?"

I frown. "I actually don't know much. He was a year ahead of Justin."

"Oooh," Joanna says. "A college man!"

"Actually," Patti says, "he's not in college. He told me that his dad needed his help, so he didn't go."

"That's right," I say, remembering. "His dad's one of the lobstermen. I think it's a whole family operation. Uncle. Cousins, too, maybe."

"Rough," Joanna says. "To have to give up college to go into the family business."

"I don't know," Oliver says. "He can always go later. I think it's kind of noble. Pitching in for the family." He grins. "Of course, I'm totally incapable of going into my family's businesses, so it's easy for me to talk."

"Mandy's kind of in the family business this summer," Patti points out. "That lighthouse is practically a family member."

"Yeah," Oliver says, tucking a strand of hair behind my ear. "And I think it's really sweet."

"Okay, now we need to know all about *you*!" Joanna says, setting her sights on Oliver. Gotta give the boy props. He's not running screaming into the night.

"Not much to tell. Here from California. And," he adds, putting his arm around me, "having a much better time than I thought I would."

"So . . . how'd you meet?" Patti asks in a singsongy voice.

I squinch my nose at her. My way of warning her not to get too—well, let's just call it "cute."

"Candy Cane," Oliver tells them.

"That job I didn't want?" I say. "It turned out to have some surprise perks."

"Is that what I am?" Oliver asks, pretending to be offended. "A perk?"

"You're a lot perkier than I am," I quip.

"Definitely perkier than Joanna," Patti grumbles.

"What?" Joanna glances up from her cell. "What are you saying?"

"Quit with the texting already!" Patti complains. "We're getting the dish on the new guy!"

I shake my head, but Oliver seems amused.

"Speaking of dishes," he says. He starts emptying a shopping bag he brought with him. Wrapped sandwiches, cut veggies with some kind of dip in a plastic tub, and more of those giant cookies.

"Oh, my hero!" I squeal. I grab one of the sandwiches. I wave it at the others. "I can guarantee all of this is super delish!"

"Oh good," Lexi says as she joins us. "I didn't miss the food!"

Oliver scoots over to make room for her. "Pops insisted I bring enough to feed an army, so dig in."

"Oliver's grandfather is an insanely good cook," I promise them. "Your taste buds will be in ecstasy."

Lexi picks up a sandwich and unwraps it. "It's true. Ol' Freaky is a freaking brilliant cook."

Everyone freezes. All eyes flick to Oliver. I carefully study the sandwich in my lap.

"Freaky?" he repeats. He looks around, but now everyone's avoiding his eyes. "Mandy?"

I swallow my bite of mozzarella, pesto, and arugula sandwich. "It's, uh, kind of a nickname. It's stupid. Just kid stuff."

"Oh." Oliver looks down and fiddles with the laces of his sneakers. He clears his throat. "Look, I know he's kind of eccentric, but he's actually—"

"He's awesome," Lexi says, cutting him off. "He knows all this stuff about art, and building things."

"If people would get to know him," Oliver says sharply, "they wouldn't be so mean."

"That's not fair," Patti argues. "He doesn't *let* us get to know him. He's like this recluse up in the woods. The only time I ever saw him in town he practically growled at anyone who tried to talk to him."

I stroke Oliver's arm, sorry I brought him here, sorry that he had to hear this, sorry that—well, just sorry. "Patti's right," I say gently. "Until I got to know him, I thought he was kind of scary. You know how kids are."

Oliver gives a little nod and takes a sandwich. I'm encouraged by the fact that he's still sitting here.

"And now that I've been spending all this time up at the house, I see him differently," I say.

Oliver unwraps his sandwich and takes a bite. As he chews I can tell he's thinking. Mulling. I reach for the cooler with sodas and hand him a can. He pops it open and takes a swig. "It's okay," he finally says. "I thought he was pretty odd when I first got here too. And he's definitely got his moods. So I understand. And this town seems pretty big on nicknames."

He smiles weakly to show he's not mad, and I see everyone relax. My own shoulders drop back to where they belong, and my stomach unclenches. The sandwiches get distributed, and after Patti takes a bite, she says, "Oh man. Lexi's right. These are freakishly good!"

"From now on," Lexi says, "that's what we mean if we call him Freaky. That he makes freakishly good food."

Oliver laughs for real, and I know the awkwardness is definitely over.

"You think these are good," I say, "wait until you taste the cookies!"

"Did someone say cookies?"

"Hi, Vicki," Lexi says. She moves over to make room.

"That was the cutest boat," Vicki says to me, but she's eyeing Oliver. I can't tell if it's because he's so good-looking, because she's never seen me with a boyfriend, or because of the Freaky connection.

"This is Oliver," I say. "From California." I lean into Oliver and look up at him. "Vicki's in some of my classes."

"California?" Vicki says. "Cool." She reaches for a cookie, then looks around at us for permission.

"Go ahead," Oliver says with a smile. "I brought plenty."

"How'd the performance go?" I ask, munching my sandwich.

Vicki's in drama club with Cynthia, and for the last few years they've been performing on one of the stages set up in the Square on the Fourth.

"I skipped it this year," she says, then gazes at the cookie. "Wow, this is good."

"Why?" Lexi asks. "You always do it."

Vicki shrugs. "Cynthia's the one who's into it. I'd rather just enjoy the great big party, since most of the summer I'm baby-sitting."

"Then why do you do it?" I ask.

Vicki shrugs. "You know how Cynthia can be."

I'm about to ask what she means when my hand is crushed under a stranger's foot.

"Yeowch!" I yelp.

"Sorry," I hear someone call.

Normally part of the fun of the Fourth of July is the giant and crowded beach party. But tonight I'd rather not get stepped on and have a bit more private time with Oliver.

"What time is it?" I ask.

Joanna checks her cell phone. "Eight forty-five."

That gives us fifteen minutes before the show begins. "I have an idea," I whisper to Oliver. "A better place to watch the fireworks. But we have to hurry."

"Okay."

I grab a cookie and stand. "We're going to take off."

"But you're going to miss the prize announcements," Vicki says.

The ribbons are given to the boat-float winners just before the fireworks begin, along with the usual announcements, thank-yous, et cetera.

"Somehow I don't think we're going to win," I say.

"Unless there's a prize for the most foolhardy," Lexi comments. She shakes her head and picks up another sandwich. "I still can't believe you pulled it off."

"If we win," Oliver says to Lexi, "you accept for the team."

Lexi gives him a thumbs-up as she chews.

We head toward the wharf, stepping around blankets and skirting kids racing around waving pinwheels and sparklers. "Do we have time for me to grab some sodas from the booth?" Oliver asks.

"If you hurry."

"Don't move." He rushes away into the crowd. The lines at

the booths aren't bad now since the fireworks are about to start, and soon Oliver reappears carrying a take-out box. He hands me a soda. Then he holds out something else.

A lobster roll. For me.

He looks so adorably proud of himself. "I got it at Kyle's booth, as promised."

"I'm not really hungry," I say.

"Aw, come on," he says. "Kyle says theirs are the best. After all, it's a day to show our patriotism. Eating a lobster roll in Maine could be considered a patriotic act."

I smile weakly as I take it from him. My nose wrinkles at the smell. *Wash it down with soda,* I tell myself. Mask the flavor with a bite of cookie. You can do this.

He's still watching. I take a teeny-tiny bite, hoping to get mostly roll. But the reason Kyle's family has so many fans is because of how overstuffed the rolls are.

Dis-*gus*-ting.

My taste buds want to leap off my tongue, and I force myself to swallow without gagging. It's not easy. I immediately take a big swig of soda, swishing it all around my mouth as if it's mouthwash. I take another gulp of soda, trying to wash away the grossness of lobster chunks drenched in mayo. I actually shudder.

Luckily, Oliver is loving his lobster roll so much he actually shuts his eyes and practically swoons. Excellent. I take advantage of his closed eyes and drop the sandwich.

"Oops!" I say as he opens his eyes. "Clumsy me."

"I'll go get you another," Oliver says.

I grab his arm. "No! We, uh, we don't have enough time."

"We can split this one," he says, holding it out to me.

"You have it. I can have them anytime, remember? But we actually do have to hurry."

I take a huge bite of Freaky's cookie—chocolate chip with walnuts—to disguise the lingering fish flavor and grab his arm.

"Where are we going?" Oliver asks as I lead him away from the wharf.

"To the most fitting place to celebrate this day," I say.

Then he gets it. "Candy Cane!"

"Exactly. We spent the day with Candy Cane Jr., so now we should spend the evening with the lady herself."

"I like the way you think." Now that he knows where we're headed, Oliver picks up his pace. We're practically running as we reach it. He follows me around to the entrance. "We're going inside?" he asks.

I give him a smug smile "We're going to the top."

I fish out my keys, and together we shove open the door.

I've never been in the lighthouse at night. It's pitch-black, which I'd expected, and also pretty spooky. "Hang on," I say. "Hold the door open."

Even with door propped the moonlight barely makes a dent in the dark. "Take this," I say, handing Oliver the rest of my cookie. "I need both hands. Actually, finish it," I add. I anticipate some kissing before, during, and after the fireworks, and I can't bear the idea of Oliver having fish breath.

That taken care of, I carefully shuffle to the entryway bench. It's a much easier target than the lamp on the table farther in. I flip up the seat and rummage around inside. "Bingo!" I exclaim, pulling out a flashlight. I flick it on. Oliver lets the door shut and takes the flashlight as I pull out another one.

I train the light on the table with the lamp. "Over there," I instruct Oliver.

He walks to the table, then stops. "Let's not."

"Let's not what?" I ask as I stand.

"Turn on the lights. Let's pretend we're way back in time. We're in the era of Mrs. Gilhooley."

"I don't think they had these." I wave the flashlight.

"They had lanterns. These will stand in for those."

I shake my head and smile. "You're not going to make me put on Mrs. Gilhooley's outfit, are you?"

"Maybe next time."

I cross to the doorway leading to the spiral staircase. "I wouldn't want to climb these in the dark in that dress."

Something about being in the tower with nothing but our flashlight beams to guide us keeps us from speaking. Maybe it's because we're concentrating hard—it would be bad to take a misstep, and we're both self-admitted klutzes. But there's also something mysterious and private and magical about climbing with only our flickering lights that invites silence.

It gets me thinking about the footsteps of all those lighthouse keepers who made this very same climb in the dark. Oliver may be right—there is something compelling about the history of this place, once it starts to seem more personal.

But neither of us can stay quiet when we emerge into the lantern room. "Oh my," I breathe. Oliver gasps behind me.

I know this is the view tourists travel to see, but none has ever seen it like this. I quickly turn off my flashlight, and Oliver does the same with his. We carefully place them by our feet.

The lantern room is made entirely of glass panes fitted into metal frames, giving us a panoramic view of all of Rocky Point. Straight ahead the new(er) lighthouse flashes signals from its rocky outpost where the bay and the harbor join together to become the wide-open sea. Out the windows on my left side, I can see the lights from the ferry docks and the food booths. Tiny fluttering green dots that remind me of fireflies sparkle along the coast. I'm guessing they're glow sticks carried by all of the kids huddled around their parents. Across the bay, lights on the Cranston peninsula dot the shoreline.

On the right-hand side it's pretty dark in the harbor. I can make out the running lights on boats where people are holding their own Independence Day celebrations on board. I turn all the way around and look at the town—the lit homes, the streetlamps, the illuminated shop windows. "It doesn't look real," I murmur.

"Like something out of a storybook," Oliver agrees. "This must be what it looked like to all those keepers who had to make sure the lantern stayed lit."

"Beautiful."

We're both lost in the timelessness of this moment. It's as if history is seeping into me, the way it has seeped into the stones of the tower.

Boom!

We both jump. "Wh-what was that?" I stammer, clutching the guardrail.

Oliver starts laughing. "There seems to be some sort of event going on. . . ."

I look up at him, then smack my head. "D'oh! Fireworks."

"They were the reason we came up here, right?" Oliver kisses the tip of my nose. "Or were they just an excuse . . . ?"

I lay my arms on his chest, with my hands on his shoulders. "A little of both."

He lowers his head to kiss me when we're both startled by another explosion. "Kissing later," I say. I spin him around to face the right direction. "Fireworks now."

"I'm sure there's a bad joke to make but I can't—"

Boom!

We stand mesmerized by the colorful display. There's something about how gorgeous they are—but last only for moments—that gets to me. All this effort and risk just to give us a fleeting vision of something exquisite.

We're too far away to hear the music programmed to go with them, but there's something even more dramatic watching them streak across the sky accompanied by nothing but natural sounds. Just the water splashing against the rocks below and people so far away it's hard to discern what's music and what's chatter, though every now and then shrieks, laughter, and applause drift up to us.

I'm super aware of how close Oliver is, the sharp little intakes of breath when an explosion surprises him, the laughter when he realizes he startled. He keeps glancing at me as if he's enjoying my enjoyment of the fireworks as much as his own.

Best idea ever, I congratulate myself with a smile.

As the rousing finale booms and bursts and explodes, Oliver

moves behind me and encloses me by placing his hands beside mine on the guardrail. I feel his warmth against my back, welcome heat in the chilly tower. I feel protected, and think again about the original lighthouse keepers—the extraordinary risks they took every single day just doing their jobs. What did Mrs. Gilhooley feel like, living here to watch over sailors and ships, before there were real roads and everything was done by ship? How brave they must have been. And how lonely.

The applause on the beach is loud enough to hear in the tower. It's an incredible feeling knowing that we've shared this not just with each other but with all of Rocky Point. All of Cranston. All those boats. All of time, it feels like.

"Spectacular," Oliver says in a long exhale.

"I did good?" I ask, leaning against him.

"You did good."

I turn and smile up at him. It's hard to see his face in the dim light, but I can see he's gazing down at me with something that looks a lot like love. It startles me, how open he is, then I remember I've got my own neon-sign face. He must have seen that same look on me.

Then our lips meet, and his hand tangles in my hair. I stroke the back of his neck, and as the kiss grows deeper, I press against him and move my hands to his back to pull him closer. Our breathing grows more ragged, our kissing more determined, our touches more intense.

We break apart and I take in a deep breath and I hear Oliver do the same. Then he brings his face close to mine and whispers, "Now we have another special place, like the spot by the river."

"Mm," I murmur as his mouth moves along my neck. Then we're kissing again and Rocky Point vanishes.

"We, uh, we should go," I finally say reluctantly. "Mom will be waiting."

"I guess," Oliver says with a sigh.

We turn toward the archway and my foot hits something. It clatters down the stairs. "Oops," I say. "I think that was a flashlight."

"It really was just luck that we didn't drown today, wasn't it?" Oliver comments wryly. "We're quite the pair."

I giggle. "Too bad being clumsy is one of the things we have in common."

Oliver holds up his flashlight. "Should I do the honors? Since you were my eyes in the boat?"

I gesture to the stairway entrance. "After you, fearless leader."

"I'm only suggesting this because you weigh less than I do. If I trip and land on you, I think it'd be a bigger problem."

"How about neither of us trip, okay?"

"Works for me," Oliver says.

"Let's just hope the ghost of Anna Christine doesn't object to our being here. She just might push us down the rest of the way."

"You didn't tell me Candy Cane is haunted," Oliver says, sounding gleeful. "Somehow that makes it even more perfect. So who is she? I mean, who *was* she?"

I tell Oliver the sad tale of the young widow waiting for her husband to return. He'd been blown off the rocks as he made his way in a torrential storm to keep the lantern lit. I get kind of goose-bumpy telling the tale as we s-l-o-w-l-y make our way down the stairs, Oliver in front holding the flashlight, me clutching the back of his T-shirt. Two reasons: One, it's a little hard to see his tiny flashlight beam, and this clues me in to when he's on the next step. And two, if he does start to fall, I can hopefully snatch him back.

A loud clatter nearly topples us in surprise. "What was that?" I squeak.

Oliver laughs. "Anna Christine just tossed your flashlight the rest of the way down the stairs. Using my foot."

We continue down the circular staircase, the rough stone walls giving off a damp smell, the metal railing cold under my hand. I grip it so tight I'm pretty sure my hand is going to be permanently cramped.

"Made it!" Oliver cheers as we arrive at the ground floor.

I stop and soak in the atmosphere for a moment. "I'm starting to get it," I say.

"Get what?"

"The . . . I don't know . . . the connectedness people feel when they come here. Why they want to see the lighthouse." I snort a little laugh. "Ohmigod. Maybe I'm even understanding my mom more!"

"Oh, not possible!" Oliver teases.

"Shut up," I say with a laugh. "But speaking of Mom, I need to get to the Square. Do you want a ride? Or are you hitching with Lexi and her gang?"

"I'm not sure I can find her now," Oliver says. "Your mom won't mind? It's kind of out of the way."

"Are you kidding? How can she not give the boy who loves Candy Cane as much as she does a ride?"

"I think she'll like me even more if I convince her daughter to love Candy Cane too."

I slip my arm around his waist. "I'm getting there."

We walk in companionable silence, soaking in the tangy salt air and ocean breeze. We stay close to the shoreline, figuring we'll head inland after checking to see if any of my friends are still at the beach so we can say good-bye. We help each other up and over the uneven rocks, feeling the spray around our ankles as water splashes the boulders.

The parties are all breaking up. People call to one another, parents corral or carry kids, and the booths are being dismantled. We arrive at the dock and continue along the beach, but it looks as if everyone has already left. We link pinkies as we wander slowly among the departing crowds, sand and seashells crunching underfoot.

Suddenly I stop.

"Do you see them?" Oliver asks.

Moonlit night. Oliver. Holding hands. A tiny soft laugh sneaks out of me. We're actually acting out one of my images from the romantic montage that flipped through my brain the very first time Oliver came to Candy Cane.

Amazing.

Reality is so much better.

*O*ther people may be in Rocky Point on vacation, but I'm not one of them. I'm back at Candy Cane (mama, not junior) way too early.

Today when I shove open the reluctant door, I'm filled with the memory of last night. How romantic it was. How special. How *Oliver.* But I also discover I'm feeling a weird kind of letdown. Cynthia talks about this—how after a show closes she gets blue. All that work and excitement and build-up and then . . . it's over. And real life begins again.

And me being me, I'm also more than a little worried that despite last night, now that there's no project for us to work on together, Oliver and I won't be . . . well, won't *be.*

I try to shake off my anxiety as people straggle in. From the looks of them, they were up as late as I was last night. But they're cheerful enough and seem to get a kick out of the photos of the various keepers lining one of the walls. Once they move off, I get up and study the keepers too. They all have such interesting faces. "Why did you take this job?" I ask each one of them. None of them answers—which is probably a good thing. In my mom's notes I read about Keeper Abe McCarthy, who couldn't take the isolation and went kind of crazy. Don't want to follow in Abe's footsteps!

I cross back to my desk, trying to picture Oliver. What's he doing right now? I swivel my desk chair back and forth, imagining him . . . where? How *will* he spend his time now that he's not here measuring or at home building? I grin. He's probably measuring and building something new.

I step through the Keeper's Café screen door since I overslept and didn't have time to pack a lunch. I'm startled to see Mrs. Gallagher behind the counter. She shoots me a giant smile. "Hello, Mandy. Loved your boat last night!"

"Thanks," I say as I take a seat at the counter. "Is Celeste out sick?"

"No, no," Mrs. Gallagher assures me. She drops a menu in front of me. "It's one of her days off. I volunteered to be her relief."

"Oh," I say. A sudden flash of anxiety rushes through me. Could Oliver be with Celeste? I tell myself to calm down, and order a salad.

After lunch, with all the visitors in town for the Fourth, I'm busy enough that I am forced to give up my obsessing. When I close up Candy Cane, there he is, sitting on the bench, a spanking new bike leaning against the picnic table.

"What are you doing here?" I ask forcing myself to not skip across the grass.

He unfolds in that languorous, relaxed way of his and stands. "Habit. I got so used to meeting you after you were done that my feet just took me here." He gives me a quick peck. "Or maybe it was my lips that lead the way."

"Ha-ha." I nod toward the bike. "That looks new."

"It is. It's a lot faster than walking, and I figured it would be better than asking Mom for rides all the time."

I unlock the shed and retrieve my own trusty steed. Together we start walking them toward Weatherby.

"All day I felt weird," Oliver says. "Like there was something I was supposed to be doing. Then I remembered—we already did it!"

"I know exactly what you mean."

"Do you have to go straight home? I thought we could go hang by the river again." He gives me a sidelong glance and waggles his eyebrows. "Pops made snacks. . . ."

"Well, in that case, how can I say no?"

I give Mom a quick call at the library, and then we ride to Oliver's house. We stash the bikes, he makes a quick trip to the kitchen, then I follow him to "our" spot by the river. Not so long ago I felt so nervous around him, and today I feel at ease in a way that's new to me.

"So what did you do all day?" I ask as we settle onto the flat rock.

"Not much. Got the bike. Ran into Celeste."

I stiffen. So they *were* together. I wasn't just being paranoid. "Oh yeah?" I say, forcing myself to be super casual. "Where?"

"Over at the bookstore. She was looking for used textbooks. Did you know she's getting an engineering degree?"

"Nope." Great. Ethereally beautiful and mathematically inclined. I could just picture them bonding over graph paper.

"Were you busy today?" He hands me an aluminum-foil packet.

"Pretty busy." I keep my eyes on the packet as if it requires great skill to unwrap it. Then my eyes widen, and my head snaps around to look at him. "Is this what I think it is?"

Oliver smiles proudly. "A homemade bloob pocket. I don't know if it will be as good as the ones you get in the booths, but I figured since you didn't get a chance to have one yesterday . . ."

I grin at him, all jealousy evaporating as I take a huge bite. He remembered not only my bloob pocket obsession *and* my nickname for them, but also went out of his way to bring me one.

"Ohmigod," I say, though my mouth is so full it comes out more like "mowfigumph." I swallow and ask, "How is this even possible?"

He shrugs. "Pops is a genius."

I give him a blueberry-pastry-flaked kiss. "*You're* the genius for getting him to make them."

"Okay, I'll take the credit."

After some more blueberry-tinged kissing, we lie on our backs, fingertips touching, listening to the sounds around us. I just hope my allergies don't kick in to ruin the peaceful setting. My sneezes have been known to make cats run for cover.

Oliver lets out a long, contented sigh. "This place is really great."

"How come you never visited before?" This is something I've been wondering.

"Mom and Pops didn't get along. He divorced her mom when she was still pretty young. From what she says, it sounds like that breakup was ugly, and she was really angry at him for a long time. That's probably why she and Dad worked so hard to avoid the usual divorce drama."

I roll over onto my stomach and pluck a strand of grass from the ground. I split it in two, then pull up another one. "So why now? It doesn't seem like she's really taking time off."

Oliver flips over onto his stomach too, his shoulder grazing mine. I lean my head against his shoulder, smelling laundry soap, sunblock, and what I now call *eau de California*. "A bunch of things, I guess. My dad's mom got sick last year, and I think that reminded her that Pops is getting up there in years."

"He looks pretty healthy to me," I say. "A little creaky maybe."

"Yeah, he's fine. But, you know . . . I think the whole mortality thing hit her."

"Is your grandma okay?" I ask.

"Not great, but hanging in." He rolls away from me and rummages in his sack. Pulling out a bottle of water, he takes a swig then offers it to me. As I take it he adds, "She also . . . I think Mom understands him better now."

"Because she's grown-up now?" I wonder if once I'm an adult I'll understand Mom better too.

"No because . . . well, Pops split just as he was getting super successful. Which her mother resented like crazy."

I hand him back the water bottle. "Understandable. She was with him when he was nobody, and once he got famous . . ."

"Exactly. But the same thing kind of happened with us. Mom hit it big and things just soured."

I sit up. "So you're saying being successful ruins marriages? That would just suck."

He sits up too. "No, it's not that. It's . . . it's more that it was a huge change. Change makes things . . . complicated. A couple will either work it out or they won't. If there were already serious cracks in that foundation . . ." He shrugs.

"I get it."

"With Mom it wasn't like 'Oh, now I'm rich, and I'm going to trade you in for a shiny new model.' It was more that her priorities changed. Pressures changed. Daily life changed. I think she stopped being so angry when she started to look at things from Pops's point of view."

"Makes sense, I guess. . . ."

"Also Pops wanted to see more of the world, paint different kinds of pictures. Nana was a total homebody. Shy. Never wanted to leave her hometown. Liked it that way. They never compared goals. Until it was too late. I think a bit of that happened with my folks too."

I swivel around to face him. "You and your mom talk a lot, don't you?"

He shrugs. "I guess. Don't you? With your mom, I mean."

I tug at the grass. "Mostly she just tells me what I'm doing wrong."

"Oh, that can't be true."

"Believe it."

Oliver stands and holds out a hand to help me up. He pulls me into a hug. "It's easy to talk to you. I've never talked so much to a girl in my whole life."

"Must be this place," I say, looking up at the canopy created by the trees and the happy blue sky, and listening to the sound of the water and the drone of unseen insects. Like a tiny little bubble of peace. "Because I've never talked so much to a boy in my whole life either."

He tightens his hold. "*Our* place," he whispers as he moves aside my hair and brushes my neck with his lips. I shut my eyes and allow the tingles to spread through me.

After a few more kisses, he says, "Want to go see *Far Far Away*? It's supposed to be really good. It's playing—" He stops when he sees my frown. "Sorry, do you have plans? Am I taking up too much of your time? I always do this—just assume—"

"No! No, that's not it." I don't want to tell him I already saw that movie and kind of hated it. "You're definitely not taking up too much of my time."

That's when it hits me. Time. Our time together has an expiration date. I grab him in a fierce hug. "I—I want to spend as much time as possible with you," I say, my voice suddenly cracking.

"Wh-what's wrong?" he asks. I can't answer; I can only shake my head. His body tenses. "Oh. Right."

He peels me off him and takes a step back. "You're thinking about . . ." He rakes his hand through his hair. "I've been trying *not* to think about that myself."

I can't look at him. "But don't we have to think about it?" My voice squeaks like a mouse's.

"Why?"

He catches me off guard with that one, and my head snaps up. "What?"

His face mirrors the misery and confusion I'm feeling. "Do we have to focus on the end? Can't we just . . . I don't know . . ." His shoulders rise, then drop again as he searches for words.

I blink back the threatening tears as I try to come up with an answer. "Stay with the micro?" I say softly. "Avoid the macro?"

A smile begins in his eyes and spreads to his lips. "Something like that, yeah."

I have told myself time and again not to overthink. *Today*, the *micro*, is fantastic. I'd only ruin it if my brain kept going for the macro, the big picture, the future. Stick with what's in front of me. No matter how much it might hurt later. Do I really want to give up what's so fantastic now?

"It's a deal," I say, and seal it with a kiss. I lean away from him, our arms around each other's waists, our hips pressed together. "I'd love to see *Far Far Away* with you." Why spoil things by telling him the movie he's looking forward to seeing is a tedious bore? I'll just sit in the dark next to him and be happy to have both him and air-conditioning.

We fall into a kind of routine, if something that makes me feel different than I've ever felt before can be called "routine." Each day he meets me at Candy Cane. Sometimes we go to the movies; sometimes we grab a bite to eat; sometimes we go to "our" place by the river. I confess, I make him pick the movies and the places to eat. Since he loved *Far Far Away* (gag) I know we have different taste. I don't want him to not like what I pick. I've sat through some clunkers, but it's a sacrifice I'm willing to make.

On my days off he shows up at my house and says, "So which Rocky Point should it be today?" remembering that first day at the river when I told him about there being multiple Rocky Points, all in biking distance. "You choose; you're the guest" is always my answer. After a week or so he stops asking. We just go.

Today he arrives at my door on his bike with a huge grin on his face and wearing an enormous battered backpack. A castoff of Freaky's, I assume.

"What are we up to today?" I ask.

"Hubbard Island! A full day of hiking, biking, bird-watching—the whole nature experience. I read about it in my guidebook, and I figured what better way to see it than with a native, right?"

My insides fall to my feet. A whole day trapped on an island doing the outdoorsy. So not a good look for me. "Uh, I'm not a native of Hubbard Island. . . ."

"You know what I mean," he says with a laugh. "Grab whatever you think you'll need and let's go. I checked the ferry schedule, and the next one leaves in about twenty minutes."

Tell him, my brain screams. *Tell him this is not something you want to do*. But somehow what comes out of my mouth when I look at his face all lit up with excitement and expectation is just "Sure."

Oliver waits on the porch while I go and try to figure out what I should bring as a survival kit. I check the bathroom medicine cabinet and find some allergy pills. Should I take one now in a preemptive strike? But this is the kind that makes me drowsy. I tuck them into a pocket in my backpack just in case. A pack of tissues—an absolute necessity. Bug spray. Sunblock. I sigh. This is why I'm not a big fan of the great outdoors. I have to pack an arsenal to fight off whatever Mother Nature has in store for me.

I leave a note for Mom telling her where I am. She's going to be pretty surprised; like the lighthouse, Hubbard Island is another of those Rocky Point attractions I've never been particularly attracted to.

Of course, Oliver changed my mind about Candy Cane, so

maybe he can change my mind about Hubbard Island, too.

I push through the screen door and Oliver jumps up. "Ready?"

"Ready."

I hope.

*T*here are two ferries from Rocky Point, one that goes to Cranston, the peninsula just next door, and the other to Hubbard Island. The one to the island is a lot more touristy, and we're not the only ones walking our bikes onto the deck. I can tell today is going to be one of Maine's rare scorchers.

I have to admit the ferry ride over is nice, with the breeze from the water cooling us, and the boats bobbing on the bright blue water with the evergreens of Hubbard Island in the background. It's not exactly romantic to be packed in with dozens of other cyclists with our bikes between us, though. *Keep an open mind*, I tell myself.

We disembark with everyone else and push the bikes up to the rustic cabin serving as a visitors' center. "I'll be right back," I tell Oliver, standing my bike near an information kiosk filled with brochures, maps, and scenic postcards. There's even the one of Candy Cane that I'm selling at the lighthouse. Before Oliver can ask me where I'm going, I scurry around the building to find the restroom. I don't know when the next chance to do this will be.

When I come back around, Oliver is sitting beside our bikes, studying a map.

"So where should we go?" Oliver asks.

"You're the one with the map; you tell me," I say.

"Yeah, but you're the one from here."

"The last time I was on Hubbard was probably in the fifth grade," I say.

"Oh. Like people who live in New York never go to the Statue of Liberty. You don't do the tourist things."

"I guess. . . ."

"Okay, so . . ." He squints at the map, then shrugs. "Let's just follow a trail."

Thank goodness I've been biking to Candy Cane every day. I'm in much better shape than I was at the start of the summer. Even so, I'm sweating pretty quickly since the path Oliver picked is mostly uphill. I know somewhere on the island there are supposed to be spectacular views, a waterfall, and good spots to swim where the water is warmer than in the bay, but I have no idea where they are. Besides, views are views. I can see them most anytime.

Oliver can't, I remind myself. It's why he's so big on all this.

The path is too narrow for us to ride side by side. This is not good. It means nothing distracts me from the driplets of sweat snaking down between my boobs, the stickiness of my hair on my neck, and how uncomfortable this dumb bike seat is. I totally wore the wrong clothes. I'm overdressed but underprotected. If he had let me know beforehand, and I didn't have to race for the ferry, I'd have been better prepared.

I try to take my mind off my discomfort by watching Oliver ahead of me. Only instead of getting my focus off the stupid gnats flying in my face, seeing his ease on his bike annoys me. I really really really want to take a break, but I don't want him to think I'm a total wimp. Besides, he's so far ahead of me that he'd never hear me if I asked him to stop. He's not even checking to be sure I'm keeping up with him.

Is that good boyfriend etiquette? I don't *think* so!

Oliver finally slows to a stop when we reach a fork in the path. And for the first time since we started riding he turns around. His big grin irritates me. Is he not even sweating? Do boys from California not sweat? In Maine we're not very used to the heat, since we only have it a few weeks a year. I'd like to see him try to get through a Rocky Point winter. I'd definitely win that contest.

"Which way should we go?" he asks cheerfully.

I'm about to say "Whichever," because seriously, I don't care, but instead what comes out is a giant sneeze. Then another. And another.

Uh-oh.

I sling around my backpack and fumble for my tissues. Just in time. "AAAAA-choo!"

Birds take flight, squirrels scurry, and Oliver still has that giant smile on his stupid face. "You okay?" he asks.

"Fine." Only now that my allergies have kicked in, they're *all* attacking at once. My eyes itch and water. I swipe at a tear trailing down my cheek. Before I turn into a dripping mess, I tell Oliver, "Just pick a direction. Let's go."

Oliver looks a little startled by my tone but starts riding again. I feel around in my backpack for the allergy pills. It may be too late, since they take a while to work, but I'm desperate. I realize that Oliver has the water bottles, so I pick up my speed.

Bad move. My streaming eyes make my vision fuzzy, and I miss seeing the root Oliver has just swerved around. I hit it hard and go flying.

I let out a shriek. The world blurs as I tumble up, down, and sideways. I land hard, scraping various parts, slamming others. I can hear the bike's chain whirring, and feel something poking my ankles. I lay stunned, staring up at the patch of blue between the thick pine trees.

Have I mentioned that I'm really not the outdoorsy type. *And* a klutz?

At least this got Oliver's attention. As I sit up checking for broken bones, he turns and rides back. "Are you all right?" he calls.

No. I'm embarrassed and bruised, and I have gravel burn on my hands. Along with pine needles and leaves in my hair. "Yes. I'm fine."

Why do my brain and my mouth come up with different answers to questions?

He drops his bike and rushes over. "You sure?"

He reaches for my bike, but I yank out my foot and kick the bike away from me. "Yes, I'm sure," I snap.

His head pulls back like a turtle's. "Ooo-kay."

I sigh. "I'm fine. Just . . . feeling stupid." I start to stand, and he instantly tries to help me. But I'm so sweaty and gross the last thing I want is for him to touch me. I step out of reach and again his head does the turtle thing. To cover, I bend over and brush the dirt off my knees and twist around to do the same to my backside.

"Can you check my bike?" I ask. "Make sure it's okay?" He's the micro guy, right? That should be a good task for him and give me time to pull myself together.

He picks up my bike and straddles it, checking the alignment, the handlebars, and the seat position. When he steps off and kneels down to examine the chain, I go through his backpack. Water. Excellent. I take the allergy pill and wash it down, then use the water to clean off my scrapes. Nothing too serious, just some stinging.

By the time I'm done, he's given my bike the thumbs-up. "Ready to get back up on the horse?"

"Huh?"

"The old saying? If you fall off a horse, you're supposed to get right . . . Forget it."

"Right." I yank the handlebars away from him. "Lead on. To wherever it is we're going."

He gives me another one of those quizzical looks, so I fake-smile at him, wondering about the condition of my face. Red and puffy eyes? Equally red and puffy nose? My allergies are making me itch from the inside out, and it's not a fun feeling. Come on, modern medicine. Work fast, please!

I follow Oliver, and now what had been minor discomfort has transformed into actual aches and pains from the fall. I just hope we come to a place to picnic soon. Is he planning to bike the entire island?

The path widens, and he slows down so I can pedal up beside him. We pass a clearing, surrounded by tall pine trees. "How about we stop here?" I suggest.

"No view," he says. "We can do better."

We bike a ways more and come out of the woods to actual picnic grounds. Although a family has claimed one table, and a foursome sit at another, there are still a few empties. "Here?" I slow down.

"Not special enough," he says, and continues pedaling.

I push hard to catch up. My muscles are burning—that ride to Candy Cane hasn't gotten me in as good a shape as I thought. Realizing I'm going to have to do this ride all over again to go back just adds to the cranky. "Who are you? Goldilocks?" I ask.

"Huh?

"When are you going to find the one that's *just right?*"

"I just wanted . . . Fine. Let's stop here." He abruptly stops by a large tree and leans his bike against it.

"Great," I say.

Only not so great. He's right. There's nothing special or scenic about it. We could be in the woods near his house.

"Where's the other water bottle?" he asks, rummaging through his backpack.

"I took it when I fell," I say as I pull it out and take another gulp.

"Don't swig it. That's all the water I packed."

"Are you kidding?"

"Aren't there, like, concession stands?"

I gape at him as he spreads a picnic blanket. "At the dock, yeah. But this is a nature preserve. You know, where they preserve nature? Didn't the guidebook explain that there aren't any food booths here?" I shake my head. "Not exactly a completist now," I mutter.

"You don't have to be so snotty about it."

"Snotty?" I start laughing. "Yep, that's me. Snotty. And drippy. And sweaty. And scraped up and bruised."

"Have a sandwich," he grumbles.

I take it from him, but only because Freaky made it and anything Freaky makes is delicious. As soon as I'm holding it, the smell tells me it's fish. "I'm not hungry." I drop the sandwich onto the blanket.

"Fine. More for me."

Bad move. Claiming I'm not hungry means I can't exactly ask if there's anything else to eat. I pull my knees up to my chest and hug them. We sit silently as Oliver scarfs down his sandwich. I hope he doesn't hear my stomach rumbling.

"So what should we do?" he asks, wadding up his napkin and sandwich baggie. He stashes them into a plastic bag. He clearly thought ahead about garbage, why not water?

I shrug and rub at the bicycle grease around my ankle.

I hear him sigh, then say, "How about swimming? I read that there are—"

I cut him off. "I didn't bring a suit."

"Why not?" He sounds annoyed.

I'm annoyed right back. "You didn't exactly give me much time to get ready."

"So what did you pack?"

I get up and go to my bike. I pull my backpack off the handlebars and stomp to the picnic blanket. I flip it upside down, dumping out my stash: Sunblock. Which I just now realized I forgot to apply. Isn't that awesome? Bug spray. Which we will definitely need as it gets closer to dusk. I'm betting that's when he'll want to take the return ferry. Tissues. Eyedrops.

Oliver studies my supplies. "You have allergies."

"Yup."

"This is all you brought with you? For a picnic on Hubbard Island?"

I kneel down and repack my backpack. "I'm not an idiot, you know. I brought what I needed. And you know what? This picnic is over."

I stand and sling a strap over one shoulder. I stomp back to my bike, slip on the other strap, and walk the bike around to face the right direction. The one leading back the way we came. "I'm taking the ferry back. Now," I announce, hopping on. "And don't you follow me."

"Wow. Overreact much?" Oliver calls behind me.

My body stiffens and I clutch the handlebars. *Don't respond*, I tell myself. *Just walk away*. Well, *bike* away.

Which I do. Muttering the whole time.

The ferry ride back to Rocky Point is dismal. I waited until the very last minute to board, hoping that Oliver would show up and apologize. Then I fumed over the fact that he didn't follow me, even though I told him not to. I waited just a moment longer, debating if I should wait until he *did* arrive, whenever that might be. Finally I just scurried aboard, practically as they were pulling away. I was lucky I didn't wind up in the water. That would have been the perfect ending to a completely rotten day.

By the time we approach the dock, it's sprinkling. I bounce back and forth between worrying about Oliver and thinking it serves him right. You have to prepare for a trip to Hubbard. He pores over those guidebooks—didn't that part stick? Had he checked the weather, brought rain slickers, or enough water, for goodness' sake?

I bike home in the light rain. With each street I get more and more depressed. Sleepy too. The allergy pill has finally kicked in. Another reason I'm glad I'm not on that stupid island. But a creeping feeling starts to take over that *I* should be the one to apologize. All Oliver wanted was to spend the day with me. To have fun. To see the sights.

I push harder on the pedals. Of course, he could have asked me first!

I slow as I make the turn onto my street. Even if he had asked, I would have said yes anyway. That's what I've been doing all summer. Seeing the movies he wants to see. Having him decide on our outings. No wonder he didn't ask me.

"I'm such a jerk!" I mutter as I carry my bike up the porch steps. I let the screen door bang shut behind me. I hope Mom's not home; she hates when I do that.

I've never been in a fight with a boy before. Other than Justin, but brothers don't count. A boy who means so much to me. I go into the bathroom and peel off my wet and dirty clothes. I sit on the edge of the tub, dabbing at my scratches and scrapes with toilet paper. Then my head drops and I cover it with my hands. Misery washes over me, and the tears finally come for real.

I avoid looking in the mirror in the entryway when I arrive for Candy Cane duty. I know what I'll see. Red eyes from crying, a stuffy nose from allergies, and the face of a girl who for no good reason left her boyfriend on an island, and probably lost him forever.

That's a girl I seriously don't want to see.

I didn't try texting Oliver last night. If he didn't respond, I didn't want to wonder if it was because the text didn't go through or because he hated me. Besides, I didn't know what to say.

I didn't even try Cynthia. There would just be too much to explain, and with her all caught up with camp—I've only been getting super-short texts—she barely has time to talk.

"What is wrong with me?" I moan to the empty room. Thankfully, it doesn't answer back.

It's busy enough that it's only when my stomach rumbles so loudly it turns the head of a little boy sitting on the bottom step of the lighthouse tower (I know, I know; I'm supposed to tell him not to sit there) that I realize it's past lunchtime. I consider skipping it since it means I have to face the celestial Celeste. I'm sure she's never been mean to someone who was just trying to be nice to her. But my stomach refuses to be ignored, so I force myself to deal with her perfection.

"Hey, Mandy," she greets me. "Lemonade?"

I nod and take a seat at the counter.

"You going to wait for Oliver to order?"

My head jerks up at this. "Is he coming?"

She looks confused. "How would I know? Aren't you meeting him? It seems like he's always here on the days you work. Though not always for lunch, I guess. . . ."

I fiddle with the salt and pepper shakers. "Just me." I can feel her eyes on me. I wish she'd stop looking. "Salad please. Chicken."

"You got it."

She disappears, and I notice some of the tourists from this

morning sitting at booths. A big group with a baby in a high chair is probably having lunch before checking out Candy Cane. Still, it's pretty sparsely populated. From what I've seen, the boys mooning over Celeste tend to show up just before she's getting ready to close. I wonder what they order.

Celeste returns with my salad, then leans against the back counter, arms crossed. "So you want to tell me what happened between you two?"

I plunge my fork into a tomato. For some reason I can't lift it to my mouth. "I was a total jerk and now he hates me," I blurt.

"He said that?"

"Well, no. But I know he does."

"Do you?"

I let out a shaky sigh. "*I'd* hate me. I treated him really badly, when all he wanted was to explore Hubbard Island."

"So what was the problem?"

"Where do I begin?" Then it all comes out: my allergies and general lack of interest in the so-called great outdoors, his not asking me about going, my not bringing the right things, his better biking skills. Celeste listens patiently. I'm too embarrassed to look up, so I'm well acquainted with every leaf of lettuce and slice of cucumber in my salad by the time I'm done.

"Yeah, you were a jerk all right," Celeste says. "But not because you were so snippy."

"Great." Just what I need. To feel worse.

"The real problem is that you haven't been yourself. You've been whoever you imagine he wants you to be." Her eyes flick over my shoulder. She taps the counter in front of me. "Hang on."

She picks up the coffeepot and goes to refill a customer's cup. I stare at the sickeningly sweet pastries in the case on the counter. That doesn't make any sense.

"I *have* been myself," I tell Celeste as she comes back around the counter. "And myself is annoying and whiny."

"Why didn't you just tell him you didn't want to go to Hubbard? You could have found something else to do. Something you'd *both* think was fun."

I open my mouth to say something, but since I don't know what to say I close it again.

She replaces the coffeepot, then starts rolling silverware into paper napkins. "I bet this isn't the first time either. I bet you've been seeing the movies he wants to see. Going to the parties he wants to go to."

"We haven't gone to any parties," I mumble.

Celeste grins, making her look like a wry fairy. "My bad. That woulda been me."

"You?"

"I know the syndrome all too well. I thought I had to pretend to like the stuff my boyfriend liked—my *ex*-boyfriend that is."

This is fascinating. Not only is Celeste telling me personal things, as if we're, I don't know, equals, but she's admitting she screwed up with a boy. "Why?"

"So he'd like me, of course! Why are *you* doing it?"

"But you—you're—you're perfect!"

This cracks her up. "You're kidding, right?"

I stare at her blankly. She shakes her head and continues. "*Any*way, if it's the right guy for you it's because he likes the real you. Not the you who pretends to be into professional wrestling and Xbox."

"He feels like the right guy. . . ."

"Jeffrey—that's my boyfriend now—he's not into engineering. He's an English major, and he loves those scary movies that I avoid like the plague."

"But you get along anyway?"

She smiles a soft, almost private smile, obviously thinking about him. "Yeah . . . ," she says a little dreamily. "Yeah, we do." She comes back to earth and points at me with a fork. "You don't have to be someone's clone to be close to him. Same thing with friends, too. Sometimes it's your differences that help keep you together."

"Complementary, not opposites," I say, remembering Oliver's words.

She comes around the counter and sits on the stool next to me, leaning on an elbow. "Here's a really tough question. Have you *ever* been yourself around him? Be super honest."

Panic tightens my chest. Has the whole thing been a sham, and the girl Oliver likes—or *liked*, past tense—never even existed?

But as I think more, I know the answer. "Yes. Plenty." Building Candy Cane Jr. At "our" place by the river. Up in the lighthouse tower watching the fireworks. I've been *me* when it has really counted.

"Good. Because from what I've seen, Oliver's really into you. Glad to know it's actually Mandy he likes. Not some imaginary girl, not some Cynthia clone."

This startles me. "What do you mean?"

She shrugs as she slides off the stool. "Hey, I went to Rocky Point High too. This is a small town. Sometimes it seems as if . . . well, look, never mind. Maybe I'm wrong."

"You are," I insist. "Cynthia's my best friend since we were little kids. If we're alike . . ."

"That's the thing. I don't actually think you are. But I could be totally off."

"You are."

I don't want to end in a fight. She's being so nice. Not to mention that hearing she has a boyfriend is super reassuring— and that I never had any reason to be worried that she might be into Oliver. And she says Oliver likes me. These are all things that make me want to hug her, not get into an argument.

I take a long last sip of lemonade. Sweet and tart. Kind of like relationships, I guess.

"Do you think he'll talk to me?" I ask.

"Only one way to find out."

"That's what I was afraid you'd say."

$\mathcal{T}$his would be so much easier in an e-mail. But I can't count on Oliver finding Wi-Fi somewhere any time soon. So here I am, pacing in the raggedy front yard, my bike leaning against a crooked tree, trying to work up the courage to knock.

What's the worst that can happen? I ask myself. Bad question. The list is enormous, and all of it makes me want to grab my bike and get out of here quick. *Try again,* I tell myself. What's the *best* that can happen?

"You can do this," I mutter for about the millionth time. The problem is each time I tell myself this, another self counters, "No you can't." Once again I wish that Cynthia were here, not just to give me advice but also so we could come up with a script together that I could follow. We would have even practiced.

I take in a deep breath to fortify myself, stride to the front door, and knock before I can talk myself out of it. Maybe he won't be home. I can't tell if this possibility is a relief or a problem.

I decide I'll try one more time, and if no one answers, I'll chalk it up to "not meant to be." It will suck, and tears spring to my eyes just imagining never being with him again, but what else can I do?

I knock more forcefully this time. I start hyperventilating as footsteps approach, then my breath catches in my throat when Freaky Framingham flings open the door. He looks as startled to see me as I am to see him. "Oliver didn't say you were coming over. He's not here. He and his ma went to the farmers' market."

"Oh. Okay."

"Nah, it's rude of the boy to not be here. . . ."

"He didn't know I was coming." I fiddle with the end of my braid, not sure what to do now.

"Oh. Well, they shouldn't be too long. Got muffins in the oven," he says, turning and heading toward the kitchen.

I could back out now, but that would be bad, right? Even though I'm not exactly sure if that was an invitation, I follow him inside.

I cross the living room, wondering if this is going to be the last time I'm ever here. My throat feels thick, and no matter how much I swallow, the lump won't go away.

I hover in the archway that leads to the kitchen, watching Freaky remove two muffin tins and place them on top of the oven. The smell is tantalizing.

"You just cool a bit," he tells the muffins. He gives me a quick glance over his shoulder. "They're for tomorrow's breakfast."

I nod. The warning is clear. Hands off.

He studies the muffins a bit longer, then sets up some racks on the counter. He taps the tops of a few. "Gotta be patient," he says, I think to me, and not the muffins this time. "Don't want to leave half of them behind in the tins."

He crosses to the fridge. "Kids drink soda, right?" He pulls out a can and holds it out to me.

I take it from him, hoping it will clear the lump in my throat. Freaky dumps the muffins out of the tins and onto the racks, then carefully turns them right-side up. He has a surprisingly delicate touch. He gives me another one of those sideways glances.

"Should probably test them," he says with a twinkle a lot like Oliver's—at least when he's not mad at me. "Wouldn't want to serve subpar muffins to the family."

I manage my first smile since Hubbard Island. Freaky chooses two muffins (he dubs them Lumpy and Lopsided) and puts them on plates for us. I've had dinner here a gazillion times, but I still feel a little nervous being here by myself. Not because I think Freaky is a freak anymore; I just don't really know what to say to him. Or if he knows what a superjerk I was to Oliver.

If Oliver did tell him, Freaky doesn't seem to be holding it against me. His twinkly blue eyes watch me as I take a big bite.

My eyes widen as the flavors collide in my mouth.

"New recipe," Freaky says. "Threw in some shredded coconut and added a little almond flour."

I swallow and lick crumbs from my lips. "Amazing."

"Oliver and his ma seem to go for my baking," he says. "So I want to keep up a steady stream."

"Who wouldn't go for your baking?" I say. "Or anything else you make," I add before taking another bite.

Freaky holds up his lumpy muffin and studies it. He breaks it into two, then pops one half into his mouth. "Hurt feelings come out in all kinds of ways," he mutters as he chews.

My stomach lurches. "Wh-what did Oliver say?" I ask. And what could it have to do with muffins?

Freaky looks at me, startled. "Oh, sorry. So used to talking to myself, I forgot I had a listener. Even with the kids staying here."

If I'm going to get Oliver to forgive me, I should try to find out what he might have told his grandfather. "So Oliver . . . ?" I prompt.

He frowns, as if he's trying to remember his train of thought. He waves a hand when he figures it out. "It's not Ollie. His ma, well, even though she certainly appreciates what's put on the table, she resents it too."

"Why?" I hope that's not impolite, but I figure since he opened up the door by telling me something this personal he won't mind. Between Alice asking me to call her by her first name, and Freaky telling me his problems with her, I feel awfully grown up.

"I didn't do any of this"—he gestures around the kitchen— "when she was small. So something about my doing it now irks her." He pops the second half of the muffin into his mouth. "She eats it all, mind you, second helpings too, but it bothers her."

I have no idea what to say. But this is definitely a conversation I never expected to have with freaking Freaky Framingham. "So if someone's mad at you, what's the best way to make them stop?"

His face twists up, and he slaps the table with a loud "Ha!" I startle and bounce a little in my chair. "I've been trying to figure out the answer to that one for most of your young life. Longer."

I trace an invisible line on the table in front of me, keeping my eyes glued to my finger. "I—I was really mean to Oliver."

Freaky gets up and pours himself coffee from a stainless thermos. The mug he's using is chipped; I wonder if he makes pity purchases too. He leans against the counter and squints into the mug, like a fortune-teller reading tea leaves. "Sorry's a hard thing to say. Sometimes, though, you can tell how important a thing is by how hard it is to do." He crosses to the table and sits down again. "But it's not just saying the sorry. Any fool can say words. It's how you back up those words that counts."

"Yeah . . . ," I murmur. "So you keep trying new recipes? To find the one that will make everything okay?"

He reaches over and pats my hand. I'm so surprised I don't even react. "I knew there was something about you I liked," he says. "That's it exactly."

I grin. "That would be such a cool story. A baker searching for the one perfect recipe to solve all the problems of the world."

He looks impressed. "I like that." He gets back up and starts to move the muffins from the cooling rack to a platter. "Sometimes it doesn't even matter if you get the recipe right. Sometimes what matters is that you just keep trying."

It's so weird that I'm having this conversation with Freaky Framingham. "How come the people you're supposed to be able to talk to are the ones who are the hardest?" I ask, thinking of my mom.

"Depends," he says, his back still to me. "Afraid to disappoint them, maybe? Fear that what we're going to say will make them think differently of us. Or prove something we were afraid they already thought."

Since Mom already thinks Justin is perfect and I'm the problem child, Freaky's theory makes a lot of sense. If she knew I'd behaved like such a brat, the worst thing would be if she chalked it up as typical Mandy. Sometimes I wonder if Dad hadn't died when I was eight and Justin was eleven if he and Justin would have fought like me and Mom, and Dad would have beamed at *me* the way Mom does at Justin. We've been getting along better lately, and I guess our current truce still feels fragile.

"Oliver and his mom talk a lot," I comment.

Freaky comes back to the table for his coffee mug. "Yeah, they're good that way."

I hear the sound of tires on gravel, and my heart speeds up.

"Sounds like they're home," he says. He gets up and heads out to the living room. I hear the door open, then he says, "Ollie, Mandy's here."

I grip the edge of the table to keep from fleeing out the back door. The pounding in my ears blocks out any response Oliver has, so I have no way of knowing how he reacts to this info.

Then he's in the doorway. And then I'm standing up. And then we're staring at each other.

"Hey," I say softly. Probably too softly for him to hear. I clear my throat. "Uh, so hi."

He doesn't say anything. Not a good sign.

I force myself to jump right in. "Okay, so I'm sorry. Super sorry. Colossally sorry."

Freaky was wrong. The hard thing isn't saying sorry—the hard thing is the gap between when you say it and when the other person answers.

Oliver crosses to the fridge and pulls out a soda. Even his back looks angry.

"Um . . . I'm trying to apologize here," I say, shifting my weight and then shifting it back.

I hear him pop the can, then he takes a swig. "Yeah, I got that." He turns around. "I'm trying to figure out what you're sorry for."

"For—for all of it. I mean, you're obviously mad at me, so clearly I have reasons to apologize, right?" I'm so confused. Doesn't he think I owe him an apology?

"Yeah," Oliver says. "But what I'm trying to figure out is what happened. You were acting like I was the one who did something wrong, but I can't for the life of me figure out what."

"That's part of what I'm saying sorry for." I sit back down and rest my forehead on my hands. "I messed up, didn't I?"

"I don't know! Did you?"

I raise my eyes to meet his. Now he doesn't look angry; he looks genuinely confused. And upset.

"You did everything right," I explain. "Well, except for maybe where you didn't ask me if I wanted to go, you just . . . well, that part doesn't matter," I add quickly when a flicker of temper crosses his face. I plow on. "I should have told you. I'm not really big on the communing-with-nature kind of scenario. Allergies. Falling down. Well, you saw. It wasn't a pretty picture."

"Why didn't you just tell me?"

I throw up my hands. "You didn't give me a chance. You were all excited, with a big picnic and guidebooks."

"Big whoop."

He still sounds mad. He comes closer to the table. "Why do you think I'd want to do something that wouldn't be fun for you?"

He's got me there. I pick up tiny muffin crumbs with my fingertip.

He slides onto the chair across from me, where Freaky had just been sitting. "Have you been doing that all along? Only pretending to like stuff? Humoring me?"

I can't respond, knowing he's not going to like my answer.

"So this whole thing? It's all been fake?" He stands up with such force the chair wobbles. He grabs it and rights it with a thud.

"No!" I'm on my feet too. "None of this is fake. None of the real parts."

He glares at me like I just said something really dumb, which come to think of it, I just did. "I mean, the important parts, the parts that make things real." Ugh! Why is this so hard?

"So what *were* you pretending? The things that you don't consider"—here he uses air quotes—"important?"

"Movies," I blurt. "I hated *Far Far Away* when I saw it the first time and even more when we saw it together."

His eyebrows rise. "Really? I thought it was—" He stops himself and shakes his head. "But why would you do that? And why do you keep making me pick what we do? That's why I didn't ask you about Hubbard. I thought you liked being surprised. I figured that's why you always have me choose."

Huh. That would have been a better reason than the actual one. "I—I was afraid you wouldn't like what I picked," I admit. I finally look directly at him despite the tears welling in my eyes. "And then you wouldn't like *me*."

We hold like that for a moment, and I'm stunned as I watch all the angry drain out of him. Stunned and relieved. He does that sideways thing with his mouth. "Sardonic," I think, is the SAT word for it.

"Are we done fighting now? Apology accepted?" I ask.

"On one condition," he says, making his way around the table.

"Ooo-kay," I say cautiously.

"From now on, you have to be more honest with me. If you don't like something, tell me. If you want to do something different, tell me. It's been a lot of pressure to keep coming up with things for us to do."

I cross my heart with my index finger. "Absolutely. Scout's honor." Exactly like Freaky said, I have to back up the words with actions.

"I have an idea of something to do," I add. Then I hurl myself into his arms.

When Oliver comes to pick me up the next day at Candy Cane, I actually have an activity in mind. "Can we go through the exhibits?" I ask.

He gives me a skeptical look. "That's more my thing, right? Our deal was—"

I cut him off. "I really want to. That night in here, it got me thinking about what it must have been like to have been the keeper in the old days. I want to learn more about it."

Oliver grins. "Cool. Where should we start?"

I glance around the lobby. "How about right here?"

"I have an idea," Oliver says as I shut the door and lock it. I don't want anyone thinking the lighthouse is still open. "How about you make up a story about whatever we're looking at, then I'll tell you the actual history. I'll bet my true stories are just as interesting as your made-up ones."

I smirk. "Too bad there's no one here to act as judge," I tell him, "because I will so win this bet."

He points to a series of framed pictures hanging above the case. There's a diagram of Candy Cane, identifying the different parts. Beside it is a poster with the headings "Daymarks," "Flash Patterns," and "Foghorns," explaining what each one is.

"Is this a test?" I ask. I put on my best schoolteacher voice. "Daymarks refer to the distinct shape and color scheme of each lighthouse so that a sailor knows where he is during the day when the light's not visible. Flash patterns"—I stop, trying to remember—"are the distinct way the light flashes for a particular lighthouse. Kinda like Morse code, but not. Foghorns—self-explanatory, right?"

"So the question is," Oliver asks with a grin, "who decided Candy Cane should have the red spiral around the tower?"

I grin. Over the years I've entertained Cynthia with variations of this story. I think back until I find the one she liked the best. "Okay, a long time ago, a nearsighted elf was on a mission for Santa in Rocky Point. He accidentally crashed into the original all-white tower. After he came to, the evil lighthouse keeper had him tied up in the tower. He recognized the elf for a magical being, though not quite clear on what kind. Using magic, the elf made the red swirl around the tower. When Santa and his reindeer search party flew over Rocky Point, Santa instantly recognized the giant candy cane as a distress signal, since candy canes are often used as markers up at Santa's workshop. You know, where there may be a message, or something to investigate.

"Using elfin magic, they turned the evil keeper into a buoy and put him out to sea. But it turned out that the elf had fallen in love with his candy-cane tower—and the lighthouse keeper's *non*evil daughter—and so he became the new lighthouse keeper of Rocky Point."

Oliver is smiling broadly. "Okay, that's a much better story than the lighthouse board making the decision, even if they did get into a whopping argument over this particular design. Practically Hatfield and McCoy about it."

"Well, I have to confess, I didn't make it up on the spot. It's from the archives."

"What archives? The historical society?"

"Why would they have a story about Santa Claus in . . . never mind. No. When we come up with a good story, Cynthia and I always say 'put that one in the archives' so that we'll remember it."

"I like it."

"Next?" This is fun. Today his idea of fun and mine are completely in synch.

There are a number of small items in the display case, but Oliver brings me over to a woman's battered shoe. It's obviously from the 1800s from the style, and judging from the large hole in the toe, the dirt, and the fraying fabric, had seen some tough times. "Don't read the label," Oliver says, suddenly clamping his hands over my eyes.

"I wasn't!" I protest, laughing.

"Well . . . ?"

I pull his hands off my eyes. "Got one," I say. "But I think it's going to have a tragic ending."

Oliver holds up his hands in surrender. "So be it. Gotta go where the muse takes you."

I'm tickled by the idea that he thinks I have a muse. "There was a young lighthouse keeper who saved a boatload of passengers after a wreck in a storm. Unfortunately, he lost his glasses during the rescue, but there was a girl he just knew was beautiful no matter how blurry her face. Her graciousness, her charm, her humor, her halo of hair, it all added up to perfection to him. All too soon, a party arrived on land to bring them the rest of the way to their destination.

"Only as they were leaving did he finally muster up the courage to try to speak to her. He ran after the group, realizing he couldn't call out her name because he didn't know it.

"But he was too late. As the driver of the carriage helped her up into her seat, her shoe fell off. Before she could try to retrieve it, the horses took off. He was left holding her shoe. After that, he made inquiries and carried the shoe around, hoping to find the lovely young lady who fit into it."

"Did he ever find her?"

I shake my head. "If he had, there'd be a pair here."

Oliver nods approvingly. "Nice twist on Cinderella. Though a lot sadder . . ."

"So what's the real story?" I ask. "Some lighthouse keeper's wife had it in her sewing basket?"

"Nope. According to the label, it was found in the wall of the keeper's house."

"Wow. If I had known that I would have come up with a murder mystery! That's so creepy!" I edge him out of the way to read the label.

My eyes widen as I read. I had no idea that there was a custom in the 1800s to place an old shoe worn by a loved one who had died into the walls of a house to protect the family from evil spirits. This shoe had been found during the renovations of the keeper's house. The hole in the toe was put there on purpose—it's supposed to allow the spirit of the original owner to flow out and keep the house and family safe.

I turn to smile at Oliver. "That's so cool. I didn't know that there were superstitions on display."

"All part of history," Oliver says. "So the point for this story goes to . . . ?"

"I think this point may go to you."

"Then we need a tiebreaker." Oliver's eyes narrow while he thinks. He snaps his fingers. "Got it!" He takes my hand and leads me to the next room.

I stand in the center, hands on hips. "Well?"

His palms are together in front of his face, the tips of his index fingers tapping his smiling lips. "Right behind you," he says.

I turn, and I know exactly which display he wants me to make up a story about. "The dog collar."

"Yup."

This is a true story that I know, because the dog collar is one of the favorite displays among the kiddies. I try to empty my mind of the facts and focus on the collar, trying to let it tell me a story. "Fog," I say, as images begin to come.

"Fog?" Oliver repeats.

I wave my hand at him to get him to be quiet so I can formulate the story. "This once belonged to the dreaded ghost dog of Rocky Point."

"Good start," Oliver says. He leans on the display case in that way he does, weight on an elbow, ankles crossed.

My voice goes low and creaky, my scary-story voice. "They say in these parts that fog can be a living thing. Ask any sailor and lobsterman and they'll agree—it can be a malevolent force with a mind of its own."

"Spooky." Oliver shudders appreciatively.

"When the moon and tides are right, a howling goes up. All then know the cursed fog is forming into the giant hound, a creature fearsome to behold!"

I let out a howl. Oliver covers his mouth trying not to laugh.

"The creature is impossible to fight, since it's made entirely of fog, yet it can devour men and ships whole." I point at the dog collar. "This is the only hope for mankind. As long as the dog collar is in the hands of good and not evil, the fog dog can be contained. The collar owner says the magic words . . ." I pause, trying to think of where to take this.

"Woof," Oliver moans. "Wooooooo-oooof!"

"Exactly. Those magic words! Then the fog shrinks down to fit into the collar, and then vanishes."

"Excellent story!" Oliver holds his bare arms up for me to see. "Look. Goose bumps."

"Yeah, it was pretty good."

"Archive worthy, I'd say."

I turn and look at the dog collar. "The real story is good too," I say. "That brave dog, ringing the fog bell when his master had slipped and broken his ankle trying to get to it." I shake my head in amazement. "That dog even got the right ring pattern."

"See?" Oliver says. "There are good stories all around you."

I look around the lobby at all the carefully preserved objects, the photos that capture a specific time, place, and face. "Okay, you convinced me," I tell him. "History isn't just the boring dates and wars that we learn about in school."

Oliver's face lights up. "In that case, how about we poke around the historical society?"

I laugh. "You really know how to get on my mom's good side."

"I'd rather be on *your* good side."

"Would that be this side?" I turn one way. "Or this side?" I turn the other way.

He laughs and gives me a kiss first on one cheek and then the other. "Both."

We head out of the lighthouse and bike to the Square. We

lock the bikes in the rack, then enter the hushed library. Mom is at the check-out desk, talking to a family with several kids and a large stack of books. She smiles when she notices Oliver and me, but she looks tired. Once the group moves away, Oliver and I step up to the desk.

"Hi, Mom," I say. "Can Oliver and I check out the files up in the society office?"

Mom tries to hide her surprise but isn't very successful. "This must be your influence," she tells Oliver. "Because she's never wanted to go up there before."

"It didn't take too much convincing," Oliver says.

I squirm a little. It's a little weird to realize my mom may have more in common with my boyfriend than I do.

"This way," I say to Oliver. We tromp up the stairs to the office in the attic. It reminds me of Freaky's, minus the paintings, though there are framed documents and photos leaning against the walls in similar stacks. There's an old card table with some boxes and a phone on it and the cluttered desk that Mom and Mr. Garrity share, and that's about it.

"What do you want to look at?" I ask him.

He shrugs with a grin. "I'm a completist, remember? I want to look at *everything*."

"Oh, right!" I gaze around the room. "Well, there's probably something you'll like in every nook and cranny. Just start somewhere."

"Do you know where they keep the info about the keeper's house? I'd love to see the changes over the years."

"Not a clue," I admit. "Why don't you try over there." I point at the filing cabinets along one wall. "I'll start with Mom's desk."

"Sounds like a plan."

Oliver studies the file-drawer labels as I pull open a bottom desk drawer and find a thick folder labeled KEEPER'S HOUSE.

I pull it out. "Found something."

Oliver joins me at the desk and flips open the folder. "This is all about the renovations when they turned it into the café." He carries it over to the table so he can lay it flat.

While he looks through the folder, I riffle through the papers on top of the desk. "These are all current bills for the lighthouse. Insurance. Estimates for repairs. An electric bill." I look up at him. "Some are marked past due. That's bad, right?"

He pulls a paper out of his file. "This explains why the second floor of the Keeper's Café is closed. They couldn't afford to make the repairs to make it safe for the public. Floorboards and staircase problems."

"They're probably waiting for more of the summer visitors and their cash to kick in so they can reopen it," I say, realization dawning. "No wonder Mom seems stressed."

"I guess this is why she's having you volunteer." He holds up another piece of paper. "Last year they paid someone to be the greeter. They save money this way."

"And why Mrs. Gallagher volunteers in the café on Celeste's days off."

I pile the papers back into what I hope had been their original order. In my usual clumsy way, I manage to knock a standing file off the desk. I slide onto the floor to put it back together. It seems to all be memos between the historical society board and various committee members. My eyes widen when I get to the most recent one. My head snaps up. "This says they're closing Candy Cane!"

"What?" Oliver puts down the folder and rushes over. He drops beside me and scans the memo. He turns to look at me, his forehead scrunched with concern. "They can't afford to keep it open anymore."

The disappointment that rushes through me is as surprising as it is overwhelming. Tears spring into my eyes. "But—but they can't!" I grab the paper back from Oliver, and he starts looking through the other memos.

"They are really behind with some pretty big bills," he says. "And there are all kinds of regulations they won't be able to meet if they can't make certain repairs and get additional insurance."

I keep shaking my head. "This can't be happening."

"It looks pretty definite," Oliver says. "Only a major influx of cash—and I mean *major*—will make a difference."

Oliver and I sit on the floor in silence. His hand snakes over to mine and he squeezes it. I'm just dumbfounded. I haven't always loved Candy Cane, but she's been part of my life forever. Literally. I may not have gone to the Candy Cane celebrations very much over the last few years, but it makes me so sad to think no little kids will be going for their first school visit, or that Mom won't be putting on Mrs. Gilhooley's dress for the Lupine Festival and the Fourth of July.

I lean against Oliver. Candy Cane brought us together. Just like Martha Kingston and Abner Rose. When she saved the sailor from drowning and he recuperated in the upstairs room at the keeper's house, they fell in love there. Like my parents. There's just something about the sweet little lighthouse that seems to shine a light on romance.

"She never said a word," I say. I turn to face him. "Why wouldn't she tell me?"

Oliver shrugs. "Doesn't want to worry you? Hoping for a last-minute save?"

"I guess. . . ." It does explain why she looks so worried all the time.

We gather together the last of the papers and return them to the desk. Just as we're shutting the drawer, I hear footsteps.

Mom pokes her head over the top of the stairs. "Closing time," she announces. "Find anything?"

Oliver looks at me, and I give my head a tiny little shake. This isn't the time to ask her about the closing. She might not like that we snooped.

Oliver grabs a book about lighthouses from one of the bookshelves. "Is it okay if I borrow this?" he asks Mom.

"Of course," she says. "Would you like to join us for dinner? You can let me know your secret for getting Mandy interested in our history here."

I roll my eyes.

"And maybe help me figure out how to get her to stop doing that," she adds with a laugh, lifting her chin toward me.

"Whatever," I grumble, and push past them to clomp down the stairs. Behind me I hear them laughing. How can she make jokes with all that's going on? The more I find out about her, the less I feel like I know her!

$\mathscr{M}$om shakes her head with a smile. "That imagination of yours, Mandy." Over dinner Oliver told her about the game we played at the lighthouse.

I always thought she said this in disapproval. Now I recognize she's saying it with some parent combo of admiration and amusement. This is another gift Oliver gave me.

"I've always loved that elf story," Mom says as she scoops ice cream. "And that's why you came into the library? To get more material?"

"Kind of," I say.

Mom returns the ice cream container to the freezer. "To me history *is* a collection of stories. It's not always taught that way, I know," she says in my direction, "but once you scratch the surface, it all becomes alive, and rich, and fascinating." She sits back down and dips her spoon into her bowl.

"I was wondering, Mrs. Sullivan," Oliver says, "would you like to keep Candy Cane Jr.? I mean, that is . . ." He flushes a little as his voice trails off.

I squeeze his knee under the table. I know this is his way to try to make up for the fact that it looks like she may be losing the real Candy Cane.

All through dinner I tried to figure out a way to bring up the awful subject. But it never seemed quite right to bring up something so upsetting. Maybe she didn't tell me because she's too devastated to even talk about it.

"That's so sweet of you, Oliver," Mom says. "But don't you want it?"

"Well, it's not like I can take it home with me on the plane," Oliver says.

"That'd be quite a sight," I say with a laugh, focusing back in on the conversation. "You could wear her, like you did in the boat."

"I'd like to see him try going through airport security," Mom jokes.

"Can you see me fitting into Mom's car like that?" Oliver says. "We'd have to cut a hole in the roof for the lantern house!"

"The car rental company would have a lot of questions," I say.

We're all laughing now. "Perhaps if Mrs. Gilhooley explained things . . . ," Mom says.

I haven't seen Mom laugh like this in a long time. I give Oliver's knee another squeeze. He puts his hand on top of mine and pats it.

"Are you sure your grandfather doesn't want it?" Mom asks.

Oliver shakes his head. "I kind of think he'd love for me to get it out of the garage, actually. But it would feel weird to just toss her."

"Well, I'd love it. It would make a nice addition to the historical society office. Thank you."

"Maybe if you can get the second floor of the Keeper's Café open, it could go up there," I say, hoping this will open the imminent closing as a topic of conversation.

Mom's face shadows a moment. "That would be a lovely idea, yes." She reaches for our empty bowls.

As we pass them to her, I ask, "Do you think you'll be able to reopen it?" I know I'm kind of pushing it, but I go there anyway.

Mom takes the stacked bowls and carries them to the sink. "Did Mandy ever tell you that her father proposed to me at the lighthouse?" she says with her back to us.

Okay. The subject is obviously off-limits. For now.

"No," Oliver says.

She turns and leans against the counter. "That lighthouse has been very special to me for so many reasons, but I think that's the biggest."

"Even bigger than your wedding there?" I ask.

Mom has a wistful smile on her face. "In a way . . . I guess because it was so private. The wedding was fantastic," she adds, coming back to the table, "but the proposal was . . . magical."

She smooths out her napkin, then gives us a mischievous look. "I probably shouldn't tell you this, but we snuck in late at night. I was already a volunteer for the historical society so I had a key. Anyway, it was incredibly romantic up there in the tower, with the stars up above and all of Rocky Point below."

I look down so she can't see my blush.

"Sounds perfect," Oliver says, and I know he's remembering the Fourth of July too.

She stands and gathers our napkins. "I do wish we could still host weddings," she says.

"Why can't you?"

"The costs are just too high. We wouldn't turn a profit. Catering, insurance, the extra people required. Marketing to get clients. We're having enough trouble." She waves a hand. "Never mind.

Let's get back to convincing Mandy that the real stories about the lighthouse are nearly as interesting as the fabulous ones she invents."

"You should tell Oliver some of the local legends and ghost stories," I say.

She grins. "How easily do you scare?" she asks Oliver.

I lean back in my chair, trying to grapple with the mom sitting in front of me. She still has those worry lines between her eyebrows, but I've never heard her call my stories "fabulous." Mostly she tells me to stop daydreaming and get to my homework. I'm discovering all sorts of new things this summer—and not just about boys!

*H*ey, Mom, is it okay if I go with Oliver and his mother over to Cranston?"

Mom looks up from the front-porch swing. "Sure, honey." She closes her battered paperback and peers at me over her reading glasses. "Something happening over there?"

I perch on the arm of the swing. "Just some shopping, I think. But Oliver's mom is going to show Oliver the house where she grew up. And where his grandfather keeps his boat."

"He goes all the way over to the Cranston wharf?" Mom looks puzzled. "Why doesn't he dock over here somewhere?"

"According to Oliver, Freaky only fishes alone and doesn't want anyone asking to tag along."

"Funny," Mom says. "Your dad was like that."

I slide off the arm to sit on the seat beside her properly. "Really?"

"Some people like to fish with friends. Your dad thought it was the perfect time to think. Alone."

"Did that bug you?" I don't think I'd like it if Oliver wanted to spend time doing something that he wouldn't want to share with me. Though, come to think of it, there are probably plenty of things Oliver enjoys that would drive me around the bend. Okay, never mind.

"At first," Mom admits. "But frankly, sitting still for such a long time? Definitely not my cup of tea."

"Oliver also said that Freaky doesn't like attracting attention or—as he put it—'feeling the prying eyes upon him' every time he wants to go out on the water."

"Sounds like Freaky."

"Mom!"

"You started it," Mom says.

I push the floor with my feet to set the swing in motion. "I really have to come up with something else to call him! But Mr. Framingham doesn't seem right."

"Ask Oliver. Or his mother."

"She told me to call her Alice. Do you think he'd be okay with me calling him by his first name?" I try to remember what it is. John, I think.

She shrugs. "Only way to know is by asking one of them." She tilts her head and looks at me sideways. "You're spending a lot of time over there. You sure they don't mind?"

"I—I don't think so. . . ." I turn to face her. "Do you think they don't like it? Alice always invites me to stay, and Freaky always makes enough food to feed the whole town. . . ." It hadn't occurred to me before that maybe I was wearing out my welcome.

"I'm sure it's fine. I just miss you, is all."

"Really?" It's out of my mouth before I can stop it.

She tugs on the ends of my braids. "Of course, silly." She leans back again and adds, "Don't worry. I understand. I know there are more fascinating ways to spend time than with your boring old mom."

I'm not sure what to say. I mean, she's not wrong. It's not that she's boring. Well, she kind of is, but only in that way that moms are. Though these last few weeks I've been seeing her kind of differently.

But compared with Oliver? Sorry. No contest!

A horn honks, and we both look out at the street. Oliver's mom pulls up.

"Will you be home for dinner?" Mom asks.

"Probably not." I shift my weight to one foot and fiddle with the strap on my bag. "You don't think they mind, do you?"

"Of course not. How could they mind having you around?"

I lean over to give her a quick kiss. I realize when I straighten back up that it's been some time since I've done that. The surprise on her face shows me just how long.

"See you," I call as I race to the street. I climb into the backseat and we take off.

Cranston is a bigger town than Rocky Point and a lot more twenty-first century. As we approach the outskirts, where several big-box stores claim space, Oliver's mom suggests we check out her old house first. "Then," she says, turning off the highway to take a smaller, wooded road, "we can get to the stores and the farmers' market."

But as we drive around for a bit, she grows perplexed. "The roads look right," she says, "but the houses are different."

"Uh, Mom, it's been a while," Oliver says. "It looks like there's been all kinds of building around here."

She drives up one street and then circles back around and drives up it again. Finally, she stops the car in front of a cleared piece of property with houses on either side. "Oliver, go check the numbers on the mailboxes," she says.

"I think it's gone," she murmurs as we watch Oliver jog first to one side of the grassy plot then to the other.

He climbs back into the car. "Seven forty-one Moosehead and 745."

"That's it," she says, nodding. "That's what's left of the place. We were 743."

"Oh man . . . ," Oliver breathes.

"It's fine," she says, patting his knee. "In a way it's heartening to know that things actually do change. Even in Cranston."

"Do you want to look around anyway?" Oliver asks.

"Nah," Alice says. "There's a pretty view of Candy Cane, but it's not like you never see the lighthouse." She gives me a wink over the seat. "And I don't think I'd even recognize your grand-father's boat in the marina down there." She turns the ignition key. "Let's just head into town."

We drive to Main Street (do all towns have a Main Street?), and as Oliver pokes around in a hardware store, Alice and I wander through the bustling farmers' market. I spot a brightly colored poster stapled to a telephone post. The state fair! I had forgotten all about it.

I see Oliver crossing the street carrying a huge shopping bag. I wave wildly to attract his attention in the crowd. He grins and crosses over.

"Looks like you found what you were looking for," I say, eyeing his haul.

"Yep," he says.

I wait for him to elaborate but he doesn't. "That's all you're going to say? Wow, you really are becoming a closemouthed Mainer."

He laughs. "I'll tell you later. Maybe. I'm still trying to decide if it should be a surprise."

"Okay, now you *have* to tell me. Because if you don't, I'll make up a wild story, and then the truth will just be boring."

His mother joins us, carrying a large bag of her own. "I think your grandfather will approve of my selections," she says. "At least I hope so. He's awfully finicky about his veggies."

"Hey, Mom, do you mind if Mandy and I take the ferry back?" Oliver asks.

"Of course not. It's a beautiful day for it."

As we stroll back to the car, I point out the state fair poster. "We should definitely go," I say. "My friend Cynthia will be back by then. We can get a whole group together."

"Sounds fun," Oliver says.

Alice drops us off at the ferry dock. Oliver does a quick check of the schedule. "Oh good. We'll be back in time."

"For what?"

"Pops asked me to drop off some film to be developed. I forgot to do it on the way here."

"He's a photographer, too?" Will I ever stop being surprised by ol' Freaky?

"Not in the way you're thinking. He takes photos to use as references for his painting, and he refuses to use a digital camera."

"Ah."

We buy our ferry tickets, then board, claiming spots at the rail on the top deck. As is typical in Maine, the once bright and sunny day turns darker. "Is it going to rain?" Oliver asks. "Should we go below?"

"I think it's just fog," I say. "Let's stay up here."

I like fog. Other people think it's gloomy. I think it's romantic. Mysterious. So much of Maine is pointy and sharp. Fog softens the edges.

I gaze at Candy Cane as the pink-hued fog starts to roll in. "I can't believe it's going to be closed down," I say.

Oliver pulls me into his side. "I know."

"She didn't even tell Justin." I called my brother to find out if maybe she had confided in him, but he was as shocked as I was.

I bang the railing with my palms. "I wish there were something we could do about it."

"Maybe there is," Oliver says. I turn to face him. "I don't know what, exactly, but if we put our heads together . . ."

I nod slowly, hoping some idea comes to mind, but right now my brain is full of the stacks of bills raining down on an empty lighthouse-shaped bank.

"If it closes, it really will become haunted, " I say. "All that will be left of it will be the past. No new memories will get made there."

Oliver weaves his fingers through mine. "If it had been closed, we probably would never have met," he says softly. "I hate to even think about that."

I slump against him and gaze forlornly at Candy Cane. "She just looks so lonely out there," I say, then straighten up sharply. "The postcard!" I've never paid attention to the lighthouse from the Cranston side. But the person who painted the image used on the postcard sure had.

"I'm going below," I tell Oliver. "I have to check something."

I scurry down the metal staircase, gripping the handrails. The fog makes things wet, and I don't want to slip—as it would be oh so me to do. I hurry to the bow on the lower level. "I don't believe it," I murmur.

Oliver comes up behind me. "What are you looking at?"

"The view!" I say excitedly. "Look at the angle. Whoever painted the Candy Cane postcard painted it from a *boat*. From this side of the bay."

"You're right," Oliver says, leaning on the railing.

"I always wondered why it looked different from all the other pictures I've seen."

"The artist could have been a Cranston local. Or a visitor."

"We'll never know," I say. "The postcard lists the artist as anonymous. I just may have to make up a story about it."

"Do you want to stay here below?" Oliver asks.

"Nah, let's go back up on deck. But how about a lemonade first?"

Oliver digs into his pockets and comes up empty.

"I've got money," I tell him. "My treat."

I buy us a lemonade from the snack bar and pick up two straws. "So are you going to tell me what was in that huge bag?" I ask as we climb the stairs back up.

"Maybe . . . If you ask really nicely."

The weather has driven most of the passengers below so we have the deck pretty much to ourselves. With the thick fog it's as if we're in our own world. A world made up of just Oliver and me, with a soundtrack of lapping water, gull cries, and the mournful foghorn.

"How about a lemonade bribe?" I ask, peeling first one straw and dropping it into the oversize plastic cup, and then the other.

He smirks. "Depends on how good the lemonade is."

We lean against the rail and sip on our straws. I release mine as a small giggle escapes my lips.

"What?"

I wipe my mouth with the back of my hand. "Nothing." I don't want to tell him that we're acting out the second fantasy image from my romantic montage. Sharing a lemonade with two straws. I lean into him and kiss the side of his neck, where he tastes salty, then the side of his face, then his lips.

"My next project," he whispers.

I pull my head back so I can look at his face. "What?"

He clears his throat. "The stuff in the bag. It's for my next project. This bribe is working better than the lemonade."

I laugh. "I see. So what *is* your next project?"

"I'm going to make another scale replica. But no rowing is involved this time."

"Small enough to take home?"

"Maybe. Or give to the historical society. Your mom seemed so happy to get Candy Cane Jr. The keeper's house I made for the boat, it wasn't all that detailed. So I'm going to pick a specific keeper, and make an accurate replica of the keeper's house when he or she lived there. I thought I'd show it at the craft fair."

"Which craft fair?" I ask. There are agricultural contests at the state fair, but I can't remember if they have an arts-and-crafts thing too.

Oliver looks surprised. "The Good-bye to Summer Festival."

The lemonade cup slips right out of my hand and splashes into the water. "Ohmigosh! I'm so sorry!"

"That's okay," Oliver says, peering down at the waves. "I was done anyway."

Good-bye to Summer is the town event held just before Labor Day weekend. I must have blocked it out this year. Because this year I won't only be saying good-bye to summer.

I'll be saying good-bye to Oliver, too.

August

*D*on't dwell," I tell myself.

The realization that Oliver's departure is a fact, and not some tragic twist in one of my more dramatic stories, sits like a lump in my stomach.

"But how can I stop?" I ask my reflection in the mirror. I know we made a deal and that I was the one who insisted we stay focused on the micro. On the todays we have. Not the tomorrows we won't.

But my brain keeps flipping to the next page on the calendar, where it says September. When Oliver and his mom will be back in sunny California, and I'll still be here in Rocky Point, getting ready for another deep freeze.

"Today," I murmur. "Stay focused on today. And only today. No looking ahead."

I cross to my desk and glare at the *actual* calendar. My eyes widen. "Yes!" I cheer. I've been so busy with Oliver that I completely lost track of the days. The big purple circle filled with exclamation points—Cynthia's coming home!

*C*ynthia phoned when she got in last night. We couldn't stay on long; I could hear chaos in the background and Mrs. Crowley calling for Cynthia to come help unpack. We made plans for a sleepover and then hung up. We'll catch up tonight—I'm already planning on zero sleep!

To add to my good mood, a Lighthouses of Maine tour group arrives just after I open. That's twenty tickets sold, and I'm willing to bet they'll buy souvenirs and maybe even eat in the café. They swarm through the lighthouse, upstairs and down.

After an hour or so, I'm writing in the ledger the number of magnets (four) and postcards (fifteen) sold. With most of the tour group in the café, it's quiet enough that I hear the conversation wafting in from the exhibit room behind me.

"Not much to look at in this one," a man says.

"Sure, it's pretty with those stripes and all, but . . ."

"Why is it even on this tour?" a woman complains as the trio enters the lobby. "It's not exactly significant."

I slam down my pen. "Not significant?" I stand and cross to the portraits of Martha Kingston and Abner Rose. "It was significant to *them*. She was the keeper's seventeen-year-old daughter. Her widowed father had gone inland for supplies when a terrible squall kicked up. Martha kept the lantern lit and nearly froze to death because she wouldn't leave the tower. She slept fitfully beside the lantern to make sure she didn't fail in her duty.

"Despite her efforts, a small fishing boat crashed on the rocks below, the sea churning so fiercely that despite seeing the light, the few men on board lost control. She left her post to help them out of the freezing waters. One man—Abner—caught sick and stayed behind at the tower to be nursed back to health after the others traveled by land to parts unknown. You may have guessed their ending—they married and became the next generation of keepers—but you may not know that Martha was one of the first suffragettes in Maine. Abner supported her in this, convinced by his experience that women are just as capable as men."

I'm on a roll now, reading aloud the framed letter thanking the then-keeper for the aid and assistance provided back in 1894 and another from the 1920s from a little kid who lived in Cranston who said that after his daddy died, he could go to sleep at night because the light from the giant candy cane made him still feel safe. I finish up and turn to face the stunned trio. "That all seems pretty significant to me."

I hear applause form the entryway. I spin around. "Cynthia!" I shriek.

"Mandy!" she squeals, and we fling ourselves at each other.

Out of the corner of my eye I notice my captive audience dispersing. I see that they have been suitably chastened as they shuffle out the door. "More souvenirs to choose from in the Keeper's Café," I call after them.

"Those were cool stories," Cynthia says.

"They weren't stories," I say. "They're facts. History."

"Really? I guess your mom made you memorize stuff for the tourists."

"Actually, no. Not Mom. Oliver and I—"

"That's right! The boy!"

She hops up onto my desk, scattering the research I'm doing for Oliver's new project. I bend down to gather the papers, avoiding Cynthia's swinging feet. Weirdly, I don't really feel like talking about Oliver. Not yet.

"Is he as freaky as Freaky?"

I stand and look around for a safe place to stash the clippings. I give up and shove them into my backpack. I straighten up again. "Freaky's not all that freaky."

Cynthia feigns a look of horror. "Uh-oh. Did he convert you to his cult?"

That had been one of my better Freaky stories, one I'm a little ashamed of now.

She hops off the desk and grabs my arms and waggles them. "Oh no! The aliens have replaced Mandy with a pod person! What have you done with my best friend?"

I giggle and shake her off. I hold my arms straight out in front of me and stomp around the lobby. "Not pod person," I intone in a gravelly voice. "Zombie. Must. Eat. Brains." I stalk Cynthia, moaning, "Brains. Braaaaaains!"

We collapse in a heap on the steps to the tower. She slings an arm across my shoulder. "Missed you!"

"Missed you back!"

"Did you really?" She knocks her shoulder into me a few times with a big smile on her face. "Or were you so busy flirting that you forgot all about li'l ol' me?"

I realize she doesn't know how serious Oliver and I are—she still thinks we've just been playing some kind of flirting game. "Actually . . . ," I begin.

She stands and wanders the lobby, picking things up, putting things down, riffling brochures. "Any of the Regulars turn out to be interesting? Or was Oliver the only crush-worthy boy this summer?"

I stand and straighten the things she's mussed. "Patti's been seeing Kyle."

"Who?"

"He was ahead of Justin at school. Blond curls. Works for his dad. Lobster dudes."

"Oh, right! Him. So she found her summer fling after all."

"I guess. . . ."

"Is she going to break his heart when she goes? Leaving him behind and all."

"Hard to say."

"Or maybe he'll break hers. . . ." She turns to look at me, smirking. "Hope she's still in that fling-only/nothing-serious zone the way she was when I left."

"Why?"

She looks at me as if I asked a dumb question, and speaks to me as if I'm a child—and a not very bright one. "Because in three weeks it's over."

I swallow and turn away, fiddling with the pages of the ledger. Luckily, a kid comes in to ask if we have a bathroom. I send him to the café, and the interruption lets me change the subject.

"How was camp?" I ask. "Were you the lead in, like, *everything*?"

An odd expression crosses her face, a mix of embarrassment and something I can't quite identify.

The door to the café opens, and one of the trio I had regaled with Candy Cane lore comes in with two tour members in tow. "Tell them the stories you told us." She turns to her friends. "She has a real knack. Makes the experience so much richer. The history comes alive."

"Uh, I . . . okay." I glance at Cynthia, and she tips her head toward the door, indicating she's going into the café. I nod, then launch back into my impromptu lecture.

Finally, the tour group leaves and Cynthia returns. "Man, the food's as bad as ever there." She wanders the lobby. "You must have been so bored."

I shrug. "Sometimes."

"Seriously? What do you do when no one's here. Play games on your phone? Does it even work here?"

"I manage. . . ."

She glances at me with a questioning look, then smiles. "I'm going to lay out and catch some rays till you're done."

"I thought we weren't meeting till after dinner?"

"How could I pass up spending quality time with my girl before Mom gets into her back-to-school frenzy?"

Before I can tell her that Oliver's going to pick me up, she's out the door. Well, I wanted them to meet. No time like the present.

I love Cynthia to pieces. She's the sister I always wish I had. I've been envious of her in the past, but today I'm outright jealous. Does she have to be so effortlessly gorgeous and allergy free?

I glance at the clock, ticktocking till my worlds collide. Cynthia disappeared somewhere, but she knows I finish up at four, which is exactly the same time Oliver will arrive.

"Please like each other," I murmur as a mantra. "Only not too much," I add just as the big hand reaches twelve and the little sticks to four.

Cynthia sails into the lobby. She must have gone home, because now she's wearing a bright blue sundress that perfectly complements her skin, hair, and eyes, not to mention her show-stopping figure. "Freedom, Free-ee-dom!" she belts out. (It's from the musical *1776*, which she performed at a previous July Fourth festival.) "Ready to go?"

"Uh, not quite."

I peek out the window. Yup, there he is. I grab my bag. "Okay. Listen, since we were going to meet after dinner . . ."

"I know, I know. You can't even be in the house while Mom makes her fish stew."

"Well, because of that," I explain as we leave the lighthouse, "Oliver's here." I pull the door shut and lock it.

"You have plans?"

"Not exactly. He just comes to meet me after work. Some-times we go to—"

"Every day?" Cynthia asks.

"Pretty much." We turn and start walking.

"Which Rocky Point today?" Oliver calls. Then he realizes Cynthia isn't a Candy Cane visitor and that she and I are together. "Oh, hi," he says.

"Well, if it isn't the flea market find," Cynthia teases.

"What?"

She laughs. "That's where we first saw you. At the Lupine Festival flea market."

"That's right." He smiles. "I hope I'm not one of Mandy's for-lorn unbuyables." I told him about my "pity purchases." He kisses the side of my head.

I squirm. Cynthia squirms. Oliver looks back and forth between us and takes a step away from me. I can tell he's wondering what's wrong. I'm wondering the same thing.

"Mandy said you're just back from camp," Oliver says.

"It wasn't *camp*," Cynthia corrects him. "Not like canoeing and making lanyards. It was professional performing-arts training."

"Right, Mandy said."

We stand there awkwardly. "Want to . . . ," I start.

"Should we . . . ?" Oliver says at the same time

"How about . . . ," Cynthia also says.

We all give nervous laughs. "Someone go first," Oliver says. He takes my hand.

"What did you mean before?" Cynthia asks. "Asking 'which Rocky Point'?"

"Oh, it's an idea of Mandy's. That there are multiple Rocky Points."

"Are they each equally dull?"

"We don't think so," Oliver says, and squeezes my hand.

Cynthia raises an eyebrow at me. "My my my. I guess someone's been doing a good PR campaign for sad little Rock Bottom."

"Aw, that's just mean," Oliver says with a grin. "This place is cool."

Cynthia's still looking at me. "Yeah?"

"Well, it's not so bad. But you have to admit," I say to Oliver, "there's not a whole lot to do."

"Are we going to just stand here looking at the oh-so-not-exciting view, or are we going someplace?" Cynthia says.

"I thought we could do some more research at the historical

society," Oliver tells me. His eyes flick to Cynthia. "Unless there's something else . . ."

"What kind of research?" Cynthia asks.

"Info about the keeper's house," Oliver says.

"He's building a replica," I say.

"Didn't you already make one?" Cynthia asks. "I saw those photos you posted."

"This one will be more detailed," Oliver explains. "I'm double-checking the floor plans so that the scale works and that it's completely accurate."

I wish that didn't sound so nerdy. I know Oliver's more fun and interesting than he's sounding.

Cynthia pokes me. "I can't believe you did the boat parade. So dorky!"

"Yeah, well . . . it turned out to be fun," I say, glancing at Oliver. "Lexi worked on it; did I tell you?"

"And that girl . . ." Oliver snaps his fingers a few times, trying to remember the name. "Vicki Jensen. She said she wished Mandy had asked her to be part of the crew."

"She did?" Cynthia says, crossing her arms.

This is getting tense. "Hey, you probably don't want to hang at the historical society—"

"You *do*?" Cynthia is looking at me more and more like I'm someone she doesn't know. I don't like how it feels.

"It makes Mom super happy. She hasn't been on my back since I started poking around up there." I don't want to get into the whole Candy Cane closing problem right now. The situation is already awkward.

Cynthia nods slowly. "Ahhh. Smart girl."

Now Oliver is looking at me quizzically. What is with me? I'm making it sound as if the only reason I'm going through the files is to suck up to my mom.

"I'm helping Oliver with the research." Now I sound like I only do it to make him happy.

Cynthia smirks at him. "He really did indoctrinate you."

"What does that mean?" Oliver says, just short of snapping at her.

"Hey, don't be offended," Cynthia says. "Be flattered."

I need to end this before it turns into an actual fight. "You want me to bring anything over for tonight?" I ask Cynthia.

"Nope," Cynthia says. "I've got plenty of movies to catch up on. And maybe we can do a little makeover." She flips the end of my braid up and down. "Someone hasn't been using conditioner."

I brush her hand away.

"I think Mandy is exactly the way she should be," Oliver says, putting his arm around me. "Why do girls think putting on more makeup makes them somehow more appealing?"

"Well, builder boy, we like to achieve our full potential."

This is so not going the way I had hoped. Here are my two favorite people in the world (well, Justin goes in that category too), and they're not getting along. At all.

I get that he's a fox, but seriously, Mandy. He's so . . . I never thought of you as going for the dweeb."

"He's not a dweeb," I protest.

We're up in Cynthia's bedroom, where the primary topic of conversation has been how *not* for me Oliver is. It's not like I didn't expect something like this tonight. It was obvious that she thought he wasn't exactly cool from their brief interaction. And I fielded similar comments from Oliver at the historical society, though it was the fact that she was "pushy and shallow" that bothered him. It made it hard to concentrate on our attempts to brainstorm solutions to the Candy Cane problem.

"What do you really know about him?" Cynthia asks.

"What are you talking about? I've spent nearly every day with him; I've hung out with his mom, his grandfather . . ."

"Right. *Freaky*."

"He's really not a bad guy." I pick at an imaginary spot on one of her bedposts. "You just have to get to know him."

"Yeah, like that'll ever happen." She finishes brushing her hair and hops onto the bed. "What I mean is, do you have any idea about Oliver's life at home? Where he actually lives. Where he'll be going in just a few weeks."

I stare down at a pillow and stroke the fringe.

"Remember Arabella Swenson?" she says.

The name chills me. Bella Swenson is the cautionary tale for all of us thinking of having a summer romance with someone from away. The guy she was gaga for turned out to have a steady girlfriend back at home. Though I wonder how serious it really was if he was fooling around with someone else all summer.

"And Billy Winston," she adds.

The boy version of Arabella. But even worse, since that girl's boyfriend came up to spend Labor Day weekend, and poor Billy had to see them all over town together.

"Why are you ruining this for me?" I ask.

"I'm looking out for you," Cynthia says.

"Well, don't." I stand and flop down onto the air mattress. "Since when are you the boss of me? I'm a big girl."

Somehow I don't think I'm helping my own argument.

*T*he next morning Cynthia goes into the bathroom, and I pretend to still be asleep. I hear her sighing heavily—it wouldn't be the first time she used this tactic to try to wake me. I just roll over, bringing the sheet up and over my head.

I lie there wondering what I should do. We had planned to spend the day together, since I don't have Candy Cane duty, but now I'm not so sure. Does Cynthia even want to? Do I?

"I know you're awake, Mandy," she says. "Your feet are doing that thing they do when you're anxious."

Busted. When I worry, my feet seem to have a mind of their own. Banging together or toes wiggling or bouncing up and down. I yank my feet back under the sheet.

"I'm sorry we had a fight," Cynthia says.

"Me too," I say. I push the covers back down and sit up. "You'd like him if you got to know him."

Cynthia winds a strand of hair around her index finger. That's what she does when *she's* anxious. "Maybe. But there's still the fact that he lives—"

I cover my ears. "La-la-la-la-la-la," I babble.

She throws a pillow at me, but at least she's laughing. "Okay. No reality speech. At least not this morning."

I climb off the air mattress and onto her bed. "Yeah, we should at least have breakfast first." I squinch my nose. "Oh, wait, is your mom still on her health-food-only diet?"

Cynthia flops back down onto her bed. "Ugh. Yes."

I flop beside her. "Then I guess we'll be going out."

I want to say, "Too bad we can't drop by at Freaky's—we'd get an awesome meal." But this isn't the time to push it.

Now I just work on Oliver's attitude toward *her*.

A few times during the summer there are gallery nights in a bunch of neighboring towns, including ours. Everyone gets dressed up, and it's like a town date night. When we were kids, we felt very sophisticated wearing nice clothes, sipping lemonade from little plastic cups, and nibbling on squares of cheese stuck on frilly toothpicks. We were allowed up past our bedtimes, which made it even more special.

A few nights after the dreadful first meeting between Cynthia and Oliver is the last gallery night of the summer. We decided to make it a girl's night. So no Oliver, no Kyle, and Joanna even promised to leave her cell phone at home. I felt a little bad, since Oliver hadn't been to any of the earlier gallery nights. Something always had come up with his mom or his grandfather. But I could use some quality girl time. I also don't want to be one of *those* girls. The ones who ditch their friends because of some boy.

We only have two actual galleries, but displays are also set up in the Square for local artists, and many shops stay open late. And because this is Maine, there's a lobster roll booth at one end of the Square and a booth selling all things blueberry at the other. Guess which side I'm planning to hang around.

"Cynthia!" Lexi cheers as we climb out of Mrs. Crowley's car in front of Scoops. Patti, Joanna, and Vicki all snap their heads in our direction.

Cynthia is quickly surrounded and peppered with so many questions she can't answer any. She holds up her hands to get everyone to quiet down and announces, "First things first!"

I think she's going to ask them about me and Oliver or maybe Patti and Kyle, but instead she asks, "What are the Scoops front-runners?"

We all laugh. "None of us agree," Joanna says.

"You'll have to catch up on the tastings," Patti says. "The vote is coming up soon."

Scoops is packed, but we cram inside with everyone else. As we push toward the counter, Cynthia says hi to a few more people. Harried "taste ambassadors" (a worse job title than "greeter," though their paychecks probably make up for it) bustle around carrying tiny pink tasting spoons.

Cynthia and I make it to the front, where Patti is holding a cone and a tasting spoon. She lifts the spoon. "Peach coconut," she explains. She finishes it and licks her lips. "Mm." Then she gazes adoringly at the cone. "But I'll always be true to mocha chocolate chip."

I drum my fingers on the counter. "Should I risk it and get a pecan graham cracker cone, or just a taster?"

"You've had the other four new flavors?" Joanna asks.

"Oliver and I have been known to detour past Scoops," I admit with a grin.

"I'm surprised you bother," Vicki says. "With all the deliciousness that Freaky makes. That Fourth of July picnic was wicked good."

Cynthia turns with a triple chocolate cone in her hand and a surprised look on her face.

"He doesn't make ice cream," I explain, then order a pecan graham cracker in a cup. Live recklessly, right?

"Ooh," Lexi says, stepping to take my place at the ice cream counter. "You should buy him an ice cream maker. See what he comes up with."

"What are you guys talking about?" Cynthia asks.

"Freaky is amazing in the kitchen," Vicki explains.

"Seriously?"

"Seriously," Lexi confirms. "We decided we could still call him Freaky because he's a freaking good cook!"

"Uh, and not because he's, you know, kind of a freak?" Cynthia asks.

"We should make space," I say, noticing the line growing huger outside. We file out.

"But he's not," Lexi says behind me. "I mean, yeah, he's a character, but he was super helpful whenever we had questions about making the boat."

"Oh, Cynthia!" Vicki squeals as we reassemble our clump on the sidewalk. "It's so sad you missed the boat parade. Their entry was adorable!"

Patti starts laughing. "I can't believe Oliver was so stubborn."

"Believe it," I say as we traipse down Main Street toward the Square. The night is clear, perfect late-summer weather. Warm enough to wear dresses—which we all are, along with bug spray— without the mugginess that sometimes creates an ick factor.

"What do you mean?" Cynthia asks.

"Didn't you tell her?" Lexi asks me. My mouth is too frozen from pecan graham cracker to respond, so I just shake my head. "It was hilarious. He refused to cut holes in the tower in order to see. It wasn't accurate, he said."

Cynthia smirks. "Not too bright."

My eyes flick to her, but she's focused on licking the drips on the sides of her cone.

"Have you met Oliver yet?" Joanna asks, tossing her napkin into the garbage can.

"They're such a cute couple," Vicki agrees.

My mouth thaws enough to allow me to smile.

"We should totally think about doing a boat together next summer!" Patti says.

"One that doesn't involve rowing blind!" Lexi says with a laugh.

"I hear you've been going out with Kyle," Cynthia says to Patti. "So how's that going?"

Patti smiles with a slightly wicked grin. "It's been an excellent . . . diversion."

"Ah, keeping it light," Cynthia says.

"Exactly."

Cynthia sends a smug look my way, which I ignore.

"It's going to be hard, won't it, having Oliver leave soon," Lexi says sympathetically.

I smile softly at her. I know she truly likes Oliver, so she feels bad for me. I shrug and leave it at that. I swallow and say brightly, "So, Cynthia, tell us all about camp!"

"Yeah, superstar, how many hearts did *you* break?" Patti teases.

"Did any big Broadway directors snap you up?" Joanna asks.

"What shows did you do?" Lexi asks.

Cynthia takes a swig of her bottled water. "We didn't do full shows," she explains. "We did scenes from *Les Miz*, *Wicked*, and *Rent*."

"And I bet you were the star in each one," Vicki says.

Cynthia tucks her chin as if she's being modest, but I can tell something's wrong.

I'm probably the only one who notices, but Cynthia's eyes aren't matching her smile. When she looks up again, her eyes are locked onto mine. She's sending me a message: Change the subject.

"We should all go to the state fair over in Franklin," I suggest.

"That would be so fun!" Vicki says.

"But we can bring our guys, right?" Patti asks. "It'll be fun to smooch at the top of the Ferris wheel."

"Will Oliver still be here?" Lexi asks.

I take a last lick of my spoon and nod. I glance around for a garbage can to toss it in.

"Great, so he can come too," Patti says. "Kyle would feel weird being the only guy in a group of girls." She bangs her hip into Joanna's. "Bringing a virtual Sam doesn't count. At least, not to Kyle."

"Ha-ha," Joanna says. They make silly faces at each other.

Vicki slides her arm through Cynthia's. "Looks like we're the only single ones here. We should find us some boys to flirt with. There's lots of visitors tonight!"

"I have better things to do than moon over boys," Cynthia says. She slings her arm across Patti's shoulder, so that they make a linked threesome. "Not when I've got my girls."

"Well, it's gallery night," Joanna declares. "Think maybe we should go look at some art?"

"If we must, we must," Cynthia says.

"Yeah, I could use some fizzy water," Vicki says. "We can get freebies."

We arrive at the Square and head inside Paterson's Gallery. Joanna and Patti make a beeline for the beverage table, while Vicki drags Cynthia around in search of flirting partners.

I spot a table with snacks. I wiggle through the art lovers (or, at least, art *observers*) to get myself some crackers—that pecan graham cracker ice cream was a tad too sweet. I need to balance it out with something salty.

"Yes, that's an Oliver," a voice says, stopping me.

Hearing Oliver's name, I glance over. An overdressed man and a woman in a long flowing summer dress stand in front of a large painting of what looks like the Cranston marina.

"A John Oliver," the man says with admiration. "Those are rare."

"Some say he destroyed many of them after some terrible reviews in San Francisco and New York."

"That's too bad."

The woman cocks her head, studying the painting. "Yes and no. It would be wonderful if there were more of them in the world, of course. But being so rare makes them incredibly valuable. I managed to snag this at an estate sale down east. It's already sold. And for a pretty penny, I tell you."

Too bad this John Oliver wasn't also a lighthouse keeper. Now, *that* would make a great story to tell tourists. I could combine the Artists and Artisans tourists with the Lighthouses of Maine tourists.

"No one to flirt with here," Vicki whispers as she and Cynthia join me. "Let's go."

We gather Patti and Joanna and find Lexi outside. "They've lined the Square with Brad Ainsley sculptures," she says, pointing.

"Cool!" I turn to Patti and Joanna. "Have you seen his stuff?"

"I don't think so," Patti says as Joanna shakes her head.

"They're hilarious," Cynthia says.

We wander down the row of sculptures. We're near the side of the Square by the lobster booth when I see one I remember from the Lupine Festival exhibit.

"Oh, look!" I point toward it. "It's Ship-nado!"

The girls laugh as we approach it. "Good title," Lexi comments as we surround the ships-trapped-in-a-vortex structure.

"Mandy!" a familiar voice calls.

I turn and see Oliver waiting on line at the lobster roll booth. I wave and turn back to the girls. "Do you mind if he just comes over to say hi?"

Cynthia looks peeved, but everyone else is fine with it. I gesture him to come over.

He holds up a finger to say "one minute," then turns back to order his lobster roll. "Just for a sec, I swear," I promise the girls.

Oliver lets a group of kids wearing college T-shirts pass, then crosses over to us. "Hi, everybody! Don't worry, I wouldn't dream of horning in on your girls' night. Just wanted to say hi."

"Are you with your mom?" I ask.

"She's over at the bookstore."

"Anyone else?" Cynthia asks.

"If you mean Pops, no." He looks around at the bustling, cheerful scene. "Not exactly his kind of thing."

"I bet," Cynthia says.

"Those look wicked good," Vicki says, nodding toward the lobster rolls. "I'm going to go get one."

Lexi and Patti join her, while Joanna goes in search of something to drink.

"Don't you want to get that to your mom?" Cynthia asks, nodding toward Oliver's hands, each clutching a fully loaded lobster roll.

"Actually, it's for Mandy." He holds one out to me. My stomach heaves.

"You eat seafood now?" Cynthia stares at me.

"Why wouldn't she?" Oliver asks.

"Because she hates it, that's why."

Now Oliver stares at me. "Is that true?"

"Uh . . ."

Cynthia throws up her hands. "This is ridiculous. You actually pretend to like fish just because of some boy?" She stomps away.

Oliver gapes at me. I dig my toe into the dirt and stare down at it. "So, uh, I guess I never got around to telling you . . ."

"Our deal was that you stop doing this!" He tosses the extra roll into a trash can, totally exasperated.

"You keep buying them without asking—"

He whirls around and points at me. "This is why you're always dropping them! You're not *that* clumsy. No one is. It's because you hate them."

"Well, kinda, yeah."

"You would have saved me some bucks if you had told me the truth."

"And been a lot less hungry." I smile weakly, hoping my little joke will help.

"Do you pretend with Cynthia, too?"

Okay, joke's not helping. "Pretend what?"

"Pretend to like what she likes. Pretend to be like her. Are you ever yourself with *anyone*?" Now *he* stomps away.

I can't believe it. We have just two weeks left and we're fighting? This is . . . this is . . . I have no words for what this is because instead I have tears.

I blink hard. I refuse to cry in the Square. Refuse. Refuse. Refuse.

"Oliver take off?" Vicki asks, taking a bite of her lobster roll.

"'S cool that he didn't try to crash girl's night," Joanna says.

"Hey, just because Kyle's working the lobster booth doesn't mean he was trying to muscle in," Patti protests. "One kiss and that was it!"

I swallow a few times, trying to get myself under control.

"Mandy, what's wrong?" Lexi asks.

I clear my throat. "Allergies," I claim.

"Yeah, as in allergic to jerks." Cynthia appears behind the other girls. They turn to look at her. "You had a fight over that stupid sandwich, didn't you?"

Now all their heads swivel toward me. I shrug.

"Seriously?" Joanna asks. "A sandwich?" She shakes her head. "And I thought Sam and I got into weird arguments."

"Maybe he *is* a jerk," Patti says.

"He's not," I say. "I mean, he did overreact. And didn't give me a chance to explain . . ." I frown.

"I don't get it," Vicki complains. "Why would anyone be mad about a lobster roll?"

I sigh. "It's complicated. It's not really about the sandwich." I push my hair away from my face. "I don't want to get into it. I just want to have fun and forget it. Okay?"

Cynthia slings her arm across my shoulder. "You'll feel a lot better after we get you a blueberry pocket."

Somehow I doubt it. But it's worth a shot.

*S*o what *was* the deal with the lobster roll?" Cynthia asks.

We're up in her room getting ready for bed. I turn on the pump for the air mattress. The noise makes it impossible for me to answer. I need a minute to decide what—and if—I want to tell Cynthia.

She lies on her bed on her stomach, arms dangling over the

edge as she fiddles with her collection of flip-flops. I turn off the pump and sit, back still to her, and hug my knees.

"It was a whole thing, earlier this summer." I sigh. "Something he was actually right about."

I stand and stash the pump under her window and sit at her desk.

She sits up and crosses her legs, waiting.

"I know you don't like him, so it's weird to talk to you about it," I blurt.

She frowns. "But I like *you*," she says finally.

I drop my head. How can this be happening? That I can't tell Cynthia my every single secret, every feeling and thought, no matter how strange or silly or outrageous.

She slides off her bed, then plops onto the air mattress and puts her feet on top of my fidgety ones. "Stop that," she orders.

"Okay, so the seafood thing was part of a big fight about my not being honest with him about what I like and don't like. The same thing you got on my back about."

"Wow." She makes a shocked face. "The boy and I agree about something!"

"Celeste too."

"Celeste Ingram?"

"Yeah, she's working at the Keeper's Café."

"She knows about your fight?"

I nod. "Not this sandwich one. The earlier one." My eyes flick to her and away. I rub a nail-polish stain on the desk. "Celeste thinks I do it with you, too. That I go along with you even if I don't really want to."

"Is that true?" Her eyebrows knit together, confusion on her face. "Why would that be true?"

"I—I didn't really think I did it until she pointed it out," I say in a small voice.

She stands and throws up her hands. "Why would you copy me? I don't want you to do that! If anything, I want to be more like *you*!"

Shock gets me to my feet. "No way!"

"You've got this great, wild imagination! Everybody likes you without you even trying! You—"

"What are you talking about? You're the interesting, cool one. I'm just the sidekick."

We stare at each other, eyes getting wider and wider. At the exact same moment we burst out laughing and fling our arms around each other. "How's this?" I suggest. "We alternate who's Batman and who's Robin."

"Who's Aladdin and who's the genie."

"Who's the Doctor and who's a companion."

Cynthia takes a step back. "We need to come up with all-girl examples."

I smirk. "Maybe girls don't need sidekicks. They can be *equal* besties!"

We hug each other again, then flop down onto the air mattress.

"Look, I like to imagine a summer romance, but really? Not into it," Cynthia says. "Why would anyone want to get involved knowing it will end?"

Before I can protest she adds, "But maybe I'd change my mind if I met someone who affected me the way Oliver affects you."

I settle down and she continues. "I do think he's in the nerdy category, but to each her own. It would be a lot worse if we went for the same type, wouldn't it?"

"You've got a point," I say. "By the way, since I'm now in that all-honest-all-the-time zone, I have a confession."

Cynthia sits up and looks down at me, frowning. "Yeah?"

"I'm not crazy about musicals."

Cynthia pretends she's been struck in the heart, flopping back down and shuddering. "Noooooooooooo," she moans. She stops flailing and says, "Okay. I forgive you."

We lie on our backs, each drifting in our own thoughts. "You're right, you know," I say softly. "Freaky *is* kind of freaky. One minute he's weirdly nice, and then the next he can practically growl. And thinking about Oliver leaving . . ." My voice cracks as tears well in my eyes. "And now we're in a fight. Do you think that was our good-bye?"

Cynthia weaves her fingers through mine. "We just won't let it be."

"Thanks," I whisper.

We're quiet again, then Cynthia says, "I have a confession to make too."

I roll over onto my side so I can look at her. "Ooo-kay."

Tears suddenly stream down her face without warning.

I sit up, alarmed. "Cynthia, what's wrong?"

She covers her face with her hands. "It was terrible."

"What was?"

"Camp. It was awful. Nobody liked me, and I got the worst parts in each of the shows."

"But you're the best!" I protest. "You're better than anyone else here!"

"That's the thing," she says, using her hands to wipe her face. "Everyone at the camp is the best in our hometowns. And there were also people from places like New York and Boston and LA and who were getting professional lessons. How could I compete? What I'm doing here in Rock Bottom is strictly amateur hour." She gives a shaky sigh. "And they let me know."

"Just some meanies," I insist. I get up and grab a box of tissues from her dresser and hold it out to her. "Did you make *any* friends?"

She sits up and yanks tissue after tissue out of the box. "The other losers." She swipes at her face.

I sit back beside her and sling an arm across her shoulder. I lean my head against hers. "I'm so sorry. But look, you'll keep training. And now you've set the bar for yourself super high. You know what you're aiming for. Then no one can knock you down. And if anyone tries"—I make a fist and shake it at her—"they'll have to answer to me!"

She laughs. I laugh. And everything's just fine.

*T*he next morning Mom picks me up at Cynthia's, and when we arrive back at the house, Oliver is sitting on the steps, his bike parked nearby.

"Morning, Oliver," Mom says cheerfully as we head up the walk to the door.

Oliver stands. "Hi, Mrs. Sullivan. Mandy," he adds a bit tentatively.

I don't say anything. Is he here to yell at me some more? Make it an official breakup?

Mom goes inside and we're alone. Well, alone-ish, considering we're standing in my front yard. Next door Mrs. Jackson picks up her newspaper from the bush where the delivery boy tossed it. Thunder the dog walks Mr. Martin past us.

"Your pals adore you, just so you know," Oliver says.

Interesting start. "Yeah?"

"Yeah. They ambushed me at Scoops."

"They went back?" He looks confused. "Never mind. What do you mean?"

"Basically they told me off," he says. "That I was a jerk. That you're the best thing that could ever possibly happen to me. The one with the New York accent—"

"Joanna."

"She suggested I choke on a lobster roll."

I cover my smile. That's so Joanna. "I never told them what the fight was about. Not really."

"Cynthia had filled them in, I suppose."

"Look," I say. "I know you're not crazy about Cynthia, but she's my best friend, whether you like her or not. And you haven't exactly been very nice to her."

"She hasn't exactly been nice to me," he protests hotly.

I run my hands through my hair, exasperated. "You told me to be honest, right? Well, this is me. Sticking up for my friend. The way she sticks up for me."

We both cross our arms and glare at each other as if we're in a staring contest. Oliver folds first. His body sort of collapses, as if he were a balloon losing air. "Point taken."

"I can like you both, right?" I ask softly. "Even if you don't like each other."

"Of course." He winks. "Theoretically anyway."

"Well, that's my theory and I'm sticking to it." I tip my head toward the screen door. "Want to come in?"

He smiles. "Sure."

As we settle onto the front-porch swing I say, "Just so you know, that fish thing. It really was the last thing I didn't mention. I didn't know how to after all those sandwiches."

"You've been lucky. Every time you've stayed for dinner, Freaky made something *other* than fish."

"I've wondered about that." I tilt my head, considering. "Do you think he knows about my fish aversion?"

"You always complain about this being such a small town," Oliver says. "Maybe everyone knows. Everyone except me, that is."

"You're from away," I tease. "We Mainers don't open up the gossip pipeline all that easily."

"Not to outsiders anyway." He touches his ears gingerly. "All last night my ears were burning."

I smack his arm, laughing. "Ego much?" Then I bring my legs up and curl into his side. "Okay, since it's all about the truth now, yeah, you were definitely a primary topic of conversation."

He rests his hand on my leg and stretches the other along the top of the sofa swing. He uses a foot to gently make the seat sway. We both let out long, contented sighs.

Even though Cynthia scared me, mentioning the possibility of Oliver having an at-home girlfriend, not one single molecule of me believes it. For one thing, I don't think he'd get all on my case about not being honest if he was keeping that kind of secret. Besides, I know this boy. *Really* know him. Maybe even better than I know myself, since I seem to still be figuring out how to actually be Mandy, plain and simple.

I know another thing too.

I love him. Truly and really. I love him. Simply and with no reservations.

And shockingly, given my usual state of insecurity, I know he loves me, too.

Not wish. Not hope.

Know.

I also know he's leaving. Every time I think of it my heart squeezes. But I keep focused on the micro. Today. This minute.

Which is just about perfect.

I haven't been to a state fair since I was . . . I guess about your age," Oliver's mom says.

Alice is driving Oliver, Cynthia, and me to Franklin to meet up with Patti and Kyle, Lexi, Joanna, and Vicki. I sit in the backseat with Cynthia, all too aware of the tension she and Oliver are both pretending doesn't exist.

It makes for a weird drive.

"How about you girls?" Alice looks at us in the rearview mirror. "Do you come every year?"

"When we were younger," Cynthia says. The state fair is one of those things that's super fun when you're a little kid, and great to do when you're older and can go to the nighttime events. But when you're not dating, and can't drive, it's less of a "thing." Cynthia hadn't been all that pumped for this outing, but she wants to hang with Joanna and Patti before they head for home.

"It'll be fun," I say, hoping I'm right.

The fair is set up in the same spot every year since the 1890s. It features a midway with games and delectably junky food, a track where there are tractor pulls, a Native American dance performance, a crazy-cars parade (I'm relieved Oliver didn't know about that—he would have come up with some outrageous float for us to build in forty-eight hours!), vendors, a petting zoo, 4-H exhibitions, and lots of rides.

"It's really nice of you to drive us," I tell Alice as she navigates the crowded parking lot. Trailers and trucks surround the wire fence draped with banners announcing the fair and various attractions. Oliver, Cynthia, and I slide out of the car. Oliver leans back into the window. "Thanks, Mom," he says.

She takes a look at her watch. "How about I pick you up at seven? We can meet at"—she scans the lot—"that light at the far corner." She glances at her cell phone on the dashboard. "It looks like there's a really good signal here, so if there's any problem . . ."

"I know the drill," Oliver says. He pats the car and then she drives off.

Leaving me standing between my boyfriend and my best friend. Who aren't exactly fans of each other.

"We should look for the others," I say. I figure there's safety in numbers.

As planned, the girls (and Kyle) are just inside the entrance. We buy our tickets (Oliver buys mine—so cute!), and Oliver immediately starts poring over the map and schedule of events. No surprise there. His complete (or is that "completist"?) absorption gives me a chance to chat with the girls as we decide what we want to do in a far less scientific and organized way than Oliver's.

By the time Oliver looks up from his papers, everyone has scattered. "Where'd they all go?" he asks.

"Don't worry. Plans and backup plans have been made," I tell him.

Everyone has a different strategy for a day at the state fair. Patti seems to always be hungry, so she dragged Kyle to the food booths on the midway before doing anything else. Cynthia never eats until after she rides the most gravity-defying, stomach-churning thrill rides, so that's where she and Vicki immediately raced to. Lexi and Joanna are into the carnival games, no matter how rigged they seem to be.

Me? I have something else in mind entirely.

Oliver pretends to pout. "And why wasn't I consulted?"

I grin and slip my arms around his waist. "You complained that it was a lot of work having to come up with things to do all summer. Today, I'm in charge!"

He wads the map and the schedule into a ball, tosses it into the air, and catches it. "I put myself entirely in your hands."

"Oh, really?" I run my hands up and down his back. "Sure you won't mind?"

"Oh, I'm sure," he says. He leans down and lets his lips ever so lightly brush mine. "In fact," he says, his voice husky, "I wish you'd never let go."

I quickly duck my chin, staring at my vivid blue high tops. My eyes fill with tears, and I clutch the back of his T-shirt, willing them to disappear. He pulls me closer and his arms come up around my shoulders and his head tucks into mine. I'm completely enveloped, and it makes it worse and better and worse.

"I know," he says shakily. "But we can't . . . dwell."

I laugh and wipe my face, breaking the circle he made around me. "Don't dwell. That's exactly what I'm always telling myself." I push him lightly in the chest, making him stumble back.

He looks at me in surprise. "What?" he asks, hurt all over his face.

"I was doing so good!" I wail. "Not dwelling. Not thinking! Just . . . being. And then you have to be so sweet and . . ."

He grabs one of my flailing hands and brings it to his chest. "You've been great. Probably a lot better than me."

"Really?" I squint up at him. We're having this intense and personal conversation at the entrance to the state fair at high noon. Well, it is what it is. At least we're surrounded by strangers, not neighbors.

He nods solemnly. "Really."

"Is it bad of me to be happy that you're having as much trouble with this as me?"

He smiles. "Very bad." He gives me a ridiculous, lip-smacking kiss, complete with a loud *mwah!* I giggle and push him away.

"Come on," I say, tugging his hands and walking backward so I can pull him in the right direction. "There's something I want to do first."

"Hey, you're in charge. I'll follow you anywhere."

I bang into a garbage can.

"Except for maybe there," he jokes.

"Very funny." I turn around and we walk side by side, hands in each other's back pockets.

We stroll through the crowds, taking in whiffs of fried goodies, and somewhere under there the scent of animals and hay. We pass the thrill rides as I lead Oliver to the area where the calmer, gentler rides are set up.

"This is where we're going?" Oliver asks as I buy tickets for the carousel.

"If we don't do anything else all day," I say, "I want us to do this."

He shakes his head and smiles that twisty smile that he uses when he's humoring me, but I don't mind.

The merry-go-round's tinkling music slows down as it comes to a stop. I gesture toward the horses. "Pick one," I say as we step up onto the platform.

He walks among the horses and poles and chariots and finally settles on a light brown horse with a dark brown mane and tail.

He pats its backside. "Hello there, Trigger," he says. He swings up onto the saddle.

"Scoot back a little," I tell him. I grip the pole and in a completely awkward way manage to seat myself in front of him. We don't really fit, but that's okay. Oliver wraps his arms around me and rests his pointy chin on my shoulder. This is the third fantasy scene from my romantic montage from all the way back in June. And now it's real. Like everything else has been. Maybe more real than anything else in my life till now.

Why did I eat that last funnel cake?" Patti moans. She sits on the curb, holding her stomach. People stream throughout the parking lot—families with kids leaving, older teens and adults arriving—as we wait for Oliver's mom.

"You're not going to hurl in my car, are you?" Kyle asks anxiously.

"Aren't you glad you're riding with us?" I whisper to Cynthia.

"No lie," she agrees.

"Are you sure you don't want this?" Oliver asks me, holding out a stuffed lobster he'd won at ringtoss. "Or does your aversion to seafood extend to toys, too?"

"Uh, every kid in Maine has one of those," I tell him. "You keep it."

Lexi and Joanna each chomp down on their grilled corn on the cob, while Cynthia fiddles with her ridiculous oversize sparkly sunglasses. She pushes them up onto her head. "I think they work much better as a tiara, don't you?"

"Definitely," Vicki says. She's wearing her own absurd pair.

"You guys don't have to wait for my mom to get here," Oliver says.

"Yeah, they do," Kyle says. "No food in the car. Dad will kill me." He waggles a finger at Patti. "And no puking."

"I'll do my best," Patti says, standing.

"There she is," Oliver says, pointing at the silver car coming into view.

He waves her down, and we say good-bye to the group. I hear Kyle anxiously asking Patti if she was really ready to get into a moving vehicle as I slip into the backseat after Cynthia.

"Have fun?" Alice asks as she winds her way around the lot.

"Yeah," Cynthia says, sounding a little surprised.

"We never made it to the 4-H exhibits," I say to Oliver. "Hope that doesn't offend your completist sensibility."

"His what?" Alice asks.

As we head away from Franklin, I explain the completist concept, which has Alice nodding and laughing. Cynthia just watches the streets go by.

Once we're on the highway, Oliver asks, "What did *you* do all day, Mom?"

"Actually, I finally went to the lighthouse," she says. "It really is charming."

"Oliver did a good job with Candy Cane Jr., didn't he?" I say.

"He certainly did." Alice smiles at him. If she weren't driving, she'd probably ruffle his hair.

Alice takes an exit, and we're back in more familiar wooded terrain. "What do you think your mother will do now that the lighthouse is closing?" she asks.

Oliver looks over the seat at me and then at his mom. "How do you know about it, Mom?" he asks.

"She and I have discussed it quite a bit. She knows I'm a financials person, so we strategized possibilities."

"Mom hasn't actually mentioned it," I admit. "Oliver and I found out about it by accident."

"Candy Cane is closing?" Cynthia asks. "It's not much, but it's the only reason tourists come to Rock Bottom. Why would they close it?"

Her tone tells me she's surprised, but it's not that big a deal to her.

"There's just not enough money for upkeep," Alice explains. "The thing is, a business like that can't survive on just a summer economy. There's too much competition." Her eyes catch mine in the rearview mirror. "I know Candy Cane is special to you, but you have to find a way to make it special to outsiders."

"The only way it will work is if it's generating income year-round," Alice continues. "Which means locals have to support it, and not only with fund-raisers. Not to mention needing a large influx of cash, pretty much immediately."

"There's the auction at the Good-bye to Summer Festival," I say hopefully.

"Every penny of this year's auction will have to go to existing bills. There won't be anything left over for next season. In fact, it may not be enough to cover what's already owed."

I shut my eyes. "We can't just let it close," I murmur.

I feel Cynthia pat my hand. "We'll think of something," she says to my surprise. "We always do."

I call this meeting of Operation Save Candy Cane to order," I say.

We're not in the library, because I don't want Mom overhearing us. She still hasn't told us about closing, and also if we don't come up with a plan, I don't want her to be disappointed. But we need the Internet so we're on one of the benches nearby. Oliver and I sit on the grass with Lexi. Cynthia, Celeste, and Vicki share a bench with Justin on Skype.

I lay out the problem. Everyone's shocked, of course, but no one has any ideas. "I don't know if anyone would want it," Oliver says, "but I'll donate the keeper's house replica I'm working on to the auction instead of the art fair."

I beam at him. "Thanks."

"What would bring more tourists?" Vicki asks.

"Not just tourists," Justin says from my laptop. "Oliver's mom said we need more year-round attendance."

I look around the Square, watching people go in and out of the stores. "They stay open all year, so why can't Candy Cane?" I ask, gesturing at Main Street.

"Too bad the food at the café is so bad," Celeste says.

"It might actually make more sense to close the café to save money," Justin says. "It probably costs more to run it than it earns."

I write that in my notebook as something to suggest.

"People go for those replicas and restorations," Lexi says. "Maybe the Keeper's Café can be turned back into what it looked like in the 1880s or something."

"That would probably take a lot of money," I say, but write that idea down too.

I tap my chin with my pen, trying to think of what made the most impact on the visitors. "Stories," I say.

"Stories?" Celeste repeats.

"That's what can make Candy Cane more special," I say. "The stories."

"Brilliant!" Oliver says, already getting where I'm going with this.

"Like the ones you told those tourists the other day?" Cynthia asks.

"But more!" I'm getting excited. "We . . . we act them out! We tie them in to holidays! We do stories based on history and made-up ones too!"

"From the archives!" Cynthia says.

Oliver laughs. "Yeah, *your* archives *and* the ones at the historical society."

"This could work," Justin says. "Something that people in town can do all year long."

"Everyone's always trying to find things to do with their kids," Vicki says. "I should know. I babysit a lot, and there's not much to choose from."

"School groups too," Celeste adds. "I remember going on trips for stuff like this in Cranston. Why not here in Rocky Point?"

My head keeps nodding with each idea.

"Then maybe we'd want to keep the café open," Celeste continues. "So they have somewhere for lunch."

"I'll get everyone from drama club to act in them," Cynthia says.

"But you'll always be the star," I promise.

"I can build anything we might need," Lexi says.

Oliver frowns.

"What?" I ask. Everyone's so excited. Why is he looking so down? "You don't think it's a good idea?"

"I want to help too," he says. "But this will all happen after . . ." He stops himself and shakes his head. Then he puts his hand on top of mine and smiles. "This is good."

He feels left out. Candy Cane means a lot to him, too. "You can help us put together a proposal. Your mom's input would be great! Then we'll give it to Mom to bring to the next meeting."

"We still have to figure out a way to bring in money *now*, though," Lexi says.

"At least enough to keep it open to put these ideas into place," Justin says.

"Yeah . . ." I stare down at my list. It is definitely not long enough.

"At my school they do auctions where people donate not just stuff but also services," Oliver says. "Massages, dance lessons, whatever. Maybe you can do something like that?"

"Freaky should donate catering services," Lexi says. "I'm still thinking about those sandwiches from the Fourth of July."

"And cookies," I add. "Mmmm."

"Somehow I don't think that's going to happen," Oliver says with a laugh. "But I suppose I could try."

"Listen, this is a great start," Justin says from the screen. "But I have to get to class." He signs off, and I reach up and shut the laptop.

"So I guess we're done for now," I say. "Keep thinking, though."

"Will do!"

"For sure!"

Lexi, Vicki, and Celeste take off, leaving me with Cynthia and Oliver.

"You know, I'm kinda surprised you're all in on this," Oliver says to Cynthia. "Knowing how you feel . . ."

"Just because the lighthouse doesn't matter to me," Cynthia replies huffily, "doesn't mean I don't care what happens to it. Not when it means so much to the people I love best."

Oliver's eyes widen a little, then he says, "Sorry. That was wrong of me." He looks down at his clasped hands. "And that makes it extra great of you to be involved."

Cynthia looks from me to Oliver to me to Oliver. She grins. "Truce?" she says.

He looks up with a grin and shoves his bangs out of the way. "Truce."

We're all systems go on Operation Save Candy Cane. Celeste and Cynthia have been working on getting auction donations. The two of them together pack a powerfully persuasive wallop—both beautiful, and with Cynthia's outgoing energy, how could they miss? Oliver has nearly finished his little keeper's house replica to donate to the auction, and he and Justin are putting together the proposal for Oliver to give to his mom. Vicki's asking the parents of the kids she babysits what might work to bring them to the lighthouse. I'm doing some of everything.

And for now, in case our plans don't work, we're keeping it all from Mom. Who still hasn't mentioned this little bit of HUGE NEWS about closing Candy Cane.

Today I'm up in the attic again, rummaging through Freaky's files for Oliver. He decided to make his model from the year when the lighthouse keeper's daughter, Martha Kingston, saved Abner Rose. He picked it because, just like me, they remind him of us: brought together by Candy Cane. We're going to write up the story too, in a fancy font, and print it on thick paper to include with the model. I'm poking around for anything that might be useful. We've already been through everything at the historical society about it.

I pull out a thick folder that seems to be full of articles and pictures that could be potentially helpful. I cross to the window for better light and—unsurprisingly—trip over something. The folder flies out of my hands, scattering pages everywhere.

"Oh, great," I mutter. I get on my hands and knees on the dusty floor and start collecting the papers. I crawl under a table that has paintings leaning against it, hoping I don't knock them over.

I reach for an article titled "Women Lighting the Way," which could have information about Martha Kingston in it. Then I stop, hand in air.

I'm looking at a painting—well, part of it—leaning with the image facing the table. The image and the signature. A signature that rings a bell.

John Oliver.

I crawl back out from under the table and squeeze past the sofa with sprung springs and the chair missing its upholstery. I come around to the paintings. All of them are stacked picture side in.

Carefully, soooo carefully, I pull the paintings out and slide them into what are hopefully safe places to rest them. I don't look at the others; I'm after that John Oliver.

I take a deep breath before turning it around. Could Freaky Framingham actually own a valuable John Oliver painting? Why would he just stash it up in the attic?

I turn it around and gasp. I actually stumble backward a little, thankfully not into anything that could fall over.

"It can't be . . . ," I murmur.

I'm looking at a very familiar image. Candy Cane. In the fog.

The picture on the postcard sold all over Maine. The one I've been selling all summer.

"I was right!" I exclaim.

This painting—the original that the postcard had been made from—includes the bow of a boat. The boat the artist had been on to capture the image. It had been cropped out, along with the signature, when it was made into the postcard.

I shake my head several times, unable to believe what I'm seeing. I turn and look at the paintings that had been resting in front of this one. My mouth drops. They're *all* signed John Oliver.

Something clicks in my brain, and I feel so wobbly I actually sink to the floor to process.

"You looking for something particular?" Freaky stands in the attic doorway.

How does he sneak up on me so easily? My head snaps up. "It's you! You're John Oliver. Why doesn't anyone know?"

He frowns and steps into the attic. He frowns more deeply when he sees that I'm sitting among his paintings. "I don't want them to. And you're not going to tell."

I stand carefully and gape at him. "But someone *must* know— this postcard is sold all over Maine!"

"Direct deposit. An account in Boston."

"Is Framingham your real name?" Has he been living under an alias all this time?

A small smile plays on his lips. "John Oliver Framingham is the full handle."

I look down at the painting. "Why would you keep it hidden up here? It's so beautiful."

He stops as if he doesn't want to get closer. He leans against an old dresser. "It's the one that was my breakthrough," he says. "Oliver's ma was too young to remember it. I never let her in the studio because of the chemicals. I suppose I've got what they call a love-hate relationship with it. Brought me into the limelight, but then trapped me in endless requests for lighthouses. I had to get out of Maine, find new vistas, new subjects. Some took. Most didn't."

I study the painting. "You painted it from a photo you took from your boat from the Cranston side."

He nods.

I frown, thinking. "This is why none of the recent paintings are signed. You don't want anyone to know."

He nods again.

"But it's so sad," I tell him. "They're just . . . wasted up here." I turn back to the paintings. "If I could paint this beautifully, I'd want everyone to know. I'd hang them all over the house just so I could see them."

"You ain't me."

I glance at him again and see pain etched on his face.

He takes a step closer, as if maybe he's a little less afraid of the paintings now. "They're from a time when . . . Well, let's just say I'm not very proud of the me that painted them. It was a very selfish time. I didn't know that then. I know that now."

He must be talking about leaving his family, about the things Oliver's mom was angry about. "I wish they didn't make you feel bad," I say softly. "Because I bet they made a lot of people really happy. Just looking at them."

"Maybe." He doesn't sound very convinced. He rubs his face with one hand, then sighs. "Well, let's put them back."

Together we drag the paintings back to their position. I pick up the file I found for Oliver and follow Freaky out. When I get to the door to the attic, I turn to gaze at the backs of the paintings.

"I'm trusting you, girlie," Freaky says with a sharp edge to his voice.

"I won't tell anyone," I promise. "Even if I think you're wrong. Totally and completely."

"Won't be the first time," Freaky says, a touch of humor returning to his eyes.

Then he does something absolutely unexpected. He ruffles the top of my head, just like Alice does to Oliver.

Before I can react, he lopes down the stairs, leaving me gaping behind him.

*T*he thing about having a lot at stake at this year's Good-bye to Summer event is that it doesn't give me time to dwell on the Good-bye to Oliver aspect. Each time I start to get morose, someone calls about Operation Save Candy Cane, and I have something new to do.

This is where Oliver's micro nature comes in super handy. He's amazing at list making, and has even drawn up charts of what has to be done by when and by who.

The project also gives us something to focus on when we're together other than his imminent departure. Still, every now and then I catch him looking at me sadly, or nervously. I know my own face reflects the exact same miseries.

We made a pact to not talk about it until after we get through Operation Save Candy Cane. Which doesn't leave much time for good-byes. He's leaving before Labor Day weekend, like a lot of the Regulars who need to get ready for school, get back to work, and otherwise return to their "real" lives. The lives that we in Rocky Point aren't actually part of.

And here come those tears again.

I wipe them away as I reach for my chiming phone. Five new texts. "Whose brilliant idea was this again?" I mutter. Oh yeah. Mine.

"What idea is that?" Mom asks, coming into the kitchen.

"Just some more ideas for the auction," I say. I told her about finding contributions for the auction since she has to register them all, but not that it's part of a larger plan to save Candy Cane.

I hold up my phone. "Cynthia and Celeste got Kyle's dad, Mr. Marcus, to donate a bucket of bait, and Ms. Hughes three hours of after-school algebra tutoring. And we're all donating baby-sitting hours."

Mom's eyes crinkle, and I think she might be about to cry along with that smile. She comes over and kisses the top of my head. "Have I told you how amazing it is that all of you kids are helping this year? It means so much. I just hope . . ."

I glance up when she stops speaking. She's blinking rapidly. Uh-oh. "Hope what?" I ask.

She shakes her head and crosses to the sink. "I hope you're not running yourself ragged with this on top of everything else you're doing."

"'S cool," I say. Funnily enough, it actually is. I think I may have the micro gene too. I'm really loving pulling all this together. Cynthia says it's like that with shows, too—it's a huge amount of organizing, but everyone works as a team, so it's fun and culminates in something to be proud of. I hope that's how I'll feel after tomorrow. Only then will we know if we actually managed to save Candy Cane.

Problem is, even with the additional auction items, Alice thinks we still won't raise enough money to make a dent in the amount that's actually needed.

Mom starts washing the breakfast dishes. Oops. That was supposed to be my job this morning, since she had to race out to a meeting. I jump up from the table. "Sorry, Mom," I say, stepping beside her at the sink.

"Nah, it's fine," she says. "You've been working hard. You deserve a break."

"You sure?" I ask. "You've been working hard too." Like, around-the-clock hard.

"I actually find it soothing," she admits. "Nicely mindless." She glances sideways at me. "Do you have plans with Oliver today?"

"I might go hang over there later. He's finishing up his keeper's house model."

My phone buzzes, and I cross back to the table. Another text from Justin. *Proposal finished.*

The water turns off, and I feel Mom looking at me. "Mandy . . . ," she begins very gently.

I can tell by her tone that I don't want this conversation to happen. Certainly not now. It's either her confession about Candy Cane closing, or it's something about Oliver leaving. I don't want to get into the first one because maybe it will all be fine. I don't want to get into the second because, well, just because.

I hold up my phone. "I need to answer this in an e-mail," I tell her, and quickly leave the kitchen.

Up in my room I pop Justin an e-mail, telling him to send the proposal to Oliver *and* to me, since Oliver's Internet connection is so wonky.

I read through the proposal. It's really great, but there's a big problem. These are all ideas to sustain Candy Cane once repairs are made and bills taken care of. Nothing we suggest can happen without a major flow of cash first.

I lean against the back of my desk chair and twirl my pen in thinking mode. Slowly an idea begins to take shape. An idea so perfect—and perfectly outrageous—that I throw down my pen and race out of the house before I can chicken out.

I bike to Freaky's in record time. I leap off the bike and hear it crash to the ground, but I don't care. In moments I'm banging on the front door.

Oliver opens it. "Hey!" he says with a big smile. "Do you want to—"

I cut him off. "I need to talk to your grandfather." If I wait another second, I just won't have the nerve to do what I'm here to do. "In private," I add.

He takes a step back, probably pushed by the force of my determination. He's so surprised he doesn't ask a single question; he just points toward the kitchen and says, "Shed."

I rush outside and find Freaky doing something with the big collection of tools in his shed. I know he doesn't like being interrupted, and if I make him mad, he's more likely to say no, but we're down to the wire here.

There's so much at stake for me, for Mom, for Rocky Point, the words force themselves out all on their own. "The painting of Candy Cane," I say. "Please. Would you be willing to sell it?"

"What?" Freaky stares at me as if I just sprouted a second head.

"At the auction. To save the lighthouse. "

He nods. "Yeah, Alice and Ollie mentioned the lighthouse is closing. It's a sorry thing, to be sure."

"But we can stop it from happening! Oliver, and my friends, and my brother, we're all trying to come up with ideas. But none of them will work without something drastic."

"And my painting somehow figures into this?"

"A John Oliver painting would probably raise enough money to keep the lighthouse going for at least another year, maybe more, while we try to find other ways to bring in funds." I launch into the whole scheme, but he quickly holds up a hand to stop me.

"That's all very well and good, but I'm not interested in selling." He turns back to his work table.

Tears spring into my eyes. "But you don't even like the paintings. They make you sad just to see them. You could do so much good if you'd just . . ." My voice chokes up and I have to stop.

How can I get him to understand how special Candy Cane is? Not just because of all the time Oliver and I have spent together there, but because of *everything* that's happened there—the people, the stories, the history. I'd hate to see that all disappear.

And then there's Mom. I think about losing Oliver in a couple of weeks. I've only known him for two and a half months, and already the pain burns in my chest. Mom lost my dad, the man she loved and lived with for years. That pain must have been unbearable. "My mom," I choke out. "I don't want to think . . . It's so much more than a lighthouse to her. It's like a symbol of her relationship with my dad. It would break her heart."

Tears are now running down my face, but I ignore them. They're not just from pain, they're anger, too. "You don't like those paintings because they remind you of when you were selfish. You have a chance to do something the opposite of selfish with them. Won't you do that? Please?"

"Can't you see I'm busy here?" he snaps without even turning around. "Why don't you go along and let Ollie show you his model or something."

My mouth opens and then closes again. I whirl around and stomp out. I drop onto the bench at the picnic table. I have to get myself together before heading back into the house. Even though I'm furious, I'm not going to spill Freaky's secret identity. I keep my promises. If I go inside now, I don't know what will come out of my mouth when Oliver asks me what's wrong.

I wipe my face with the bottom of my T-shirt, trying to get myself to calm down. I hear muttering from the shed. Probably Freaky complaining to himself about me.

A shadow makes me realize Freaky is now standing behind me. Just like him, I don't bother turning around.

"I hear you, girlie. I hear how important this all is, but so is my privacy."

I don't think that's a very good excuse, but I figure it's not a good idea to keep yelling at Oliver's grandfather, so I keep my mouth shut.

He sits beside me on the bench, his back against the table. "Do you know what would happen if folks hear that John Oliver is none other than ol' Freaky Framingham?"

My mouth drops and I turn to face him.

His eyes twinkle. "You thought I didn't know about that lovely moniker, huh?"

"I—I—I . . ." I shake my head.

"Those danged artist tours, they'd be crawling all over my property. I've been famous; I know what it can be like."

My brain clicks frantically, searching for a solution. I get the strongest feeling that he's trying to find a way to say yes. "What if we say it's an anonymous donation? That someone who knew about the postcard decided to give it to the historical society?"

"You think there's anything done anonymously in this little town?"

"The postcard is."

A smile slowly spreads across his face. "I think I know a way to make this work. But no one can know. Not even your mother."

"Not even Oliver?"

"How about you hold off until after they leave town. That's a big secret for anyone to keep. Think you can?"

"To save Candy Cane, you betcha!"

Then I do something as startling as Freaky ruffling my hair. I throw my arms around him.

And he even hugs me back.

*T*he next day my phone rings, and I see that at least for now, Oliver has cell service.

"Hey, you," I say. "How goes the building?"

"Just waiting for the paint to dry," Oliver says. "Then it is officially done!"

"Congratulations." I lean back in my desk chair and slowly spin in it, taking in the souvenirs of this summer that I've accrued. The plushy lobster toy Oliver convinced me to take after the state fair. The spreadsheet he devised to determine which new flavor should win the ice cream contest at Scoops. (Neither of our choices won. Pecan graham cracker? Are they kidding?).

Mrs. Gilhooley's "bib." An evergreen branch tacked to my bulletin board that Oliver pretended was mistletoe (since it's Christmasy). A sparkly rock from the river near "our" place.

"Uh, so I wanted to ask you something," Oliver says.

I stop the chair with my feet, wary. "Yeah?"

"This antiseafood thing of yours. Is it just eating it, or do you hate being around it, uh, generally?"

I turn the chair so I'm facing my desk again. "You want to go to the lobsterbake tomorrow."

A highlight of the Good-bye to Summer Festival for many (not me) is the lobsterbake held on the cove's sandy beach where everyone watched the fireworks. For those not from Maine, a lobsterbake is a super-traditional party meal, though there are big arguments about the best recipe and technique. The way we do it in Rocky Point is like this: Giant steel washtubs are placed on rocks over coal fires. Salt water goes into the tubs, then the lobsters, which get covered with a layer of seaweed. Next there's a layer of clams and mussels and more seaweed. The last to go in is corn on the cob, which is also covered with seaweed.

As you can tell, I've been to them, but only when I was forced to as a small child. It's mostly for visitors to Rocky Point, since it's pretty pricey and most of the locals are working at it in some capacity or other.

"Would you . . . would you want to go?" Oliver asks tentatively. "Mom's kind of into it."

"Of course she is," I tell him. "Everyone who comes to Maine has to experience a lobsterbake on the beach."

"Will you come too?" Oliver asks.

"To be honest, it's not my thing. I'd have to bring my own food, I'd be trapped among the creepy crawlies, I'd—"

"I get it," Oliver says, cutting me off. "So we won't go."

"No, no!" I say. "You definitely should go."

"But I'll be leaving . . . I mean, we only have a few days left. Don't you want . . . " He clears his throat. "Don't you want to spend that time with me?"

"Of course I do!" I exclaim. "It's just—I don't want to keep you from doing something I think you'd really enjoy."

"I get it. I do," Oliver says. He sighs.

I take a deep breath then say, "You know what? Let's go. Together."

"Really? But you—"

"Really." Relationships are about compromise, right? "You just have to promise not to try to make me eat anything."

"Promise."

"Or do classic boy moves like chasing me around with a squirming lobster."

He chuckles. "Do I have to promise that? Cuz that sounds like fun."

"It's a deal breaker, buddy. Promise or else!"

There's a knock on my door, and Mom barges in. She's wired, pacing back and forth, radiating a crackling energy. I've never seen her like this. It's freaking me out.

"Call you back," I tell Oliver. I put down the phone. "Mom?"

"I don't believe it," she's muttering over and over.

"Mom! What's going on?"

She stops her pacing and stands by my bed, one hand holding the headboard as if to keep herself steady. "I just got the most amazing call." She spots my phone. "Was that Oliver?" Now her face grows a bit crafty. "Is this something the two of you cooked up?"

"I have no idea what you're talking about!" Then it hits me. Freaky must have come through. He waited till we were down to the wire, but he came through.

Mom settles onto my bed and gathers herself. "I just got off the phone with Oliver's mother. It seems she has a client who owns a John Oliver that he'd like to donate to our auction!" She pops up off the bed again.

"And not just any John Oliver!" she continues. She bends down to look me straight on and puts her hands on my shoulders. "The *Candy Cane* John Oliver!"

I'm confused how to react. I'm not supposed to know anything about this. Luckily, Mom is so jazzed I don't have to come up with anything. She straightens up and shakes her head. "I'm so sorry. You probably have no idea what I'm talking about."

She perches on my bed again. "John Oliver had been a pretty famous artist from Maine, though no one is sure where he actually lived. His paintings are quite valuable. So as soon as Alice mentioned it, of course I was thrilled." She pops up again. "And then I saw it! She sent me a picture she snapped with her phone."

She takes in a deep breath. "It's of Candy Cane! The most amazing thing of all? The postcard we've been selling all these years—it's a reproduction of this very painting! I had no idea it was a John Oliver!"

She plops back onto the bed as if she needs to catch her breath. Which I'm guessing she does. Just watching her is making me hyperventilate.

"That's awesome, Mom!" I say. I get up and sit beside her. "So now you'll be able to keep Candy Cane open, right?"

Her head snaps to look at me. "How do you . . . ?" She waves a hand. "Never mind. Everyone knows everything in Rocky Point."

Not *exactly* everything.

My laptop pings with an incoming e-mail. The proposal from Justin. No time like the present, I guess.

I hit print and then turn to face Mom. "So . . . we found out that Candy Cane was in danger of closing. And we don't want that to happen. So we did this." I collect the pages from the printer, then hand them to her.

"What's this?" she asks. She looks up at me quizzically. "Operation Save Candy Cane?"

I settle beside her on the bed. "It's a proposal for you to take to whoever makes those decisions. It's all ideas about how to get the lighthouse to bring in money year-round. Oliver's mom is going to look it over too."

Mom's eyes turn shiny. "You—you did this?"

I shrug.

She flips through the pages. "You *did*. This has you all over it. The stories . . . the . . ." She holds the proposal against her chest. "I—I don't know what to say.'"

"Say it will work!"

*B*ecause of the amazing addition of the John Oliver painting to the auction at the very last minute there was some scrambling to do. It was too late to get the info into the newspaper, so we printed up flyers that the Operation Save Candy Cane crew handed out all morning. The auction will take place at four, so everyone with tickets to the lobsterbake earlier in the day can attend too. Because the painting is so valuable, special precautions had to be taken to be sure it would travel and display safely. People took turns sitting beside it in the auction tent in the Square to be sure no grubby little fingers touched it.

Tables with clipboards that listed the donated services that people could bid on lined the tent, and there were a podium with a mike and a long table where the objects up for sale would be displayed. And thanks to Justin, who understands these things, there was even an online version so that anyone around the world could bid—but this was only going to be used for the painting. It was a lot easier for Justin to get the word out in London about the surprise addition to the auction than in Rocky Point because our Wi-Fi connection is so unpredictable.

The Candy Cane painting (which is actually called *The Friend*—I'm not sure if Freaky is referring to Candy Cane or the fog with that title) was in the place of honor. Anyone walking into the tent would see it immediately on its easel in the very center at the front of the tent. I helped Alice write the crafty label description: *An anonymous art collector with a love of lighthouses and a connection to this area has generously donated the iconic John Oliver painting* The Friend *to the Rocky Point Histori-cal Preservation Society. The collector has expressly stated that any funds raised will go to renovations, maintenance, and programming of the Rocky Point Lighthouse.*

Mr. Garrity from the historical society has a background in fine arts, so he helped to make sure it was moved safely. Then Oliver, Alice, Mom, and I ambushed him with the proposal. He promised to read it over carefully and get back to us.

Even though there are lots of activities all day long—concerts at the pier, where Cynthia is singing; windjammer cruises, where Oliver is with his Mom; balloon animals; face painting; and various food-eating contests—I stay in the auction tent. I just can't bring myself to leave the Candy Cane painting. So much work went into getting this to happen; so much is still at stake.

Mom comes up to me and lays her arm across my shoulder. We gaze at the painting together.

"It's so beautiful," Mom says.

"Do you think it will raise enough money to save Candy Cane?"

"I do. I really really do." She glances around. "Where's Oliver?"

"He and his mom are on a windjammer tour."

"Ah, the full Maine experience." She grins as people start filing into the tent, picking up paddles for bidding, and reading the descriptions of the donated items.

"They're going all out," I say. "They bought tickets for the lobsterbake. I'm going to meet them over there after the auction."

"They're not coming?" she asks, surprised.

"They bought their tickets so late that they were only able

to get the five p.m. seating." The company that handles the lobsterbake keeps it all under control by doing timed "seatings," if sprawling on beach blankets and in lounge chairs can be called seating. But it's how they can serve the hundreds of people who want their share of the experience.

"Wait a second." Mom turns to look at me. "You? At the lobsterbake?"

I throw up my hands. "I know!"

She laughs and pulls me into her. "Love makes us do crazy things. Even if it's just the love of a lighthouse."

$\mathcal{M}$andy! Over here!" I whip my head around to find Oliver waving frantically from a prime spot on the packed beach. He, Alice, and Freaky have staked out a sandy break between rocks, so that they're using flat stones as end tables. Amazingly, Freaky occasionally nods at passersby. Alice concentrates on cracking apart her lobster.

I told Oliver that I had no idea when I'd really be finished at the auction, so they should just go ahead and start without me. Secretly I was hoping they'd have finished eating before I arrived so I could avoid close contact with the quintessential Maine seafood. I snacked all day, so it's not like I'm hungry—or that there would be anything here for me to eat.

I wind my way through the throngs, stopping for a moment to admire the caterers manning the fire pits. I may not like the food, but the action is really impressive. They're prepping for the next seating, so they're poking the coals to make sure they're still hot. Although the company does lobsterbakes up and down the coast, they use Kyle's family to provide the lobsters here. I spot Kyle dropping a mound of the seaweed that's stacked near the pits onto Patti, who lets out a squeal.

I make hand signals to Oliver, indicating I'm going to stop by the beverage table, and he heads in the same direction.

"Hey, you," he says, giving me a quick kiss. Thankfully, he doesn't taste like lobster.

"Hey, you." I glance around as I wait for the kids around the soda cooler to get out of the way.

"How'd it go?" He takes a step back and looks at me. "It went great, didn't it? I can tell by that grin."

I grip his arms and bounce a little. "It was amazing! Everything sold! I didn't have to bid on a single pity purchase!"

Oliver laughs. "Lucky for your wallet there weren't any broken mugs or toys donated."

We step up to the cooler, and I rummage in the ice. I pull out a soda and hand it to Oliver, then grab one for myself.

We scoot out of the way to make room for other thirsty people. "Mr. Garrity bought your keeper's house," I tell him as we head to where his mom and grandpop are sitting.

"And," I add, "they're so sure that they'll be able to raise enough money to stay open that he's going to add it to the displays in the lighthouse."

"Really?" Oliver beams.

"He said it really does show what it had been like in a particular moment in time," I say. "The write-up we gave it is going to be turned into a label card!"

Oliver clinks my soda can with his. "Congratulations to us!"

We stop to let some kids race by using their corn on the cob as swords. I glance at Freaky and Alice. "I'm kind of stunned that he's here."

"It's nice to see them getting along so well," Oliver says as we start walking again, carefully, to avoid stepping on anyone. "It was kind of tense when we first arrived."

Workers are starting to move through the crowd, collecting dirty dinner plates and handing out bowls with blueberry crumble and ice cream. Now, those I wouldn't mind having.

"They've been acting funny for the last couple of days," he continues. "Almost like they have some kind of plot brewing."

I have to look down at my feet because I'm afraid my face will reveal that I know exactly what plot they've been brewing. As much as I want to, Freaky Framingham's secret isn't mine to tell. Oliver will know soon enough.

"So . . . ?" Alice asks expectantly when we reach them.

Her half-eaten lobster creeps me out, so I stay focused on her face. "The bidding for the John Oliver is going to be extended until midnight because of so much interest from places in other time zones. The last time I checked, the bids were already through the roof."

"You done good, kid," Freaky says. "You done a good thing."

"We all did," I say.

It was hard work but worth every aching muscle and sprained brain cell.

As I settle onto the sand with Oliver on one side of me and Freaky on the other, my elation over our success suddenly gets put on hold as a thought sneaks in. As hard as putting all this together was, tomorrow will be so much harder. Saying good-bye to Oliver.

But a surprising realization surrounds that painful thought, creating a sort of cushion. The heartache that will come . . . well, it's been worth it too. To have had this summer.

I lean against Oliver and shut my eyes. All worth it.

*T*he next morning Oliver arrives at my house. We had each prepared lists (so us, right?) of what we wanted to do on our final day together.

We're sitting on the sofa swing on the screened-in porch. I look at the paper with his list Oliver just handed me. I start laughing.

"What?" he asks, a little defensively.

I place the paper beside me on the sofa and hand him my list. My list is *identical* to his. "Great minds, huh?" I say.

"'Our Place,'" he reads aloud. "'Candy Cane.'" He smiles at me over the paper. "We even wrote them in the same order."

I swivel on the seat so that I'm sitting cross-legged facing him. I waggle a finger at him. "I don't want to spend the day crying."

Oliver nods. "I don't want that either."

"So, got any ideas how to do that?"

Oliver pushes my hair back over my shoulder. "None." Then he leans away and smiles teasingly. "We could always go back to Hubbard Island. I'll annoy you so much you'll be glad to see me go."

I laugh, despite the raw feeling that's suddenly claimed my throat.

The day we spend by the river is terrible and wonderful, full of intense debates (he's still trying to convince me that *Far Far Away* is a decent movie), stories, laughter, kisses, and long stretches of comfortable silences.

When it grows dark, without even discussing it, we head for Candy Cane. I pull out my key, and together we shove open the (still) reluctant door.

"It took every ounce of restraint to not kiss you that day," Oliver admits.

I smile. He doesn't have to tell me which day he means. I know it was when we fell onto each other trying to get the door open.

"I thought that's what was going on," I say as we stand in the doorway letting our eyes adjust to the pitch-dark entryway. I stand on my toes and kiss his cheek. "I was fighting the same fight."

We only have one flashlight since the other one broke in its tumble down the stairs. I remind myself again to put it on the list of things that need to be replaced. Unbelievable as it is, I'll still have Candy Cane duty after Oliver leaves. Labor Day weekend is busy in Rocky Point. The good thing is, it's official. Candy Cane will be staying open. We made more than enough money on Freaky's painting, even before the final bid. Not only can it stay open, there might even be funds left over for some improvements.

Up in the lantern house it's a lot darker than it was on the Fourth of July. No fireworks, no bright clip lights on booths on the piers. Just the regular harbor lights and streetlamps.

"Someone built a fire on the beach," Oliver comments.

I'm looking at the sky. Tomorrow he'll be on the other side of the country. We'll share the same stars, but have a continent between us. I take in a shaky breath.

Oliver clicks off the flashlight, and I'm grateful. I don't want him to see me cry. Not when we promised. His lips find mine.

"Mandy," he says when we gently pull apart. "I know you don't want to talk about this, but don't we kind of need to?"

"Why?" I murmur, staring down at my feet, which I actually can't see in the dark.

He rakes a hand through his hair. "What's the plan? Are we going to stay in touch? Try long-distance? I might be back next summer."

"Might . . . ," I repeat.

He looks down at his feet too, our heads lightly touching.

"I—I don't want to make a promise I can't keep." His voice thick and creaky.

"I—I know." We're doing it again. That matching stammer.

He inhales and straightens up, resting his chin on top of my head. "Stick with the micro, right?"

"Micro. Right." I blink away my tears and shift my head so that we're looking at each other in the moonlight. "And right now the micro is perfect."

"So we figure it out day-to-day?" he asks.

"It's too hard to see the big macro picture."

"But we stick to our deal," Oliver says, bending a little to bring his face directly in front of mine. He grips my arms. "Honesty only."

I swallow and say, "Honesty only."

He wraps his arms around me and I melt into him. "So, being honest, this has been the most amazing summer of my life. Most amazing *ever* of my life."

I squeeze him hard and let the tears come. After all, they're honest too.

*O*liver left today. That's the lovely thought that greets me the moment I open my eyes. I feel like I'm made out of rocks. I force myself up, trying to relieve myself of the sensation of being crushed. I trudge downstairs, each step weighing a million pounds.

When I galumph into the kitchen, Mom's sitting at the table. "Hey, sweetie," she says sympathetically.

I nod, not trusting my ability to speak, and just lean against the doorjamb. I feel her eyes on me, and I'm grateful she's taking her cues from me and not asking any questions. She doesn't need to. My misery must be radiating.

"Justin will be home in time for dinner," she says.

Justin. Right. I brighten a little.

I'm trying to decide if there's anything I can possibly eat on a morning like this, when there's a knock at the door.

"So early?" Mom says, glancing at the wall clock. It's just past eight o'clock. She pushes up from the table and goes to answer the door, but calls for me a moment later.

Puzzled, I pad out of the kitchen. I'm even more puzzled when I see Freaky standing on our front porch. He's holding a large cooler. Perched on top is a teeny tiny model of Candy Cane.

"The lighthouse is from the boy," he says. "The rest from me. A . . . care package. Thought you might need it today."

Speechless, I pick up the insanely adorable baby lighthouse. Mom takes the cooler.

Freaky turns and heads for his truck so quickly our thank-yous are drowned out by his engine roaring to life. We stare after him as he drives away.

Mom plunks the cooler in front of the sofa swing and sits. "That man continually surprises me."

I drop beside her and flip off the top of the cooler. It's filled with sandwiches, dips, cookies, breads, and muffins. I place Baby Candy Cane on the sofa and pull up a jar.

"'Mandy's Tikka Masala,'" I read from the label. My eyes widen. "This is the sauce he made that first dinner I had over there."

"What is all this?" Mom asks, staring at the goodies.

I lay a hand on her arm. "It's amazing is what it is. Wait until you try it."

Mom raises an eyebrow and unwraps a blueberry scone. Her eyes grow practically as big as the treat she holds. She takes a bite, swallows and says, "You're not kidding he's a good cook."

She pats my knee. "You made quite an impression on him." She takes another bite and gazes at the scone thoughtfully. "I wonder if he'd be willing to sell these at the café." She frowns. "Not likely, I suppose. I know he's not all that interested in getting involved in community events. But still—"

I start laughing.

"What?" she asks. "The idea's absurd, I know, but he is unpredictable. Maybe he could be persuaded."

"You have no idea how unpredictable he is." I launch into the whole story. How I discovered the painting and Freaky's secret identity. I know I wasn't supposed to tell, but I can't keep something this huge from Mom.

By the time I'm finished, she's staring at me so hard I think her eyes are going to fall into my lap.

"You did all that? The proposal. The auction items. *And* convinced Freaky Framingham to go out on such a limb and be so generous?" She shakes her head. "I don't know what I'm most surprised by."

"Me either, frankly."

She pulls me into her. "Have I told you lately how proud I am of you?" She kisses the top of my head as she stands. "I think I need another cup of coffee to process all this." She opens the door to the house. "Coming?"

"In a bit."

I lean back and give the swing a tiny push. Back and forth. Back and forth. I pick up Baby Candy Cane and realize there's a small envelope taped to the bottom. Inside is a little card with a picture of a starry night on it.

No matter what happens, know that this summer was real. Not a story.

Keep it forever in the archives.

I love you.

Oliver.

I shut my eyes and feel the swing's gentle motion. He loves me back. It's real and it's been right.

My brow furrows as a new thought enters. It's good that he's gone. It hurts, yeah, but I learned so much from him. And one of the things I learned is that I need more practice at being "just Mandy." Not a Cynthia clone, not the girl I think a boy wants me to be.

Then I'll really be ready for a forever kind of love, not just a summer one. And who knows? Maybe that will happen by next summer—and Oliver really will return.

A smile grows across my face, a smile bigger than I thought possible on the day Oliver left.

I sit and swing a little while longer, then rummage in the cooler and find a cookie. I unwrap it as I head into the house. "Mom?" I call. "If I do it right, maybe Freaky will agree to sell his cookies at Candy Cane by next summer."

After all, I have a whole year to work on him.

And on myself.

Want some more summer romance?

Read on for a peek at *Pulled Under*,
A Sixteenth Summer novel,
by Michelle Dalton.

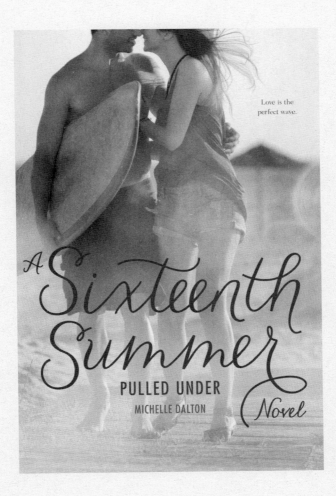

*D*ifficult questions come in all shapes and sizes. They can be big and philosophical, like "What's the meaning of life?" Or small and personal, like "How do you know if you're really in love?" They can even be evil (Yes, I'm talking about you, Mrs. Perkins), like "For the quadratic equation where the equation has only one solution, what's the value of C?" But of all the world's questions there is one that stands alone as the single most difficult to answer.

"Does this bathing suit make me look fat?"

If you've ever been asked, then you know what I'm talking about. It's not like you can just say, "No, but your butt kinda does." And it's not like you can say, "Oh no, it looks great. You should definitely wear that on the beach, where every guy you know will see you." Instead you have to find that delicate place between honesty and kindness.

I know this because I hear the question all the time. I work weekends and summers at Surf Sisters, a surf shop in Pearl Beach, Florida, where women asking you how they look in all varieties of swimwear kind of comes with the turf. (Or as my father would say, it "comes with the *surf*," because, you know, dads.)

It's been my experience that a great many of those who ask the question already know the answer. This group includes the girls with the hot bodies who only ask because they want to hear someone say how great they look. My response to them is usually just to shrug and answer, "It doesn't make you look fat, but it is kind of strange for your torso." The proximity of the words "strange" and "torso" in the same sentence usually keeps them from asking again.

Most girls, however, ask because while they know a swimsuit doesn't look right, they're not exactly sure why. That's the case with the girl who's asking me right now. All she wants is to look her best and to feel good about herself. Unfortunately, the bikini she's trying on is preventing that from happening. My first step is to help her get rid of *it* for reasons that have nothing to do with *her*.

"I think it looks good on you," I answer. "But I don't love what happens with that particular swimsuit when it gets wet. It loses its shape and it starts to look dingy."

"Really?" she says. "That's not good."

I sense that she's relieved to have an excuse to get rid of it, so I decide to wade deeper into the waters of truthfulness. "And, to be honest, it doesn't seem like you feel very comfortable in it."

She looks at me and then she looks at herself in the mirror and shakes her head. "No, I don't, do I? I'm no good at finding the right suit."

"Luckily, I can help you with that," I say. "But I need to know what you're looking for, and I need to know how you see yourself. Are you a shark or a dolphin?"

She cocks her head to the side. "What do you mean?"

"Sharks are sleek and deadly. They're man-eaters."

"And dolphins?"

"They're more . . . playful and intelligent."

She thinks it over for a moment and smiles. "Well, I probably wish I was more of a shark, but . . . I'm a total dolphin."

"So am I. You know, in the ocean, if a shark and a dolphin fight, the dolphin always wins."

"Maybe, but on land it usually goes the other way."

We both laugh, and I can tell that I like her.

"Let's see what we can do about that," I say. "I think we've got a couple styles that just might help a dolphin out."

Fifteen minutes later, when I'm ringing her up at the register, she is happy and confident. I know it sounds hokey, but this is what I love about Surf Sisters. Unlike most shops, where girls have to be bikini babes or they're out of luck, this one has always been owned and operated by women. And while we have plenty of male customers, we've always lived by the slogan, "Where the waves meet the curves."

At the moment it also happens to be where the waves meet the pouring rain. That's why, when my girl leaves with not one but two new and empowering swimsuits, the in-store population of employees outnumbers customers three to two. And, since both customers seem more interested in waiting out the storm than in buying anything, I'm free to turn my attention to the always entertaining *Nicole and Sophie Show*.

"You have no idea what you're talking about," Nicole says as they expertly fold and stack a new display of T-shirts. "Absolutely. No. Idea."

In addition to being my coworkers, Nicole and Sophie have been my best friends for as long as I can remember. At first glance they seem like polar opposites. Nicole is a blue-eyed blonde who stands six feet tall, most of which is arms and legs. This comes in handy as heck on the volleyball court but makes her self-conscious when it comes to boys. Sophie, meanwhile, is petite and fiery. She's half Italian, half Cuban, all confidence.

Judging by Nic's signature blend of outrage and indignation, Sophie must be offering unsolicited opinions in regard to her terminal crush on the oh-so-cute but always-out-of-reach Cody Bell.

"There was a time when it was an embarrassing but still technically acceptable infatuation," Sophie explains. "But that was back around ninth-grade band camp. It has since gone through various stages of awkward, and I'm afraid can now only be described as intervention-worthy stalking."

Although I've witnessed many versions of this exact conversation over the years, this is the first time I've seen it in a while. That's because Sophie just got back from her freshman year at college. Watching them now is like seeing the season premiere of a favorite television show. Except without the microwave popcorn.

"Stalking?" Nicole replies. "Do you know how absurd that sounds?"

"No, but I do know how absurd it *looks*," Sophie retorts. "You go wherever he goes, but you never talk to him. Or if you do talk to him, it's never about anything real, like the fact that you're into him."

"Where are you even getting your information?" Nicole demands. "You've been two hundred miles away. For all you know, Cody and I had a mad, passionate relationship while you were away at Florida State."

Sophie turns to me and rolls her eyes. "Izzy, were there any mad, passionate developments in the Nicole and Cody saga while I was in Tallahassee? Did they become a supercouple? Did the celebrity press start referring to them as 'Nicody'?"

I'm not about to lie and say that there were new developments, but I also won't throw Nicole under the bus and admit that the situation has actually gotten a little worse. Instead, I take the coward's way out.

"I'm Switzerland," I say. "Totally neutral and all about the chocolate."

"Your courage is inspiring," mocks Sophie before directing the question back at Nicole. "Then you tell me. Did you have a mad, passionate relationship with Cody this year?"

"No," Nicole admits after some hesitation. "I was just pointing out that you weren't here, so you have no way of knowing what did or did not happen."

"So you're saying you did not follow him around?"

"Cody and I have some similar interests and are therefore occasionally in the same general vicinity. But that doesn't mean that I follow him around or that it's developed into . . . whatever it was that you called it."

"Intervention-worthy stalking," I interject.

Nicole looks my way and asks, "How exactly do you define 'neutral'?"

I mimic locking my mouth shut with a key and flash a cheesy apology grin.

"So it's not because of Cody that you suddenly decided that you wanted to switch to the drum line?" Sophie asks.

"Even though you've been first-chair clarinet for your entire life?"

"You told her about drum line?" Nicole says, giving me another look.

"You're gonna be marching at football games in front of the entire town," I say incredulously. "It's not exactly top secret information."

"I changed instruments because I wanted to push myself musically," Nicole explains. "The fact that Cody is also on the drum line is pure coincidence."

"Just like it's coincidence that Cody is the president of Latin Club and you're the newly elected vice president?"

Another look at me. "Seriously?"

"I was proud of you," I say, trying to put a positive spin on it. "I was bragging."

"Yes, it's a coincidence," she says, turning back to Sophie. "By the way, there are plenty of girls in Latin Club and I don't see you accusing any of them of stalking."

"First of all, there aren't *plenty* of girls in Latin Club. I bet there are like *three* of them," Sophie counters. "And unlike you, I'm sure they actually take Latin. You take Spanish, which means that you should be in—what's it called again?—oh yeah, Spanish Club."

It's worth pointing out that despite her time away, Sophie is not the least bit rusty. She's bringing her A game, and while it might sound harsh to outsiders, trust me when I say this is all being done out of love.

"I had a scheduling conflict with Spanish Club," Nicole offers.

"Besides, I thought Latin Club would look good on my college applications."

It's obvious that no matter how many examples Sophie provides, Nicole is going to keep dodging the issue with lame excuse after lame excuse. So Sophie decides to go straight to the finish line. Unfortunately, I'm the finish line.

"Sorry, Switzerland," she says. "This one's on you. Who's right? Me or the Latin drummer girl?"

Before you jump to any conclusions, let me assure you that she's not asking because I'm some sort of expert when it comes to boys. In fact, both of them know that I have virtually zero firsthand experience. It's just that I'm working the register, and whenever there's a disagreement at the shop, whoever's working the register breaks the tie. This is a time-honored tradition, and at Surf Sisters we don't take traditions lightly.

"You're really taking it to the register?" I ask, wanting no part of this decision. "On your first day back?"

"I really am," Sophie answers, giving me no wiggle room.

"Okay," I say to her. "But in order for me to reach a verdict, you'll have to explain why it is that you've brought this up now. Except for Latin Club, all the stuff you're talking about is old news."

"First of all, I've been away and thought you were keeping an eye on her," she says. "And it's not old. While you were helping that girl find a swimsuit—awesome job, by the way . . ."

"Thank you."

". . . Nicole was telling me about last week when she spent two hours following Cody from just a few feet away. She followed him in and out of multiple buildings, walked when he walked, stopped when he stopped, and never said a single word to him. That's textbook stalking."

"Okay. Wow," I reply, a little surprised. "That does sound . . . really bad. Nicole?"

"It only sounds bad because she's leaving out the part about us being on a campus tour at the University of Florida," Nicole says with a spark of attitude. "And the part about there being fifteen people in the group, all of whom were stopping and walking together in and out of buildings. And the fact that we *couldn't* talk because we were listening to the tour guide, and nothing looks worse to an admissions counselor than hitting on someone when you're supposed to be paying attention."

I do my best judge impression as I point an angry finger at Sophie. "Counselor, I am tempted to declare a mistrial as I believe you have withheld key evidence."

"Those are minor details," she scoffs. "It's still stalking."

"Besides, you have your facts wrong," I continue. "It wasn't last week. Nicole visited UF over a month ago, which puts it outside the statute of limitations."

It's at this moment that I notice the slightest hint of a guilty expression on Nicole's face. It's only there for a second, but it's long enough for me to pause.

"I thought you said it was last week," Sophie says to her.

Nicole clears her throat for a moment and replies, "I don't see how it matters when it occurred."

"It matters," Sophie says.

"Besides," I add, also confused, "you told me all about that visit and you never once mentioned that Cody was there."

"Maybe because, despite these ridiculous allegations, I am not obsessed with him. I was checking out a college, not checking out a guy."

"Oh! My! God!" says Sophie, figuring it out. "You went back for a second visit, didn't you? You took the tour last month. Then you went back and took it again last week because you knew that Cody was going to be there and it would give you a reason to follow him around."

Nicole looks at both of us and, rather than deny the charge, she goes back to folding shirts. "I believe a mistrial was declared in my favor."

"Izzy only said she was *tempted* to declare one," Sophie says. "Besides, she never rang the register."

"I distinctly heard the register," Nicole claims.

"No, you didn't," I say. "Is she right? Did you drive two and a half hours to Gainesville, take a two-hour tour you'd already taken a month ago, and drive back home for two and a half hours, just so you could follow Cody around the campus?"

She is silent for a moment and then nods slowly. "Pretty much."

"I'm sorry, but you are guilty as charged," I say as I ring the bell of the register.

"I really was planning on talking to him this time," she says, deflated. "I worked out a whole speech on the drive over, and then when the time came . . . I just froze."

Sophie thinks this over for a moment. "That should be your sentence."

"What do you mean?" asks Nicole.

"You have been found guilty and your sentence should be that you *have* to talk to him. No backing out. No freezing. And it has to be a real conversation. It can't be about band or Latin Club."

"What if he wants to talk about band or Latin Club? What if he brings it up? Am I just supposed to ignore him?"

"It's summer vacation and we live at the beach," Sophie says. "If he wants to talk about band or Latin, then I think it's time you found a new crush."

Nicole nods her acceptance, and I make it official. "Nicole Walker, you are hereby sentenced to have an actual conversation with Cody Bell sometime within the next . . . two weeks."

"Two weeks?" she protests. "I need at least a month so I can plan what I'm going to say and organize my—"

"Two weeks," I say, cutting her off.

She's about to make one more plea for leniency when the door flies open and a boy rushes in from the rain. He's tall, over six feet, has short-cropped hair, and judging by the embarrassed look on his face, made a much louder entrance than he intended.

"Sorry," he says to the three of us. There's an awkward pause for a moment before he asks, "Can I speak to whoever's in charge?"

Without missing a beat, Nicole and Sophie both point at me. I'm not really in charge, but they love putting me on the spot, and since it would be pointless to explain that they're insane, I just go with it.

"How can I help you?"

As he walks to the register I do a quick glance-over. The

fact that he's our age and I've never seen him before makes me think he's from out of town. So does the way he's dressed. His tucked-in shirt, coach's shorts, and white socks pulled all the way up complete a look that is totally lacking in beach vibe. (It will also generate a truly brutal farmer's tan once the rain stops.) But he's wearing a polo with a Pearl Beach Parks and Recreation logo on it, which suggests he's local.

I'm trying to reconcile this, and maybe I'm also trying to figure out exactly how tall he is, when I notice that he's looking at me with an expectant expression. It takes me a moment to realize that my glance-over might have slightly crossed the border into a stare-at, during which I was so distracted that I apparently missed the part when he asked me a question. This would be an appropriate time to add that despite the dorkiness factor in the above description, there's more than a little bit of dreamy about him.

"Well . . . ?" he asks expectantly.

I smile at him. He smiles at me. The air is ripe with awkwardness. This is when a girl hopes her BFFs might jump to her rescue and keep her from completely embarrassing herself. Unfortunately, one of mine just came back from college looking to tease her little high school friends, and the other thinks I was too tough on her during the sentencing phase of our just completed mock trial. I quickly realize that I am on my own.

"I'm sorry, could you repeat that?"

"Which part?" he asks, with a crooked smile that is also alarmingly distracting.

When it becomes apparent that I don't have an answer,

Sophie finally chimes in. "I think you should just call it a do-over and repeat the whole thing."

She stifles a laugh at my expense, but I ignore her so that I can focus on actually hearing him this go-round. I'm counting on the second time being the charm.

"Sure," he says. "I'm Ben with Parks and Recreation, and I'm going to businesses all over town to see if they'll put up this poster highlighting some of the events we have planned for summer."

He unzips his backpack and pulls out a poster that has a picture of the boardwalk above a calendar of events. "We've got a parade, fireworks for the Fourth of July, all kinds of cool stuff, and we want to get the word out."

This is the part when a noncrazy person would just take the poster, smile, and be done with it. But, apparently, I'm not a noncrazy person. So I look at him (again), wonder exactly how tall he is (again), and try to figure out who he is (again).

"I'm sorry, *who* are you?"

"Ben," he says slowly, and more than a little confused. "I've said that like three times now."

"No, I don't mean 'What's your name?' I mean 'Who are you?' Pearl Beach is not that big and I've lived here my whole life. How is it possible that you work at Parks and Rec and we've never met before?"

"Oh, that's easy," he says. "Today's my first day on the job. I'm visiting for the summer and staying with my uncle. I live in Madison, Wisconsin."

"Well," I hear Sophie whisper to Nicole, "that explains the socks."

Finally, I snap back to normalcy and smile. "It's nice to meet you, Ben from Wisconsin. My name's Izzy. Welcome to Pearl Beach."

Over the next few minutes, Ben and I make small talk while we hang the poster in the front window. I know hanging a poster might not seem like a two-person job, but this way one of us (Ben) can tape the poster up while the other (me) makes sure it's straight.

Unfortunately when I go outside to look in the window to check the poster, I see my own reflection and I'm mortified. The rain has caused my hair to frizz in directions I did not think were possible, and I have what appears to be a heart-shaped guacamole stain on my shirt. (Beware the dangers of eating takeout from Mama Tacos in a cramped storeroom.) I try to nonchalantly cover the stain, but when I do it just seems like I'm saying the Pledge of Allegiance.

"How's that look?" he asks when I go back in.

I'm still thinking about my shirt, so I start to say "awful," but then realize he's talking about the poster he just hung, so I try to turn it into "awesome." It comes out somewhere in the middle, as "Awfslome."

"What?"

"Awesome," I say. "The poster looks awesome."

"Perfect. By the way, I'm about to get some lunch and I was wondering . . ."

Some psychotic part of me actually thinks he's just going to ask me out to lunch. Like that's something that happens. To me. It isn't.

". . . where'd you get the Mexican food?"

"The what?"

That's when he points at the stain on my shirt. "The guacamole got me thinking that Mexican would be *muy bueno* for lunch."

For a moment I consider balling up in the fetal position, but I manage to respond. "Mama Tacos, two blocks down the beach."

"Gracias!" he says with a wink. He slings the backpack over his shoulder, waves good-bye to the girls, and disappears back into the rain. Meanwhile, I take the long, sad walk back toward the register wondering how much Nicole and Sophie overheard.

"I noticed that stain earlier and meant to point it out," Nicole says.

"Thanks," I respond. "That might have been helpful."

"Well, I don't know about you guys," Sophie says. "But I think Ben is 'awfslome'!"

So apparently they heard every word.